A

GUISE

OF THE

SEA

A

GUISE

OF THE

SEA

JENNA MANDARINO

This is dedicated to my sister who shares my love of reading and writing. Thank you for pretending to be a teacher and reading all your books to me and not laughing when I said I wanted to write books.

London, 1756

Ⓗ ow in the world would I prove my husband's death?

I smoothed my hands over the embroidered pink flowers on my fine linen skirt as a footman of the carriage I'd hired opened the door. He extended a pale hand to help me down as another held a parasol overhead to escort me to the door of the law offices. I lifted my hem, hoping my petticoat would be spared from the mud and sleet of the dreary London day. Having donned my best gown for the elegant Mayfair district, it'd be a shame to ruin it.

With my every step, John's pocket watch clinked against some loose coins inside my reticule. The extra weight of the watch pulling on the drawstring around my wrist was somehow comforting. I could breathe easier knowing it was there, despite my stays pinching my waist too tight. He'd leave it in his stead whenever he took off for months at a time. As if a trinket could replace him.

I raised my chin high as a footman opened the door to the

building, exuding an air that I hoped would make me seem more important than I was. Striding forward, my pannier stuck, wedged in the doorjamb. With teeth bared, I twisted myself through the threshold. The footman holding the door behind me cleared his throat. Damn these false hips. I gave a tight-lipped smile and continued to Mr. Pilkington's office, ready to find a solution to obtain what was rightfully mine. To find a way to survive.

John was gone. Dead. My shoulders drooped before I shook my head and straightened my spine. I had already publicly mourned. Perhaps maybe not as long as I should have, but the one person I was supposed to rely on, the one man who was never supposed to abandon me, had gone and gotten himself killed on a ship somewhere off the coast of Nova Scotia on the way to Jamaica. The fool should have retired like I'd asked, begged. Having an inheritance meant he could have relaxed into the lifestyle of a gentleman and nothing more. Instead, he preferred strategizing in war after war as a captain in His Majesty's Royal Navy. I exhaled a shaky breath. Now it was time to move on and do what I always did—survive.

And that meant forgiving him. For everything.

I *was* Emme Clark, after all, and I didn't escape from squalor, hunger, and my neglectful drunkard father to only end up a resentful, penniless widow. Me, a miner's daughter, in the Mayfair district, ready to claim *my* jointure—I wouldn't lose it all now. But how on earth would I prove John's death to obtain access to his will when he had died halfway across the world with no body to prove his death?

From the other side of the large, ornately carved desk, Mr. Pilkington peered up. His white wig that perfectly matched his skin tone fell askew, and his quill hovered in the air. A big, black droplet of ink plopped onto the parchment he was poring over. "You're late, Mrs. Clark."

Withholding a sigh, I traversed through the towers of stacked books on the floor, nearly knocking them over with the hoop under my petticoat. This time I didn't hold back my sigh as I twisted sideways and walked like a bloody crab through the narrow path to sit in front of him.

Lowering myself into my seat, my wide pannier nearly caught between the chair's armrests, the solicitor no doubt used to dealing only with men. I shifted my weight, the oak creaking beneath me.

Mr. Pilkington's chest heaved as he released an exasperated breath. "I've done all the research I could about our problem, Mrs. Clark, but I cannot obtain a deed of release for your jointure without proof of Mr. Clark's death. There were no loopholes I could find in your marriage contract that would permit you to claim your jointure in the event your husband was simply missing."

No loopholes? My body shook. He had to have an answer. Otherwise, I'd have been better off saving the last of my money for... well, food, rather than his bloody retaining fee. I dug my nails into the wooden armrests in lieu of doing what I really wanted—to take one of the stupid books littering his office and throw it at him. "I came to you because I'm told you *make* solutions."

His tongue poking against the inside of his cheek, he arched a brow. "There is only one thing I can think of to resolve our little predicament."

Our? I perched myself on the edge of the chair. "And that is...?"

"Mrs. Clark, this commodore of John's fleet, Commodore Cobbe, I believe you said *he* could write you a letter certifying your husband's death." He pursed his lips, the wrinkles around his mouth deepening.

I blinked rapidly. "And how, sir, do I go about obtaining it from him when word is the *HMS Glory* is likely sailing across the Atlantic as we speak?"

The commodore who'd broken the news of John's death was long gone. I'd made enquiries on his whereabouts after my *first* visit to Mr. Pilkington's office at the initial reading of John's will where I'd learned of the clause denying access to my jointure. I'd been putting some pin money aside, saving for a rainy day, refusing to ever fall on hard times again—but it wasn't enough to live on. In truth, it was all but gone and unless there was another silver candlestick I had somehow missed since I started selling off my goods, then supper for tonight may be out of the question.

The solicitor cleared his throat and removed his spectacles. Grabbing a white handkerchief from his russet waistcoat's inside pocket, a dark blue monogrammed *EP* on one corner, he rubbed the delicate glass lenses. "Perhaps you should—" He paused, his expression unreadable as he wet his lips. "Perhaps you should follow him. With the declaration of war against the French, I fear it'd be months, if not years, before his death would be registered with the Naval office or until we could collect the ship's muster rolls. With the war, the commodore performed a personal favor by delivering the news directly to you himself."

Such a favor. I fought rolling my eyes at the lawyer. As a child,

I'd received too many lashings from my benefactor for that very gesture. Instead, I pressed my knees together, fighting to keep this façade up, this practiced and refined mask I'd worn for over a decade. I'd made it this far—I wouldn't let it crumble away now. Yes, Commodore Cobbe had *personally* come to tell me my husband John died in a French attack on his ship, but he hadn't taken the time to have it officially recorded with the bloody Naval Board.

But this wasn't the commodore's fault—it was my bloody father-in-law who had demanded there'd be a clause in our wedding contract for proof of death. With John gone for months at a time, he worried I'd say he was dead during an extended absence and flee with his inheritance. But he needn't worry, I wouldn't have gone off. Bloody bastard, John's father.

I clenched my skirt, the expensive, fine material smooth against my fingertips. "How, exactly, would one do that when there isn't a single ship bound for the West Indies?" I'd already checked every posting for both passenger and trade ships. With the tumultuous war and all the unknown dangers it brought, most didn't dare make the long voyage.

Pilkington smiled and shoved his spectacles back on. "Ah, you've done your due diligence, Mrs. Clark. Good, good. Well—" He stood, walked around to my side of the desk, and leaned against it, hands gripping the wood behind him. "Under normal circumstances, a woman could return to her brothers or even her father-in-law—if she was well liked—to be cared for until the estate was settled."

Did he think me daft? I already knew this. I understood the severity of my situation. I wasn't a *normal*, gentle widow. A fact that made me try to prove my worth all the more. My penniless, drunk father died years ago, my brothers before him. John's papa, the Baron of Rye, too ashamed of my poor *breeding,* and who had protested our marriage 'til the bitter end, would sooner send me back to Newcastle to whore than offer me a bite to eat. My benefactor, Mistress Beatrice, who took me in at ten years old, the reet ol' bat, would have taken me back. I had despised her strict rules more often than not, but in the end, she'd given me the tools—and dowry—to survive in society. Perhaps she even cared for me as if I was her own child, a poor replacement for the daughter she had lost that she had once admitted I'd reminded her of when she was deep in her wine one summer evening.

But she, too, had died years ago.

I was utterly alone, with no one to care for me.

Maybe I should have been sadder than I was. Mourned John longer. Or truly. But how could I be sad when he had been gone much of the time? I didn't have a pang of sadness after waking up and remembering he wasn't by my side in bed, because he never *was* to begin with. Being gone for months at a time meant, when he was in actuality gone, it didn't hurt as much as it should have. His death felt like another long campaign on the other side of the world fighting for the Crown instead of fighting for me, for our marriage.

How I had wanted him to put me first, just once… A heat pressed against the backs of my eyes. Despite all of that, I was grateful for him and the life he had provided.

"Under normal circumstances, things would be different, but I fear…" Mr. Pilkington gave me a pointed stare, eyes surveying me as if he was searching for any sign of destitution behind my fancy dress. The way he gawked was exactly the reason I never told people of my true upbringing.

He tapped his fingers on his desk. "As you know, your jointure is *particularly* important so that you may live out the rest of your life with *something*… at least until you remarry."

My stomach twisted behind my stays, and I bit the inside of my cheek. "Yes, yes. I know that well, sir."

"But I may have a solution to our current predicament." His words were hesitant, like he was dipping a toe in cold water, testing it. I inclined my head to one side. "If you're willing, I can get you aboard a ship headed to the West Indies. It'll follow the commodore's route. I have important investments with the captain, and it'd be mutually beneficial for you and the captain if you were to gain access to Commodore Cobbe and your jointure."

Mutually beneficial for the captain and me? No doubt the solicitor would take a quarter of my jointure and invest further with the captain. In the end, it was always about money with men like them.

What Pilkington didn't say, however, was that since I had no man left in this world who'd care for me, I must be willing to do whatever it took to claim my estate. But I already knew what was at stake. It wasn't the first time I'd been left with naught. I knew what it was to fight my way in this world. Even when I had slipped into the comforts of having married someone with peerage, parading around like a high-born lady, ordering servants about—I knew the truth all along: I could only rely on myself for my survival. John's continual leaving and death were more proof of that fact. All the people who were supposed to stay came and left instead. I wasn't enough for them—but I was enough for myself.

My heart rate picked up in pace. "Of course I'd be willing, but I hadn't found any ship daring to travel there right now. What is the name of this ship?"

"It's called the *Bluebell*." Mr. Pilkington rubbed his palms together, his mousy brown hair peeking through the edge of his wig.

I narrowed my eyes. "And you're sure it'll follow the commodore?"

Averting his gaze, he looked toward the window where rain droplets pelted the glass, and he slipped his hands into the pockets of his coat. "I am sure."

A knot formed tight in my belly. What was he hiding? "But?"

"The *Bluebell* is a privateering rig." He flicked his eyes back to me, watching, waiting for a reaction.

I didn't grow up as a child living in a hovel in Newcastle and not learn a thing or two about offering up more information than I intended. I smoothed my features and arched my brow, awaiting his inevitable "and."

"The *Bluebell's* captain is wanted by the Crown and flies under a Danish letter of marque, but if you're willing, I will make an arrangement with him for your safe passage to the Indies." His eyes were wide and seemed to ask the challenging question, "You've lost everything. How far are you willing to go to get it back?"

My heart thumped in my ears, louder than the rain hammering on the cobblestones outside that mingled with the hoofbeats of horses towing elegant carriages full of important, carefree people. I'd lost everything. What *was* I willing to do to get it back? To join a privateering ship with a wanted man as its captain... I'd heard about privateers—pirates with papers was all they were. It'd be a long voyage, living with dozens of men in destitute conditions, traveling across dangerous waters in wartime. Everything I worked for, from begging for food and stealing, to etiquette lessons with a benefactor, to finally becoming a well-to-do wife of a naval captain being groomed for an admiralty... Everything, my entire life, would be gone if I couldn't obtain proof of his death.

A sweat broke out on the back of my neck. Hopefully, the powder in my wig would hold. Heaven forfend if a too-bright red curl slipped out while in the fashionable Mayfield district. The town would be abuzz. I could only imagine what they might say: "There goes the widow who always talked a little funny and was seen selling her candlesticks last week. Now the poor lass can't even wear her wig properly." I held back a laugh. If my hair caused gossip, what would they think if they heard of me taking up with pirates?

This was *my* life, and I'd worked too hard for it to end like this. Like always, if I needed something, I'd better do it myself. So, I would obtain proof of John's death.

I raised my gaze to meet Mr. Pilkington's. "What do I have to do?"

He smiled, amusement dancing in his eyes like the flames of the candles behind him. "Do you happen to own a pair of breeches?"

I hated this bloody dock.

I'd been at this dock in the Port of London too many times. Six years... six years of marriage, and this was where he wanted to be. I should have told him how I felt, how he was making me hate him, what he was doing to me. We'd spent more time apart than together; I'd always thought that'd change once he retired. Instead, he refused, and now it was too late for us. And I resented him for that. What kind of widow resented her dead husband?

Well bugger him, and bugger this port. I shook my head, ignoring the growing warmth behind my eyes.

Bloody hell. A laugh bubbled up from deep within me. In all the times I'd seen John off, I'd never looked like this, with a trunk in hand, wearing a lad's costume. Utter rubbish. I yanked the waistband of the breeches away from my stomach for the umpteenth time. Never mind the way they kept riding up. I didn't know if I'd survive the next hour, let alone a whole voyage.

But if I acted my way into a gentle family, I could act my way onto this ship.

The gray skies told of rain to come, and the salty, snapping wind seemed to match the stirrings of my stomach. I waited for my erratic pulse to settle and watched the busy comings and goings of the port. Traders bartered around me, their arms flailing about as they argued over prices. Fishermen ambled around selling their goods, while others cleaned stinky fish while shooing away diving seagulls awaiting any fish guts and scraps they might find. Men loaded and unloaded heavy cargo and crates from sizable and pristine-looking ships. On the far side of the dock, a large military ship bobbed up and down in the lapping water, its British flag flapping in the sea breeze, looking regal as ever.

I'd never particularly liked the port. It was a far cry from the elegant tea rooms and salons to which I'd become accustomed. The docks reminded me too much of home, Newcastle being a port town, too. But the stench of smelting coal and the plumes of smoke from brick dwellings were much stronger in a city as large as London.

It was the overbearing smoke smell that'd given me the idea—if I had to wear a silly lad's costume to sail on the *Bluebell*, might as well go for it completely. My fair skin wouldn't take the continual peltering of sunlight a ship would offer anyway, so I'd rubbed soot on my face, hoping the dirtiness of a down-on-his-luck lad would hide my feminine features, and darkened my eyebrows with soot as well. I tried my best to tame my wild curls with a thin leather strip, tying my hair in a low ponytail close to the nape of my neck. I donned a black tricorn hat, pulling it low to further hide my feminine bone structure. Finally, I'd bound my breasts by wrapping myself several times with a strip of material I cut from my draperies. It chafed my skin, but it was better than wearing stays.

Pilkington said the presence of an English lady could land the wanted captain and crew in a spot of hot water if they were boarded by His Majesty's Navy while out at sea. Women did privateer, of course, though they were few and far between. But someone like me would cast suspicion over the captain, and they'd likely haul him in on kidnapping charges so they could nab him on English soil for whatever his transgressions were.

The cresting sun began to break through the thick marine layer and clouds, refracting shimmering light off the blue water. One ship, quite large but not necessarily regal, caught my attention. The weathered ship looked as though it should be laid up in ordinary, not ready to set voyage across the world. I cupped my hand over my eyes. Sure enough, a Danish flag on its main mast snapped in the wind. Below it was a unique red flag that even from a distance revealed it had seen better days. Holes let through peeks of gray sky, and sunlight shone through others. The symbol stitched across it was a sword and flintlock pistol crossed over each other.

That'd be the *Bluebell* then.

After a deep breath of the briny air, I picked up one side of my trunk and dragged it across the dock's wooden planks. Each thump at a crack in the planks scared away the screeching seagulls scrounging for food. I dropped the luggage with a loud thud next to the gangway leading to the main deck of the ship. How was my trunk so heavy? It had so few contents—the remainder of my pin money, a few used men's shifts and breeches, John's Prussian pocket watch that he adored, now stored in my reticule, and my wedding ring. The ring that had once promised me so much, love and the whole world, was now nigh better than a chunk of metal.

The life of luxury to which I had become accustomed was gone. The servants had departed when I couldn't pay them. "Friends" slammed their doors in my face when I'd come for help, and the society I so desperately craved acceptance from left me in its wake. Material possessions were left behind—I couldn't very well bring my gowns. I had had half a mind to pack some of my favorite books from our library, but the trunk was already heavy enough. Those things would be there sitting on the oak shelves in my townhouse *if* I could return to it after this journey.

I tightened my grip on my luggage handle. Scarce it may be, everything in that trunk was all I had left if I didn't receive my jointure.

I examined the ship I'd call home for the next several months. Mismatched wood hinted at its history; different types had been used to fix and patch the ship. Peeling paint and worn-out wooden etchings made up the railing. There were three masts in all, but it was smaller than the grand man o' war ship John set sail from. The figurehead at the front of the ship looked as if it had once been painted gold, but now it was marred with flaring splinters and missing chunks. Oddly enough, the carving wasn't a half-naked siren, or even a warrior charging into war, but a raven, or perchance a crow.

Well, that was ominous.

"You there, boy!" a crewman shouted.

I swallowed. Time to test out this utterly ridiculous idea—and costume. I trudged up the gangplank, struggling with the trunk. For half a moment, I'd expected him to come running and relieve me of it, but then I remembered I was dressed as a boy, not a woman.

"Miller or Clark?" the crewman barked.

I tugged the trunk around and belatedly realized the crewman was holding a ledger and quill. Quartermaster, then. "Clark, sir. John Clark."

The quartermaster's gaze swept from my head to my toes. In the growing sunlight, the ebony skin on his high cheekbones was highlighted with a warm gold. Grease stains stiffened his yellowing shirt. On one side, a black patch had been stitched into his shirt, a brick-red stain suspiciously similar to blood trailing down underneath it. I gulped.

"Bit scrawny, aren't ya?" He narrowed his eyes as he scrutinized me, shrugged, and closed his book. "Capt'n Mac said your master lost a game of cards, and you in the bargain. He'll be wantin' to meet ya after ya're settled. I'm William, the quartermaster. Follow me." There was a hint of a West Indies accent in his voice, similar to a woman's I'd once met who came from Kingston.

My gaze jumped to the sailors working on the ship behind him. They—all men, naturally—loaded crates as others scrubbed the deck, and another pair of crewmen hammered away at a chunk of missing railing. They were mostly a gang of blisters, pock scars, and grisly hair. Some looked to be perfectly normal citizens. Their wide array of clothes told me they were from all different walks of life and backgrounds, in addition to their varying races. One thing was shared, however—they all eyed me curiously, though not in a sinister manner. And that, to be sure, made me grateful for the bloody breeches. Nonetheless, I tipped my hat lower over my face and jogged to grab my trunk.

William stopped some feet away and rolled his eyes before ambling over to me and lifting the other side of the trunk for me. "Ya'll need put some muscle on you, lad. Life on a ship is hard."

Together we lugged my trunk over ropes and rigging across the slippery main deck. William, though pacing backward, seemed to know when to duck and twist from memory and had no trouble keeping his feet in place on the wet planks. I, on the other hand, felt like I was walking across the icy Serpentine bridge in Hyde Park in the middle of winter.

A putrid stench of vomit and piss hit me. "Oh, what is that smell?" I gagged and nigh dropped the trunk to reach for a handkerchief to cover my mouth before I remembered what I was wearing and doing.

William grinned, his smile wide and brilliant, and nodded to a man passed out on the quarterdeck behind him. "That'd be Jacques. The first mate."

"Is he quite all right?" I coughed and cleared my throat and lowered my voice to sound more masculine. "I mean, he must be in need of a surgeon."

"He be faring all righ', just a case of scurvy and too much rum. And perchance the lack of a good bath." The quartermaster shrugged.

Panic wrapped around me, squeezing my throat. For a moment, the man's face transformed into that of my father's. A phantom hunger pang roiled through my stomach. Would the first mate forget his basic duties as my papa had forgotten his? I shook my head as if it could shake away the dour thoughts.

We ducked inside an enclosure, and William put down his end of my trunk and climbed down the small steps. He waited, and I shoved the trunk down the stairs, nearly crushing him. I grimaced. Thankfully, he seemed more entertained than annoyed with my blunders. The corners of his lips tipped upward, and his brow seemed to be permanently arched in amusement.

"We'll be heading past the galley and gun decks. As ya're a late addition, all our hammocks were spoken for already." His eyes swept down me again. "But you're quite small. We can add a cot in the quartermaster cabin and squeeze ya in with me."

We stood in place for a moment, him waiting for me to move.

"Toward the aft, lad." His brow arched even higher.

I peered in either direction of the corridor, trying not to focus on the cannons and ample cast iron balls for using with them. Barrels and crates stood between them, mayhap holding gunpowder and more ammunition. I gulped. "The aft, right. Umm."

William laughed, the sound deep and rich. A laugh that would surely make everyone around him want to join in. "Lord, ya'll be in for a rude awakenin'." He pointed to the back of the ship. "That way, Clark."

We reached a small door, *QM* carved into the front. He pulled out a black iron ring of keys and opened the door. An unlit taper candle sitting on an overturned crate next to a narrow cot with a wool blanket totaled the contents of the small cabin. A round porthole window above the bed displayed the black clouds rolling in from the distance.

I would be sharing this extremely small cabin with a strange man while pretending to be a lad. Didn't foresee any problems there. None whatsoever.

"Put your trunk under the bed. We'll get another cot in here. But in the meantime, ya'll need to be meetin' with Mac in the captain's cabin. It's in the stern." He grinned. "That's the back." He walked out without holding the door open for me.

"I know what the bloody stern of a ship is." I pushed the door open, its rusty hinges creaking.

"What was that?" he asked, peering over his shoulder, eyes wide.

I lowered my gaze. "I said 'yes, sir.'"

The corner of his lips curled up for a brief moment. He stopped at the door farthest in the back of the ship and knocked. After someone inside called for us to enter, we walked in.

I hovered in the doorway, taking the place in. For Judas's sake! The size of it... I knew the captain's quarters would be more spacious and luxurious than anywhere else on board, but this was beyond my imagination. At the stern, a wall of windows overlooked the ocean and the back rudder. The captain stood there, looking out, his back to us. He had a hand on the hilt of a pistol in a holster, casually, like it was habit.

In the middle of the sea, I imagined, he'd have a spectacular view. At the center of the vast cabin was a dining room table set for six, an intricately carved wooden navigation table with maps and rolled parchments unfurling across the top, and a full-size bed with a fine duvet made of burgundy silk and embroidered with gold filigree.

And I was to be stuck in a cot in the tiniest room possible.

My stomach dropped. Thank the Lord. In the corner was a narrow wooden door with the word *privy* carved across it. The captain had his own private latrine. He wouldn't have to use the head at the front of the ship, something John had told me of. Out in the open. A glorified hole keeping sailors from falling over the railing. I'd be able to find some semblance of privacy, at least. Because I *would* be using this privy.

William yanked me forward into the room. "Mac, I've brought the new cabin boy, John Clark, to ya as you asked. Anything else ya be needin', Capt'n?"

The captain, a gargantuan figure of a man, faced us at last. "Nay. Thank ye. Please leave us."

William tipped his hat before he departed.

Once alone, Mac, apparently, slid his hands behind his back, standing at attention like a good navy soldier, not a scoundrel privateer. "I apologize for the need to disguise your sex, Mrs. Clark. However, given my record with the British, it's likely they'd cry foul if they discovered ye onboard. And I've no intention of adding kidnappin' charges to their long list of complaints against me."

"Please, call me Emme." I rubbed my hands on my breeches, his eyes following the gesture.

His voice was different from the various other accents I'd heard on board. A Scotsman, it seemed. Ignoring my words, he stepped toward the dining table, and a ray of sun hit the curves of his suntanned, high cheekbones, illuminating him. His sharp jawline was speckled with a day or two's worth of scruff, and his black hair glinted with undertones of gold when he moved. A perfect curl splayed across his forehead—which only called attention to the fact he didn't don a wig and kept his hair trimmed short, reminding me I was indeed a far cry from the Mayfair district. His mossy-green gaze landed on me. The intensity of his stare made the room no longer feel so spacious. Pulling out a chair, he nodded toward it. "Sit."

I stumbled into the chair, nearly tripping over my boots despite them not being as tall or painful as the shoes I was used to. He sauntered to the other side of the table, saber at his waist, smacking the side of his thigh, and sank into the chair opposite me. The chair had a coat hanging on the back, but he somehow made the chair look miniature. I supposed to be such a large man, one would need to be the captain—he'd likely not fit anywhere else if he wasn't, though several crewmen were quite large themselves. It must have been a terrible inconvenience to add one more to an already full ship. Despite my small size, another body meant another bed they may not have space for.

The captain pinned me with a cold stare as he rolled up his shirt sleeves, revealing large muscular forearms. Between the bare forearms and the billowing, open front of his shift, he had more skin on display than most men dared.

Despite the lanterns and candles being unlit, the cabin suddenly felt too hot. Thank you, Mr. Pilkington, because to be sure, I was thankful to not be wearing my stifling stays right about now. My face and neck warmed; hopefully my cheeks weren't as red as my hair.

He squinted, small lines wrinkling at each corner, and his lips twitched as if he meant to smile. Lord, if I didn't want to see what a smile would do to that face of his. But any hint of a warm welcome was completely erased as his full lips thinned into a line. Maybe I had imagined it.

Which was for the best. My husband had *just* died. While love had evaded us, he'd never been cold or callous. And he'd always looked at me like no one else of his rank ever did—like I was more. His memory shouldn't be sullied, erased, by a privateer who looked good in breeches. Besides, I didn't need any distractions. I'd need to make our encounters as transactional as possible.

"Let us discuss the details of our arrangement." His voice was even colder than his introduction. He grabbed a wineskin from his belt—despite having glasses and bottles full of an array of colored spirits sitting on a tray in the middle of the table right in front of him—and took a healthy pull from it. "I'll take ye to the new commodore. The *Glory*'s home port is in Kingston, though I do hope to rendezvous with her well before that. But it'll be one of our stops in the Indies if all else fails." He took another swig from the wineskin. "But whatever business ye have wi' him, when ye're done, ye'll need to make your own way home from the Indies. Dinna want ye aboard longer than I must." He crossed his arms, his biceps stretching the material of his shift taut.

I gnawed on the inside of my cheek. "Yes. Mr. Pilkington has provided me a purse. It should be enough for me to gain a ship home when my business with the commodore is completed." He furrowed his brows, frustration radiating from him like I was nothing more than a thorn in his side. "Additionally, Mr. Pilkington has ensured that you will receive a handsome stipend for your trouble."

Could I even trust him? I eyed the various spirits on the table. Mayhap, the crew of pirates would become drunk and belligerent. Violent even. No, no. No need for hysterics. Mr. Pilkington invested in this ship because of their profitability. I was sure there must be some professionalism on board.

"I ken well all about the stipend. 'Tis for that reason, and the fact he is an investor of the *Bluebell*, that ye're on board at all." He shifted in his seat, the wooden chair creaking under his enormous weight. I wasn't sure it could hold him for much longer, and at this point, I'd have given my entire jointure to watch it break underneath him as he fell on his arse.

But he needn't worry. I wasn't the typical gentle lady. "I won't be a trouble to you, Captain Mac. I can assure you."

Mac grinned wolfishly. "Oh, I ken. Which is why ye'll take up duties here, in my quarters. I'll have a lad fetch your things. Ye'll sleep and work here. I canna have ye mingling ower-long with the crew or working the deck. Ye might sweat off some of that soot ye so cleverly applied, and 'tis a long, lonely journey to the Indies for a ship full of men."

My insides clenched, and my palms broke out into a sweat at no longer having to worry about blushing, because the blood drained from my face. I wiped my hands on my breeches.

His grin grew wider, like he enjoyed rattling me, and he plopped his wineskin down on the table. "Never fear, we'll be making port in Limerick before setting out for the Atlantic. They'll quench their thirst there, and ye can go pick up any supplies ye might need." He leaned back in his chair and propped his legs on the table. "And only William calls me Mac. It's Captain Xander Lock to you, princess."

Bloody hell. I tried to swallow, squelching the need for the contents of my stomach to come back up. Could I truly do this? Take passage with privateers for months before we landed in Jamaica?

But I had no choice. I *needed* John's proof of death.

I must do this, because if I didn't, who would? Besides, I'd lived in horrid conditions before. People didn't forget where they came from just because they wore fancy dresses and had food in their bellies. I *would* do this. As always, I could only rely on myself.

Although, technically, I did need this haughty man to not kick me off his ship. Surely, the smart thing would be to be amenable. But the other option was too tempting. I must have thrown my intelligence away with my gowns.

I pursed my lips. "And Captain Lock, who's to say I don't have to worry about *you* getting too lonely on the long voyage to the Indies?"

For a moment, it looked like he was going to smile, but in the end, his jaw clenched tighter. He swept his eyes up and down me. "Trust me, ye dinna need to worrit. I think I can control myself around ye."

Tugging my shoulder blades together, I straightened. "I don't really look like this." *You damned fool.*

He laced his fingers together and placed them behind his head before leaning back in the chair. "I should hope not. Unfortunately, ye canna even sit here and look bonnie for me, dressed as you are, princess."

Lord, please let his chair break. He would be getting paid for this—he needn't act like it was the end of the world. I gritted my teeth to withhold a sigh. "Fine, I'll stay holed up in this cabin like a prisoner." I reached for the wineskin and took a healthy gulp. The smoky sweet Scottish whisky coated my tongue and burned as it went down. I cocked my head to the side. "But I'll be taking *that* bed."

His laugh was loud and boisterous. "Ye dinna really think I'd give up my bed?"

Folding my arms across my chest, I raised one shoulder in a half-shrug.

"You're mad." He hopped to his feet with surprising agility for an ogre his size and walked to the bed in two large strides before plopping down on it. "If ye insist though"—he patted the spot next to him—"ye may have that side. But I should warn ye, I do prefer to sleep in the nude."

The moment Lock left the captain's cabin, I exhaled loudly, able to breathe again without his stifling, overbearing presence. I tossed my tricorn hat aside and free-fell backwards onto the bed.

Devil take him—he didn't *really* intend to sleep in the same bed as me?

Closing my eyes to gather myself, I focused on breathing. No need to fret now. Heavy rolling across the deck above me dropped little bits of dust on my forehead. I peeled open my eyes, curious at the noise.

Sitting upright, I twisted my lips to the side, lost in my thoughts. To be sure, he couldn't mean for me to spend *all* my time in the cabin. Tapping my palms on my breeches, I peered around me. How could I spend months in this little room? I'd go mad.

I rose from the bed and paced to the door. I'd just have a quick gander. There'd be no harm in *looking*. Resolved, I placed my hand on the cold brass doorknob, but it twisted before I could open it myself. I jumped back as Captain Xander Lock paraded in, nearly bumping into me. My cheeks heated as if I'd been caught doing something wrong.

"Lass—" He peered behind him to the open door and cleared his throat. "Lad," he corrected before shutting the door. "What is it ye're doing that's turned your face a brighter red than madder root?"

I backed away from him, his looming body entirely too close for comfort. Had I been so close to another man before that wasn't a family member or my husband? I had to bend my head back to see his face. "I was going to... investigate a noise."

"Investigate?" One corner of his lip curled upward. "I thought I made it clear what would happen if ye mingled too much wi' the crew. But by all means"—he stepped aside and opened the door—"test out the waters for yourself."

I pressed my tongue against the roof of my mouth. "Savage pirates. Can't you lot control yourselves? I will go where I please."

Lock said nothing. Instead, he stood there with his arms folded across his chest. Would he physically stop me? Would I actually go wander around a ship full of men? I probably wouldn't have gone past the doorway if he hadn't caught me. But now I bloody wanted to skip and frolic on the deck just to watch his reaction. What happened to me trying to be amenable? The mere presences of this brute seemed to throw me off kilter

Plucking at my frock coat's sleeves, I met his narrow-eyed stare. A tense, long pause lingered between us, as if we both refused to be the one who broke first. My breathing was louder than usual as we locked eyes.

Dammit. My shoulders sagged. "Fine! I'll stay in here. For now.

I refuse to allow this little room to be the total sum of my existence for the next few months. Besides, there must be something I can help with. And won't it seem odd that a 'cabin boy' isn't out fetching you food and the like?"

He ran his hand through his black waves, tousling the lock of hair that seemed to permanently form the perfect curl over his forehead. "They willna question me, and unfortunately, lass, we dinna have a pianoforte for ye to play or any cross stitching that needs to be done. So, I dinna ken what ye could do to help while on board."

My hands balled into fists. "I can do more than..." I gritted my teeth. I nearly told him I wasn't a true lady, that I'd done my fair share of dirty, hard work before. But why would I offer such personal information freely to the likes of him? "Well, I'll just sit here, on *my* bed, and sleep away the days, then."

He exhaled, hands clenching as if he was fighting for self-control. Like *I'd* been the one offending *him*. "Ye ken, there is somethin' that most on board canna help with. Being a learned lass, I'll put the reading and daily reporting of the captain's logs to ye." He walked over to the navigation tables. "Ye see, when we capture a prize ship, we typically seize the logs in case o' important information they may be holding. Intelligence on military ships. Secret isles. They take a while to review and not many of my men can read. So, I'll have ye read them and summarize any important information ye've read that day to me."

Well, that seemed... perfectly reasonable. I nodded. "Very well, then."

Lock rubbed the space between his eyebrows. "Well, now that

that's settled. What I came here to say was we're due to depart in less than a half hour. In case ye've decided your *business* with Commodore Cobbe isna worth sticking 'round *savage pirates* for the next few months."

There was no other option. I had to do this. I took a shaky breath. "I'll be staying."

He shook his head. "Verra well, Mrs. Clark. Sorry, I mean, *John* Clark. Best get to readin'." As he departed through the doorway, he muttered something in Gaelic under his breath.

When the *Bluebell* set sail, I didn't have the chance to stand on the main deck and wave goodbye to my old life. Instead, I stayed stowed away in Captain Xander Lock's cabin. Nonetheless, as the ship creaked, and bells tolled above me on the main deck. I nearly ran from the cabin. I knew poverty, knew what hunger pangs in the pit of my stomach felt like, but I didn't know privateering. The moment the wall of windows displayed the moving landscape as the ship lurched, my equilibrium teeter-tottering, I knew it was too late to change my mind about following through on this foolish mission. For a heartbeat, I considered leaping off the bow and taking my chances in the water, but I stayed in place as nervous laughter escaped my lips whilst I read through some of the captain's logs.

And goodness gracious, there was plenty to read. At first, I took the utmost care in reading them. Even found a quill and spare parchment to scratch down some notes. But halfway through my second book, between the mundane contents—weather patterns, inventory notes, notes on crewmen—and the lulling, swaying of the ship, I fell asleep on top of the book.

I woke with a jolt, finding the purpling hues of twilight and the first wink of stars on the horizon. A wooden plate with gray mush had been placed on the table beside me, a slice of bread and a bruised pear beside it. Flashbacks from my childhood made me grimace. But as my stomach grumbled, or rumbled from nausea—I wasn't sure which—I broke down and shoveled a few scoops of the porridge in my mouth and ripped off a piece of bread with my teeth.

A mistake, a big mistake. I shoved the plate away from me, my stomach cursing the rocky waters. I exhaled, trying to keep the food down, as sweat broke out on my forehead.

After some time, my stomach—and perhaps my nerves— settled. I looked back down at my monotonous task at hand. Maybe this wasn't the perfect fit I'd originally assumed it was. What did he bloody well expect to find? A map to hidden treasure? Unlikely. Well, maybe he did expect that, because in the ramblings of my third log, from the nonsense I *could* decipher, that captain was obsessive to the point of madness, going on about trying to find a secret island with treasure off the coast of Nova Scotia. None of the 'evidence' of the treasure seemed to be of merit.

Useless… This was all mindless work.

I slammed my fist on the navigation desk. Oh, the rutting bastard. It *was* mindless work. Tasked to me so I wouldn't stray from this cabin. Groaning, I threw the book across the room. If he thought he could fool me like this… Well, he was sorely mistaken.

After I found a tinderbox to light a couple of brass lanterns and candles, I sat on the edge of the bed, foot bouncing, waiting for the Scottish arse to return.

But a tune of a fiddle started, and feet stomped on the main deck above me. It seemed he wouldn't return anytime soon, so I paced the cabin and poured myself a glass of rum from the tray on his table. After an hour of pacing and two cups later, I had a new mission—find out more about my cabin mate.

I riffled through papers on the navigation table. A creamy parchment was folded and sealed with a red wax coat of arms. I flipped it over. On the front, *Violet Grant, Castle Grant* was sprawled in elegant calligraphy. Hmm. Violet. Did the Scotsman have a lover?

In the far corner of the cabin was a brown sea chest with *AGM* carved on the front. Who the bloody hell was AGM? No doubt a poor sailor he'd stolen this from.

I gnawed on my cheek, eyes roving over the worn wood. I shouldn't... But damned if it wasn't too tempting. I ran my fingers over the lever to release the buckle lock. A peek wouldn't hurt.

The metal clanked as I unlatched it. I took a glimpse behind me before lifting the lid, hinges squeaking. I eyed the contents. A pool of red, blue, and black plaid covered everything. I yanked out the tartan, a scent of salt and oak and leather permeating the air around me. It smelled like *him*. As if he'd wrapped it around himself recently. Underneath the tartan was a broadsword with a cage as a handle. I heaved it from the trunk. Christ, it was heavy. I immediately dropped it with a loud clang.

I shrank away from the door, expecting it to break off the hinges any minute. When nothing happened, I continued my snooping and found a leather-bound book, the spine well-worn. Across the mahogany-colored leather, the title *Don Quixote* was etched in gold. Tossing it back in the trunk and digging some more, I found two portrait miniatures. One of a blonde lass, the portrait framed in an intricate silver design. The other of a baby in what looked like a white baptism gown. A sudden sharp pang struck my chest. The sneaking no longer felt light-hearted. Now I felt like a voyeur who'd spied something vulnerable. The rum in my belly turned sour, and I replaced the trunk's contents and closed the lid before I laid down in the bed to sleep.

Would he come stumbling in here, having drunk too much of his wineskin, unshed his clothes, and lie next to me? My muscles stiffened at the thought.

In the end, while I pretended to be fast asleep, Lock had neither slept in the bed nor in the nude. When he entered the cabin in the late hours of the night, he emanated what I could only describe as a Scottish noise, left, and dragged in something that squeaked across the floors. As I dared sneak a peek, I saw him adjusting a cot for him to sleep on.

After sailing nigh two days, our first stop was Limerick, as Lock had promised, a city on the west coast of Ireland, to gather supplies. I had the distinct feeling he didn't like to stay in English ports for long. What were his crimes? Why was he wanted by the Crown? So far, he'd been decent enough. But privateering was but a small step away from piracy. Moreover, his distaste for the English had been thinly veiled at best. I knew the Scottish had a long, sordid history with England, but the uprisings and the eventual fall of the Scottish at the Battle of Culloden had been, what, ten years ago now? Eleven?

Who was Captain Xander Lock?

The portrait miniatures flashed in my mind—souvenirs of memories passed, perhaps. And then the book, *Don Quixote,* a romantic adventure of knighthood and revived chivalry and all the mishaps in between. And the letter addressed to someone named Violet. They were all puzzle pieces to the mystery of Xander Lock.

Hopefully, a mystery I'd never solve, and this business with the commodore would be done sooner than later, so I could return to London, claim my estate, and move on with my life.

With chance on my side, the *Bluebell* had arrived in the mid-afternoon, so there was daylight, even if the sun hid behind thick, low clouds. I had no idea where I was, but as I strolled down the Limerick wharf, I walked with purpose, swaggering, trying my best to copy the slumping posture and gait of other sailors despite the fact that the dry land seemed to be moving.

An eerie mist hung in the air, creeping in from the sea to the shore, but the wharf roared with the same ferocity as the London docks. I could only imagine how the fog would intensify in the dark of night. Chills ran down my spine. I needed to find the Limerick transportation office to secure my return back to London. Between the disorienting mist and unknown surroundings, I didn't even know where to start. A medieval castle stood on one side of the mouth of the river, so I didn't think it would be that direction.

"Hey, Clark!" I stiffened as the thwacking of running feet stopped next to me. William offered me a wide smile. "Thought it was you. Your red hair sticks out like a sore thumb, even under your hat. Where ya headed?"

I shifted my weight from one foot to the other as I pulled a folded piece of paper out of my waistcoat pocket. *Mr. J.P. Walsh, Transportation Specialist.* Pilkington had given me Walsh's name, saying that Lock usually made berth in Limerick before heading across the Atlantic. Walsh was the man to talk to about booking passage from the West Indies back to London, and I needed to book it now so I wasn't begging passage when Lock left me in Jamaica after my meeting with Commodore Cobbe. I'd need to do it still dressed as a man, so they'd not ask questions I couldn't answer. Hopefully, the soot on my face wouldn't drip from the moisture in the air.

"I'm searching for the transportation office. I need to book passage for... my sister." It probably wasn't best to spend time with other crew members, but William didn't seem so awful. Besides, what other options did I have?

William whipped his head in either direction. "If I remember correctly, the office is due north, just past the wharf." He began walking, stopping when I didn't follow, and beckoned me over. "C'mon, Clark. I'll show you. Lest ya get yaself lost in the fog. "

Well, that was thoughtful of him. "Thank you." I nearly curtsied before catching myself and stumbled awkwardly. I grimaced. How did men show thanks?

He tilted his head to the side. "Been gettin' in Mac's whisky, have ya?"

"No. I—" How could I explain my near curtsy? Damn it all to hell. I was a man now—they could get away with nearly anything. I puffed my chest out like I'd seen the sailors do. "Yes. Don't rat me out."

"I'd be a hypocrite if I did. Mac's got the best liquor on board. I'd be lying if I didn't say I took a sip here and there." He gave his contagious chuckle, one I couldn't resist, and I laughed too. We fell into easy banter as we strolled along the cobblestone path next to the river.

As we stopped outside the transportation office, he faced me. "When I said your hair stuck out like a sore thumb, I meant no offense. It's quite the striking color."

I tugged on a strand hanging from the ponytail and brought it to my front to examine it. "Really? I always thought it was rather obnoxiously bright."

"Not at all." His white teeth shone in contrast to his ochre skin. How did he keep them so nice while living on a ship for months at a time? It seemed like cleanliness wasn't mandatory on board the *Bluebell*. He jutted his head toward the door. "Now, go on and be a good brother."

This time, remembering the situation, I tipped my hat in thanks. No more curtsies.

A half hour later, the bells to the door of the shop jingled as I exited. The setting sun was giving way to more mist, its earthy, grassy musk encompassing me. I had a letter of passage in hand— though Walsh couldn't promise the passenger ship would leave in a few months' time, saying that'd be dependent on the war. It was less than pleasing, but better than no chance at all.

William leaned against the side of the building, waiting for me. He pushed off the wall once he saw me. "Everythin' settled?" I nodded. "Good. Wanna go to one of the dock taverns we saw on the way here for a drink and a meal that ain't the gray mush the ship's cook calls porridge?"

"Aye." I nodded again, despite the unease curling around inside my stomach. No doubt it'd be like the taverns at home where my father spent all his time drinking away his existence.

As the night blackened the sky, we found ourselves a nice spot in a warm tavern full of sailors, all from different ships, including many from the *Bluebell*. A snapping fire was roaring in a wide hearth, and the ale was poured liberally by a few bar wenches. At a far table, Lock mingled with some of the crew. With a large metal mug of ale in hand, he stood, one foot on the ground and one on the bench before him. He gave a loud, deep laugh that I could hear even from across the room and over the chatter. And dammit, if he was utterly handsome before, he was devastating now with his wide smile.

What would it feel like to be the one who made him smile like that?

I shook my head. Now was not the time to get distracted by a privateer, no matter how he looked or the way his Scottish brogue sent shivers down my spine, even when he had been cold and standoffish. I hadn't been around a man like him in a long time—a man with a wild spirit, not bound by the duties of a title or societal expectations.

Gentlemen, like John, were proper and refined. Clipped and, to be honest, often dull. I didn't know Lock well, but dull could never be used to describe him. Insufferable, yes. Dull, no.

I rolled my shoulders back as I exhaled. I needed to focus, keep my head low, and stick to the shadows. Even now, I shouldn't be engaging more than I had to with anyone. I tugged down my hat to cover my face.

A barmaid served black cast-iron pots filled with steaming stew around the tavern. My old self, as a London lady, cringed when I realized there were no plates or utensils being used. A flash of my childhood, scrounging for dirty food scraps off the ground, flitted through my mind. Was I any better than them? The men around me simply tore off pieces of bread to use as forks and dug into the communal stew. I shrugged and followed suit.

After a cup of ale, I allowed myself to take a peek at the men I'd be with for the next several months. Hazy smoke clouds further darkened the dim, flickering lantern light. The aromatic pipe tobacco gave me a headache, but I suspected it was better than the body odor and bad breath I'd smell in its stead. Men drank ale and spirits while they stuffed their faces in quick, uncouth ways. Some didn't even sit while they ate. One man, scarred from pox, used his pinky to dig in his ear and then peered at his finger, sniffed it, and rubbed it on the front of his shift. Another, with a grizzly scar running from his scalp to his chin, sucked his teeth noisily with his tongue until he gave up and used his fingernail instead. There would have been a time I wouldn't have second guessed any of this behavior, but I'd been in polite society for too long now, so I dropped my gaze lest I lose my appetite completely.

I was alone with dozens of men, most armed with pistols and swords. If they found out I was a woman... My entire body shuddered. One heard of certain behaviors from sailors, and I was literally in their den.

But were sailors any different from the miners I grew up around? Surely if I could handle myself around them as a chit, I could handle myself now as a grown woman.

Turned out, my fears were short-lived as someone shouted, "How about a song?" Another man grabbed his fiddle. The instant the bow vibrated across the string, the room reawakened me from my lonesome thoughts, filling me with merriment and laughter.

The men all around me seemed to be familiar with the tune. Some clapped and others pounded their fists or mugs on the table in a steady beat. Plates bounced and ale tipped over, but no one dared to stop the music.

A smaller lad took the floor, and in a surprisingly deep baritone voice, he sang, *"What do you do with your mate full on rum?"*

I nearly fell out of my seat as the whole room shouted, *"Ain't got his senses come mornin' sun!"*

The skinny lad sang a few more lines solo. *"Kiss his wife and bed his sister. Leave him in the sun 'til he blister."*

"Ain't got his senses come mornin' sun!" the sailors called back as they beat their mugs and fists on the table.

All eyes in the room pinned on the lad as he added, *"Leave his sword in water 'til she's rustin'. Strip him down and toss him in the brig."*

Having caught on, I was ready this time. *"Ain't got his senses come mornin' sun!"* I raised my mug in the air and shout-sang the line.

Some men danced a jig and others swung their cups to the beat, beer sloshing over the sides. Despite me wanting to deny my ability of fitting in, I was enjoying myself. Ever since walking up the gangway, I was all too aware of my feminine differences—from the way I walked and sat, to the way I felt obligated to smile at every passerby. Men here slouched, cursed without apologies, and didn't exchange unnecessary pleasantries. Slouching again, despite having believed it'd been beaten out of me by my benefactor, Mistress Beatrice, years ago, was like slipping into a well-worn coat. Or in my case, breeches.

And I didn't entirely mind that.

I'd wanted to fit in with high society so desperately, to have a place to belong, that I had ignored the stuffy, strict expectations it bestowed upon me. From the too-tight stays to what I was allowed to converse about. Had I really never noticed how stifling it had been? Perhaps that was what it was to be a woman.

William elbowed my side, and ale spilled over the lip of my mug. "Watch this."

His gaze flicked to Lock, who now leaned against the wall, arms folded. "If ya ever wanna get a Scotsman to do something," he whispered in my ear, leaning in, "ya'll be wanting to make it a challenge."

He hopped to his feet and slid his sword out of its sheath. For a moment, every muscle in my body clenched. "Mac," he shouted across the room. "Hand me your sword."

Lock pushed off the wall as William paced to him. "If ye suggest what I think ye will, I'll use my saber to impale you."

William grinned, the lantern light reflecting off his skin as he grabbed Lock's proffered sword. He placed the swords in an "X" formation on the ground. "Campbell over there said the Scottish can't sword dance like an Irishman."

Lock arched a black brow, head moving to give him a clear view around the dancing men in front of him, before his gaze landed on a redhead in the corner who suddenly looked like he feared for his life.

Couldn't say I blamed him; might have pissed myself if the giant had pinned me with that stare.

Lock scratched his chin, eyes narrowed. "Ye dinna say?"

William bowed. "Aye. Swear it on me life, Mac. Now get on with it, ya old pipe blower."

I'd seen Highlanders do a sword dance once before, a few years after the fall of Culloden, at a party in London. The only Highlanders who could still wear their plaids and their kilts were those who took an oath of loyalty and served in the British military after the uprising. But what those two men had done compared nothing to this.

Despite his beastly size, Lock was very light on his feet as he pranced and hopped over the blades. His hands waved and floated in an elegant manner as he sashayed over each quadrant. I caught a glimpse of his smile. He was clearly amused, even after his earlier protests. I couldn't help but smile myself. The sight was at such odds with the cold man who'd laid out the details of our arrangement in his cabin mere days prior.

And at such odds with my own feelings toward the man.

In truth, there was something about him that reminded me so much of the type of men I grew up around in Newcastle. The type of men I had long since avoided. And yet... my heartbeat picked up in pace as I watched him hop to each section. I couldn't pull my gaze away from him and his magnetism, even as he almost misstepped and teetered on one booted foot for a blink.

I was wholly engrossed in his dance until the very end, when Lock took a deep bow and the room erupted in cheers. The Irish sailor took him to task as the fiddle changed tempo from a reel to a jig. His feet flew beneath him nearly as elegantly as Lock's had. Lock shouted in Gaelic, clearly some kind of insult, and I was laughing before I could stop myself.

Cheeks sore from smiling so wide, my gaze caught Lock's from afar. I raised my pint in salute. He quirked a brow, but nodded in return. Almost in approval, like he'd doubted my ability to fit in—nay, to *survive*—amongst the sailors. To be sure, I doubted it myself.

Perhaps the next few months wouldn't be so bad. But what did that say about me for thinking so? Cheeks flushed from ale and spicy brown liquor, I was nearly ready to dance a jig myself. Normally I never overindulged in drink, afeard of turning into my late father, but falling into the merriment was all too easy. *Focus.* I was not here to gawk at a dancing man. I fought too hard for a better life. I had no time for such frivolity. No time for a foolish, distracting man. I had my livelihood to secure, after all.

In the midst of the raucous cheer, the door creaked open. Silence rolled through the tavern like a wave. Two men in dark blue frock coats and black bifold hats sauntered through the room, weapons drawn. Royal Navy sailors.

From the corner of my eye, I noticed Lock slink back into the shadows of a far corner just as a third man walked in, his bifold hat trimmed in gold, matching the gold laced buttons and shoulder insignias on his blue coat.

The tavern was dead silent as the man's boots thumped across the floor. Coming to a stop in the middle, the man cleared his throat. "Fine evening for a drink, isn't it, gents?" He removed his hat, placing it in the crook of his arm, and smoothed back the escaped chocolate-brown strands of hair from his low ponytail. From this angle, I couldn't quite make out his pale face in the flame's light. "Such a lovely place, Limerick. So many subjects *loyal* to the Crown… I'll make short of it—we've found ourselves two men short of a full crew. I need two volunteers to join the *HMS Glory*. Meals and uniform provided, and a reliable stipend from His Majesty's Navy. If you're interested, meet with the quartermaster at the end of the dock by midnight. We sail at dawn." He replaced his hat and stomped out of the tavern, the two privates towing after him.

Once they exited, a murmur roared through the tavern. William returned to my side, sinking down on the bench next to me.

My stomach was in knots, but I didn't know why. "What was that all about?"

"The damn *Glory*." William took a long pull from his mug. "Their commodore there don't take no guff and likes to keelhaul dissenters. Probably needs to replace a few. Won't get any from the

Bluebell, no sir. Not with what happened to Mac's family."

I startled. The commodore? I hadn't recognized the man in the tavern as the same one who'd stood in my drawing room, delivering the news that'd dismantled my life; the news that John had died. In my grief, his face had turned into a blur. But now it came back into focus—the man *was* Commodore Cobbe.

A buzz zipped through me as I sat on the edge of the bench. Maybe I didn't have to journey across the ocean after all. Why, all I had to do was follow them, speak to the commodore, and all my problems would be solved. I rose from my seat.

William's brows furrowed below his hat. "Where ya going?"

I peered down, my heart beating. I wouldn't lose this chance to get the proof of death I needed to be able to move on with my life. What was it my brothers would say to me when I followed them around like a little shadow? Oh, yes, now I remembered. "To take a piss."

"Be damn careful they don't see ya and press ya into service. Ya don't want to know what that commodore did to Capt'n's family." William's eyes were wide.

I squinted, examining him and his words. A sudden chill raised the hair on my arms, but I nodded and ducked out of the tavern.

My blood rushed in my ears. But why? It was the commodore, after all this time.

Maybe it was the way William said what he did.

Once I stepped outside, I shook out my limbs, shoving down my nerves. For the love of God. I was an Englishwoman, a Naval officer's wife. All I had to do was walk up to the commodore and ask for a damn letter certifying John's death.

I puffed out air, my breath making a plume of steam mixing with the mist. The creeping fog in the darkness only added to my unease.

I slinked into the shadows, following the three men. People walking past the commodore hopped out of the way. It was fine, I told myself. There was no reason to worry. I should just walk right up to him. Why was I nervous?

I stepped into a pool of light from a lamppost and froze. A woman called out, her cry sharp. My breathing turned shallow, and I peered around, heart pounding like a blacksmith's hammer.

A woman stood in front of the commodore and his men. They were no doubt trying to catch a good rate with a lady of the night. Wait. No. A shimmer of her gown's fabric caught the light. Silk or fine beading. And there was a wink of a pearl in her ear. A dash of powder across her face.

My stomach clenched, every muscle stiff. She was a gentlewoman... and she sounded English.

The commodore's men stood at attention, but he waved them away. One shifted his weight from foot to foot like he was debating disobeying orders, but he about-faced and rushed away with the other.

"Sister." The commodore cocked his head and spoke in lower tones, but I couldn't hear what he was saying.

The woman was shouting, but I could only make out bits and pieces. "My husband... Where is he? What have you done? Children! Mr. Sinclair?" The commodore chuckled, a low, cold sound that put my teeth on edge.

I was frozen to the spot, horrified as the woman stalked forward. She jabbed a finger into the commodore's chest, and in an instant, ringing in my ears drowned out all other sounds while I watched him slide his saber from its sheath and ram it into the woman's stomach.

I couldn't move beyond the heavy breaths ripping from my chest.

I wanted to vomit up my stew and ale. My eyes were wide as the woman slumped into the commodore's arms. The woman's dying gaze met mine. She seemed to mouth *help me...*

My mouth opened, a scream scrambling up my throat, but before it could pierce the night, a large, warm hand clamped over my mouth.

A s I screamed into the hand, a muscular arm hooked around my waist. "Shh, lass," the man whispered in my ear. "Emme, it's me."

Lock.

Relief flooded my body as I sagged against him, and he hauled me back into the shadows. "That's not a man ye should be wanting to follow."

I couldn't tear my gaze away from the gruesome scene. The commodore yanked his saber from the woman, letting her body drop. He squatted over her, rubbing the blood from his sword on her skirt before peering over his shoulder and rising to his feet.

Warm tears rolled down my face. The commodore, he…

What in God's name had I gotten myself into?

As the commodore's form faded into the far distance, eventually disappearing into the foggy night, Lock released me. The moment his warm embrace left my body, chills wrapped around me.

Should I still try to follow him? My *entire* life rested in his hands. I needed the damned letter from him. Perhaps what'd happened had been some kind of fluke. There cou.d be a perfectly reasonable explanation. Witnessing the horrid act didn't change the fact I was left with naught if I didn't get proof of John's death.

"What were ye thinking?" Lock growled out, his arms folded across his chest.

Didn't he realize my life hung in the balance, and that I was at the commodore's mercy?

I balled my hands into fists. "Wha' was I thinkin'? You know I need a guide to the *Glory,* to the commodore!" My voice was sharp and high as I cried out. I was shaken. My Newcastle accent I'd tried hard to contain seeped into my words. Gone was the London gentlelady. A woman was killed right in front of me, and now this man came at me like that? "That's why I came to you! Well, there he is, reet in front of me. Figured I could 'ave my business done sooner than later. You said you wanted to rendezvous with him. Well, there's the *Glory.* Let us go." I crossed my arms over my bound breasts in this silly disguise, mirroring him.

Lock shook his head. "I dinna want to rendezvous with him to have a spot of tea!" His voice raised, and he inched closer, looming over me. "I want revenge." He muttered what I assumed were Gaelic curses. "I plan to kill the man, but I canna have my vengeance until the *Glory* is far from England and her colonies."

"Kill him? He's a bloody commodore of His Majesty's Royal Navy! You're s'posed to take me to him, not kill him. Fine. I'll go after him by meself, then." Lock said nothing, his brows furrowed over his green gaze that was just visible through the hazy fog. I growled and tried to walk around him, but he sidestepped in front of me. "Move out of my way, you Scottish brute!" I needed the commodore alive to get the damned proof of death. And apparently, Lock wanted him dead.

But why?

He shrugged and clumped out of my way. "Verra well then, by all means, take your chances wi' him like the wee lass laying in a pool of her own blood…" My eyes landed on the crumpled body in the distance. He tilted his head to the side, brow arched. "Or ye can trust me and come with me back to the *Bluebell*?"

I gritted my teeth, saying nothing. A muscle in his jaw feathered, like he couldn't believe I wouldn't just outright go with him. He shook his head before he stalked over to the body, squatted down, and riffled through the woman's pockets and purse.

"How dare you, you pirate savage! Her blood hasn't even cooled, and you're tryin' to find some coin."

"Shh, now, before someone comes to check out the noise thinkin' *we're* the ones who killed her." He rose, producing a letter from the folds of her gown, and paced back to me. Unfolding it, he brought it under the lamppost and read it in silence before handing it over. He pinned me with a pointed stare. "Tell me in truth if that's the kind of man ye think ye can do business with?"

I snatched the letter from his hands and brought it under the light. A letter of condolences from the hand of Commodore Cobbe himself, announcing the unfortunate death of his own older brother— and apparently the former commodore—to his now widowed sister-in-law. God's teeth. The woman was the commodore's sister by marriage, and she obviously suspected foul play. And he killed her for it. Good God. My guts twisted into tight knots.

If he had seen me... I shuddered. "Fine. I'll go with you. But I'm going to need to know why you want him dead."

Lock paced in front of the wall of windows whilst I sat on the bed, the fancy French duvet wrapped around me.

"Lord..." I cleared my throat, gathering myself lest my accent make an appearance again. "*Lord,* can you stop pacing?" He pinned me with a stare, head tilted slightly. "You'd think you were the one who had nigh followed a murderer."

"Nay, I just nigh had to save a lass from gettin' herself killed." He ceased pacing and jolted to the foot of the bed like a strike of lightning. "You're ower your head wi' that man. Do ye ken what kind o' danger you were in? Wha' kind o' man ye followed?"

Unable to control myself, I jumped at the harshness of his tone. I wasn't *princess* or whatever damned name he wanted to call me. No, all the playfulness was gone. His eyes narrowed to slits, his lips thin. His Scottish brogue thickened in his anger. But upon seeing my reaction, his features softened into the beauty I'd admired earlier. "I'm sorry, lass. Ye're shaken and I'm..." He sighed, his broad chest heaving. "Can I get ye—" His head whipped around. "Tea? I'm sure there's tea."

"Do I bloody look like tea will help me? I saw a woman stabbed to death!" My eyes shot to the mugs and various bottles on a table behind him. "The brown stuff. I'll take some of that."

"Rum?" The "r" rolled particularly deep as he put his hands on his hips. "I'm sure I can find a bottle of claret. Or something more to your likin'."

I scoffed and peered up at the ceiling above me. "Any liquor is fine." Yanking off my hat, I tossed it on the bed beside me, and smoothed my hair, finding a knotted bird's nest. My cheeks heated at the thought of what it must look like. I untied the leather strip that'd been holding it in a low ponytail and ran my hand through my curls.

Lock's stare seemed to scrutinize my wild mane before landing on my face. "There's fresh water in the basin if ye'd like to wash up." He grinned. "Your soot looks even more unbelievable than before, I'm afeard. I'll pour us a wee dram o' whisky."

Abandoning the warmth of the duvet, I ambled over to the water basin, a small looking glass above it, next to a straight razor and shaving brush. My face, indeed, was smudged with soot and it wasn't as neat and cleverly applied as it had been when we'd left London. Made me think of the story *Cendrillon.* The one about a girl who slept in a fireplace with cinders dirtying her until one day she married a prince. Mistress Beatrice had forced me to read it to learn French. I stole a glance at the man behind me in the mirror. Such things didn't end so happily in real life.

Face scrubbed clean, hair somewhat smoothed with my fingers, I faced the man who needed to tell me all about the damned commodore. He sat, legs perched in front of him at the dining table, drink in one hand. He slid another cup across the table.

I sank down in the chair in front of him, wrapped my hands around the cup, and pinned him with a stare. "Now, you'll be telling me what the hell is going on."

He arched a black brow, his green gaze sparkling in the candlelight. "Will I now? I should be demandin' the same o' ye. Ye were the one who had business wi' the commodore."

I raised the mug to my lips, eyeing him over the rim, and took a large sip. The smoky sweet flavor warmed me as it went down. "Yes. Business that I'll be needing him alive for." I crossed my arms over my chest. "And apparently you want to kill him."

He surveyed me. "Christ, your hair is bright as fire. I hadna noticed before wi' it tucked away under your hat. So bright, wi' all the windows in here, it'll be like a beacon to any ship behind us." He said the words with a smile, but I wanted to grab my hat and place it back on my head.

I regarded the small bubbles on the surface of my drink. "Normally, I'd wear a wig. Or curl it with a hot rod. Pin it up in a high pile on my head. Attempt to tame it." I made the admission without thinking as I stared into my drink, unable to think through my feelings.

Shaking his head, he took a sip of his dram. "So like the English to ruin somethin' that is already perfectly bonnie to begin with."

I exhaled loudly through my nose. "Is that what this is? You want to kill Commodore Cobbe because of some decade old Scottish vendetta? Purely because he's English? Bonnie Prince Charlie is long defeated now. A Stuart will never again sit—"

"Ye did just see the man kill a woman in cold blood, no?" He looked away, gaze setting on the dancing flame of a brass lantern, his tongue pressing against the inside of his cheek. "I ken well what it means to go against the British, Red. And I've no intention to do it again. This is aboot Cobbe, and Cobbe alone."

I swallowed more whisky to garner courage. Because I needed it, being too afraid to learn what I knew would be a horrible truth. "William said... well, he mentioned something about Cobbe and what he did to your family."

"Was there a question there, Red?" He inclined his head, curl across his forehead remaining perfectly in place, and his eyes turned a deeper green, like the color of what I imagined the rolling grassy hills of the Scottish Highlands would look like in spring. "Ye think me a monster? To want to kill a man? I was raised Catholic. I dinna take a life easy. Trust me in that."

Trust him? He was but a stranger. And a privateer at that.

After another hearty pull on my drink, I licked my lips. Why would he want to kill a man so badly that he'd commit a cardinal sin? "I-I just want to know that choosing to stay on the *Bluebell*, instead of chasing after the commodore, was the right decision. I need his help and you want to—"

"I'm a soldier." He let loose a heavy breath. "I've taken many lives. Never for naught. I was in *Blàr Chùil Lodair*—the Battle of Culloden."

My stomach dropped. A bloody battle, and from the stories, many Highlanders—perhaps his family or friends—died. John himself had taken part. He hadn't been directly involved in the battle, but the Royal Navy had delivered supplies to the ground troops. I remembered we'd discussed it once, debating the ethics of war, and he'd used one word that stuck with me—massacre.

He rubbed his lips together. "The numbers were against us, but

I went despite having a wife and a son."

I stiffened. Was his wife Violet—the woman he wrote the letter to? The woman in the portrait?

"Aye. Surprising to ye I had a wife. But when ye had to wait until marriage as a good Catholic lad, I was in a hurry to wed." He laughed, and it was one hell of a sound—deep, reverberating from his chest. Goose flesh broke out down my arms.

But then I realized what he'd said. *Had* a wife. My face blanched.

"Despite wanting to fight for our cause, and the danger our future held, I was selfish and decided to take a wife. I was a lad, and there was this bonnie lassie named Sophie. Love at that age." He puffed out a small laugh. "Love at that age, so dramatic, intense. There'd been some massacres of clans." He stared off behind me as he took another sip of his dram. "Redcoats takin' what they wanted, from who they wanted, when they wanted. I shouldna have married knowing what I planned to do, and the danger I'd put her in.

"There was an English lieutenant. He and I had a history. Before the battle, during the English occupation, he was first stationed in Scotland, where he met Sophie. They fell in love. He asked her for her hand in marriage, but she said no. She told him she could never marry a Protestant or a redcoat. It'd be a betrayal to her family and clan. I think she did love him. In a way. But she was the daughter of a laird—her father would have killed her for kissing a redcoat, let alone marrying one. We dinna take kindly to the English. No offense." He paused.

I shrugged, not caring about anything other than learning more about his story. I leaned on the edge of my seat, waiting for him to continue.

His chiseled features heightened in the shadows and shimmering flames, dimmed only by the haunting storm brewing in his eyes. "Shortly after she denied him, we fell in love and married. In a raid at her family's castle, he saw her—and her heavily pregnant belly. She introduced us. After that day, he had a target on my back.

"During the battle of Culloden, they captured me, and I was one of the few who survived. There were a mere hundred or so o' us survivors who weren't brutally executed by platoons, or removed of clothes and left to the elements to die a slow death. Some were sent on a ship for trial in London where the journey itself was an execution—less than a quarter of them survived the trip after the whippings, beatings, lack of food, and infection by the redcoats. I was sent to Carlisle to await trial with children and women. I didna feel much like a lad then, but during that time I was sure glad they thought of me as one. And o' course, none other than the bloody lieutenant was stationed there. He'd taken it as his personal duty to ensure I received a punishment—one he made worse after I wounded his ego by digging at him every chance I had about Sophie. Foolish. Stupid. But I was a lad unburdened yet by the heaviness and consequences of life." His eyes dug into mine. "That lieutenant is now a commodore."

I bit my bottom lip as I mused over what he'd revealed. "So you wish to… to kill him because of his maltreatment toward you?"

"Maltreatment?" He scoffed. "That's an English way of puttin' it if I ever heard one. The word ye mean is tortured."

"I'm sorry, I didn't mean to say what he did—"

"No, Red. I havena told ye everything. Ye couldna ken the extent." His hand resting on the table balled into a fist. "I wish to kill him for murdering my wife and son. The only family I had left after Culloden. My everything. Without them, I have naught."

"H-he..." I felt the blood drain from my face. Like me, Lock had lost those he loved. Abandoned with nothing. At least I, once I accessed my jointure, would have some semblance of my old life back. But Lock had been shipped away, had committed treason.

He could never go back to Scotland.

"Aye. I willna go into all the details and issues between us." He cleared his throat. "But the Highlands were a dangerous place after the battle. Thanks to the Duke of Cumberland. The redcoats—ye may think 'em admirable and honorable, your kinsmen, but most aren't. Pillaging towns, beating without cause, raping our women..."

A shudder rolled through me. The Duke of Cumberland. Or Butcher Cumberland, as he'd come to be known. Growing up, I'd seen soldiers who were less than honorable—what they'd do to their own countrymen who were doing what they had to because they were hungry—it wasn't a stretch to imagine such a scenario.

And I knew everything he was saying of the commodore had to be true because I'd watched him kill a woman, his sister-in-law, a mere hour ago. But a child too? Lock's wife and son? "I'm sorry for your loss. To lose a spouse, a child..." John's face filled my sight, and I blinked before tears could come.

"Aye." Lock grabbed the bottle off the table and refilled both of our drinks.

"What happened at Carlisle? I mean, obviously you weren't

hanged, and you're wanted by the Crown." My imagination ran wild, picturing him dressed in a kilt, taking on droves of men at a time, or conducting an elusive escape and swimming across the sea…

A lopsided smile splayed across his face. "Sheer luck. I'd been exiled and sentenced to seven years of indentured servitude in the colonies. The ship commissioned to carry us, the *Veteran,* was taken over by a French privateering ship—the *Diamant.* Took us to the French colony Martinique, and they just let us go, refusing to hand us back to the English out o' spite." I arched a brow. He laughed. "No' quite the heroic story you envisioned? Nay, isna, but it was my luckiest day. The captain of the *Diamant* began recruiting men for his own ship."

My mouth was a perfect circle. "So that was how you began privateering? As a corsair on the *Diamant?* "

"Aye." He gave a small smile. "I didna ken what the French were plannin' when they captured the *Veteran.* True to my character, and bein' fluent in French, I ran my mouth to the crew. Captain told me that only a lad as large as I could get away with saying such things, and it was time to put my money where my mouth was. He offered me a job on the spot. I couldna return to Sophie." His lips twisted to the side, his hand tapping on the wood. "But I thought I could've sent her and my son some gold." He took a deep breath. "But they had already… They were gone."

For a moment, I raised my hand to reach out to his resting on the table before catching myself and dropping it to my side. The room fell into a comfortable silence for a few beats. "H-how did the commodore, how did he…"

He rapped his knuckles on the table. "My sister sent a letter saying they were dead by fire in a raid searching for me, and Cobbe was to blame. I dinna ken all the details. Did he ken a babe was inside? I just ken, when I kill him, it'll be well deserved."

I stared openly, perhaps brazenly, examining him. My whole life I wanted someone around who wouldn't abandon me, and here was this man, fealty and loyalty embodied. Even in death, he didn't desert his family. The feelings that thought elicited within me… well, they were something I couldn't quite wrap my mind around yet. "I can't say I disagree."

I watched his thumb stroke the side of his cup. What would it be like to be bestowed with such a commitment?

"Now." His voice turned to cold mist again, sounding like my first day aboard the *Bluebell*. I snapped my gaze up to his scrutinizing face. "What kind o' business do ye have wi' a man the likes of him?"

I splayed my fingers out on the table. "My husband is dead." I peered at the table, tracing the wood's flowing grain with my eyes. "It turns out, the commodore, as well as being a cold-blooded murderer, also doesn't do his paperwork. He personally came to inform me of my husband's death when he was in London, but he didn't register it with the Naval Board or turn in any muster roll that Pilkington could find." My problems suddenly seemed inconsequential, materialistic, compared to Lock's. But there was one substantial difference— he was a man, and I was a woman. He had options for work and could earn enough to buy land for himself, even if he was exiled. I couldn't, as dictated by the law, ever purchase land. I could only own what was in John's will, gained by my jointure. "I can't have access to my jointure until I obtain proof of his death." I rubbed my lips together. "I know such a thing may sound vapid to you in light of your history with Cobbe, but I have nothing left. No way to live without the allotment written in my marriage contract. I have no family who'd take me in or..." I shook my head. "I've been completely abandoned, and his proof of death is the only option left for me to survive. I need Commodore Cobbe to write a letter declaring John's death."

I'd obtain it, even though now the thought of approaching the commodore, talking to him, made a tightness wrap around my throat and chest as if a snake coiled around me. I was absolutely terrified to go near that man.

Lock palmed the back of his hair, his tricep stretching his shirt so tight I thought it might rip. "I understand. As a woman, you dinna have many options." He tapped his thumb on his cup. "I thought the worst o' ye when I'd learnt you needed to meet with him. Tha' somehow ye were as bad as him."

"I understand." I downed the rest of my drink in one gulp. "But that leads me to our problem—you want him dead, and I need him alive. But after what he did to his sister-in-law. To your wife. I don't know how I could approach the man. What if I'm next?"

"Dinna fash yourself, Red." His full lips split into a wide smile. It was the first time he truly smiled at me. My stomach flipped. "I'm an honorable man, and I'm duty bound to bring ye to Cobbe. And I'll see ye through it. I'll no' leave ye alone in the clutches o' a murderer. Did you ye already book passage back from the Indies?"

"Yes. From Jamaica." My head tilted to the side.

He nodded, his fingers tapping his chin. "Good. I can offer ye protection and, in exchange, ye can help me kill him. Then we can bring ye to Jamaica, and we can go our separate ways, both of us havin' what we want."

My mouth dropped open. "You want me to help you kill the man?"

"Nay. But I want ye to give me a good reason to approach him without a whole garrison following in his wake. Your letter 'tis a good reason. We can meet him together." His gaze turned distant, and he took another sip of his dram. "It'll take some scheming, but I see no reason why ye canna get what ye need *before* I kill him."

"Go to him together?" My heartbeat picked up in pace, and I didn't know why.

"Aye, Red." He winked. "We're in this together now, if ye accept."

I gulped more whisky, not really tasting it. "Well, I'm not in a hurry to run up to him and very well end up his next victim."

He grinned; his mouth curled up lopsided, higher on his left side of his face than his right, and it was utterly dashing. "Then we have ourselves a deal."

5

Grunting and groaning woke me up with a start, my eyes snapping open.

My gaze found the cause of the infernal sound—a Scotsman too long and too wide for the small cot he was sleeping on. I froze, not daring to move around in the large bed. His feet hung off the end, and his shoulders splayed out wider than the whole cot. Lying on his stomach, he stretched and groaned some more, rambling in Gaelic. And for the love of God… his biceps were larger than my thighs. He sat up, revealing his bare back to me, and… and I hadn't realized the human back was made of so many intricate muscles.

He stretched his neck each way whilst I stayed perfectly still in bed, muscles as stiff as a day-old dead church mouse. I let my eyes wander, finding evidence of wars and imprisonment on his skin. Healed over marks and scars—some white and fading, others pink like he'd received them not too long ago. Demands almost leapt out of my throat, begging he tell me the stories of each and every mark. He rose from the cot and faced my direction as he stretched some more. The muscles of his chest and abdomen were chiseled in a manner reminiscent of Greek statues. In the rainbow glow of morning light streaming through the windows, every curve and mound was highlighted in gold.

I slammed my eyes shut lest he catch me spying. After what sounded like bare feet slapping on wood, I opened one eye, taking just a peek. He was pouring a ladle of water into a mug. I saw him in a different light now, not just because of his physical appeal, but standing here, I could almost see him dressed like the Highlanders in Scotland—regal, clad in plaids and kilts, fighting for his family, his country.

It was not an unpleasant sight.

Sadly, he slipped his shift on after drinking some water. I watched every mound of muscle disappear under the hem. Heat crept up from my chest and neck to my face.

The door slammed open and William rushed in. "Mac—" He stopped. "Sorry, I didn't think you'd be barely goin' at this hour."

Shite. My face. I quickly rolled to the other side of the bed.

"Aye. Have a wee bit o' whisky head this morn'." Bottles clinked for a second. "A wee sip of hair of the dog."

"Ya gave the cabin boy your bed?" William's voice sounded closer. I stiffened.

Lock cleared his throat. "Aye. Lost a bet."

There was a pause for a moment. "Righ'. Anyway, came here lookin' for the lad. Wanted to see if you wanted the other cabin boy, Miller, to show him the ropes. Shadow him a bit."

"That won't be necessary; Clark can read. I'll have him helping wi' recording inventory stores and the like. More clerical, if ye will,"

Lock said. I tried to keep my breathing steady, as if I was sleeping.

"Well, let us wake the lad." William's feet stomped closer. "I'll show him to the galley at least to fetch ya some food."

I knew it would be odd if I didn't bring him food!

"Dinna fash. Let the lad sleep. I think last night was the first time he partook in tavern festivities. Overindulged a wee bit. Let him sleep a little longer." Silence lingered for a moment. I clenched the blanket in my hands, holding myself back from flipping over to see their expressions. "I'll show him myself. We can meet at the quarterdeck in half an hour."

"As you wish, Capt'n."

Once the door clicked shut, I flipped on my back and sat up, smoothing my hair down. Lock's gaze was set on the closed door before he snapped his eyes to me. "The princess rises." I narrowed my eyes at him, and he smirked. "Ye'll be needin' more soot, and then I'll show ye to the kitchen."

I sat up straighter. "The kitchen? As in, out of this room?"

He peered in each direction. "I dinna see a galley in here, Red."

I gnawed on my cheek. "But what about what you had said? 'It's a long journey to the Indies and ye're too bonnie?'" I stood and crossed to the table and poured myself a cup of water.

Amusement shimmered in his eyes. "I dinna recall sayin' exactly that. But, aye, 'tis a long journey. And I canna pretend tha' some of these men dinna have a sordid past. Ye dinna turn to privateering instead of the Royal Navy unless ye must. But I may have embellished a wee bit. Ye'll be fine if ye stick by my side—a crew listens to their captain. But ye should remain here most times.

Besides, there'll be the readin' I need ye to do. Verra important."

I swallowed the contents of my cup in one gulp and slammed it down on the table with a thud. "Ah, yes. The readin'. Important, as you say." I gnawed on my bottom lip while he pulled his knee-high boots on over his tan breeches. "Speaking of, you didn't get my report yesterday."

He paced to the looking-glass over the washbasin, angling his head in the mirror before dipping his shaving brush into the water and smearing it over the cake of soap next to it. He coated his whole chin and neck in white cream and lifted the straight-edge blade to his face, pulling his skin taut. "Ah, aye. We were busy though, no? Dinna worrit." He slid the blade down his cheek, a grazing noise accompanying the motion. "Besides, wi' the new information, we have some plotting to do."

My jaw clenched. "Oh, but it was most intriguing. I will give you the full, detailed report tonight. I'm afraid that this report did get quite winded. You should come before the nightly festivities on deck." He paused shaving, rotating his head toward me with eyebrows raised. I folded my arms across my chest. "Wouldn't want you to miss any details after you've had a few pulls from your wineskin. You did say it was 'verra important.'"

He licked his lips and faced the mirror again, his expression unreadable. "Was that supposed to be a Scottish accent, princess?" He wiped his blade clean, sideways smile in place, before dragging another line down his face. He met my gaze in the mirror. "Aye, I did say it was important. I'll wait on the edge of my seat all day long awaitin' your full report." Dammit. Now I'd have to write a report.

I thought he'd have come clean. "Don your hat, we'll grab some parritch."

I held back a gag. "Lovely, more mush."

He arched a brow as he finished up shaving the remainder of his neck. "I'm sure ship food is a far cry from the fine roasts and seafoods ye surely grew up on. But it could be worse."

I laughed, unable to contain myself. Fine roasts? I was lucky if I scrounged up enough for a soup made of roots. I nearly said so, but I bit my tongue. He needn't know.

He must have mistaken my laughter as condescension, because he added, "I shoulda let ye follow Cobbe."

The smile disappeared from my face, my eyes widening. My breath hitched as I relived the moment the woman mouthed *help me,* the light fading from her eyes until they drooped, her gaze staring off.

"Oh, hell's bells." He plopped the razor next to the water basin and rushed over to me, eyes scouring my face. "I'm sorry, Red. 'Twas a bad jest."

"No, I'm—" I shook my head and crossed to the mirror. "I'm still in shock, that's all. I keep seeing the woman's face."

What had I gotten myself into?

What had seemed to be a simple mission to find the *Glory* and the commodore now had turned into a dangerous game of chase and possible treason. I was essentially aiding a pirate to murder a commodore of His Majesty's Royal Navy.

But I needed John's confirmation of death, and Commodore Cobbe *did* kill a woman in cold blood. So was it really the worst thing if Lock killed him after? As long as it was *after.* Now, here I was on a ship, masquerading as a man for that much longer, living in filth and grime and with strange men.

Sharing a cabin with a highlander turned privateer who looked like Adonis himself.

Lord, help me.

6

Privateering.

In these last few weeks, I'd learned that life on a ship was both faster and slower than I expected.

On one hand, it seemed like work on the ship was endless. There was always a crewmember doing some type of work. On the other hand, floating in the sea, the days seemed long and slow when there was no immediate plan.

I did stay in the captain's cabin the majority of the time, unless I was glued to Lock's side. I thought we had reached a mutual respect, or at least an understanding. But between the too close living quarters, the one bed we continued to fight over, and a secret plan between just the two of us that tended to leave us both isolated—me from everyone, and him from his brothers at sea—the tension between us had risen.

He was an arse. I absolutely despised him.

Well, not absolutely. Just sometimes. Until he smiled at me. Or I remembered the vulnerability that shone in his eyes the night he told me about his wife and son and the way his words had felt more intimate than the idea of sharing a cabin with him ever had.

Additionally, there were, to note, some moments when he'd show an ounce of civility, from bringing me licorice root to chew when we were on particularly rocky waters to pouring me a dram. Sea life was beautiful but sickening. He told me I'd get used to the rocking, and that land would be the cause of my nausea soon enough, but that had yet to come to fruition. If I was dizzy from whisky, it at least drowned out the spins from the sea. Although I was afraid of relying on the booze too much to aid me, lest I turn into someone like my father.

As difficult as it was to live so closely with someone, when I dared to go to the main deck, sea life did offer a reprieve from boredom. On the main deck, I'd find, at last, what I had expected of a pirate crew. Men maneuvered ropes and masts and sails, crewmen swept and mopped the floor, a carpenter repaired a bit of broken railing. At the helm I'd often find Lock, not a helmsman, William beside him, always engaged in what seemed like friendly conversations, if their smiles were any indication.

And I felt a peacefulness when I'd press my hands on the railing, and peer out to the sparkling blue sea while the cold wind would chap my face; the salty brine and clear air were refreshing.

But fear had me heading back to my hidey-hole in the captain's cabin sooner than later, despite the damned boy's costume I wore. It'd gotten so monotonous that some days I'd actually taken to reading the captain's logs again.

Truth be told, in the past week, there were days I'd been so bored and isolated that I may have taken to doing or saying things that I knew would irritate Lock *on purpose* just so we'd have a row, and I'd have something other than boredom to focus on—anger. And I was beginning to think he was avoiding me today.

So, smearing my bread across a pile of mush and having a wee dram earlier than usual, I read yet another log.

The door to the cabin opened, and I was surprised to see William walking in instead of Lock. His eyes flashed around the room. "Where's Capt'n? We need one more for a game of cards."

I sighed and rubbed my eyes. "He said something about checking the inventory of the water casks in the cargo hold."

His brows crinkled. "Odd. He did that yesterday." The Scottish arse. He *was* avoiding me. "Well, no worries. C'mon, lad."

I snapped my gaze to William's face. "W-what?"

He chuckled. "I told ya, we need one more."

I clutched the hem of my shift, wringing it between my hands. "I cannot. I'm busy."

"Busy?" William bent his head over the navigation table. "Reading leftover logs? What would ya be doin' that for? Useless information, them there logs."

I leaned back in the chair. "It's not normally done, then?"

He crossed his arms as his eyes swept over the leather-bound journal before me. "Nay."

I clenched my hands. "Oh, the bloody bastard."

His brow arched. "What?"

"Never mind." I chewed on my thumbnail.

"Let us go before they start the game without us." He nodded toward the door.

"I—"

"Lad, I am *still* the quartermaster." He said the words firmly, but a quick smile came after. "Besides, it's not healthy to waste away in a cabin all day. Let's get on with it."

My palms were sweaty as we headed away from the captain's cabin, navigating around ropes and rigging into the dim, tobacco-hazed lantern light in the crew's quarters. Releasing a steadying slow breath, yanking my hat low, I faced the two men seated around a barrel.

William sank onto a crate and shuffled a deck of cards, clearly worn and faded even in this light, but they clicked together like a fresh deck.

"Oh good. We needed one more. Sit, boy," one sailor ordered as he talked around the tobacco pipe in his mouth.

My lips flattened. Typically, in social situations, I was quick to offer a smile, to appease. But men didn't do that, so I didn't wipe the unpleasant look from my face as I sat on an overturned bucket with a bag of grain as a cushion.

A second sailor sipped on liquor from a wooden cup. I recognized him. The passed-out man on deck with the putrid stench. What had William called him? Jacques. Well, I was glad he had cleaned up—either that or I'd become accustomed to all the smells on board. The third man was dressed like many others here—once-white shift, worn with overuse and permanently tinted yellow, breeches with patches and well-used leather boots, and a tricorn hat that'd been shaped to his head—what made him stand out from the others was his clean-shaven appearance, short black hair, and the *lack* of dirt and grime all over him.

His black-brown eyes, further darkened by the shadow of his hat, noticed me staring. "I'm Antonio. The surgeon." He was a Spaniard, if I was reading his accent correctly.

"John." I nodded in greeting.

He scrutinized me, looking too intensely. I clenched my fingers, so I didn't smooth my hair or fidget under his stare. At last, he looked away, lighting his own pipe, seeming to swish the smoke around in his mouth before exhaling a large, aromatic gray cloud.

William dealt the hand-painted cards. Red paint faded and chipped from parts of the pattern on the back, but they still held an undeniable beauty. "Are ya familiar with Piquet?"

"*Piquet*," Jacques corrected, saying it with an "ay" sound at the end instead of pronouncing the "t" as William did.

William grumbled a response.

I fought the smile curling my lips upward at their exchange. "Of course."

"Good, then I won't feel bad takin' all your money when I win." William's eyes sparkled in the lantern, grin wide, as he clenched an unlit pipe between his teeth.

Antonio snatched his cards from the makeshift barrel-turned-table. "You mean when I win. And don't worry, lad, we can't actually play for money—it's against ship rules."

"Nay, but we can play for work duties." William smiled.

"Or women." Antonio winked, and I gulped.

Jacques whistled. "Clearly you've forgotten who won last time, *crétins*."

Despite my concerns of closely associating with anyone on this ship, I fell into their easy banter and became engrossed in the card game. They were quick to laugh and insult one another. It was quite nice to interact with men while I was dressed as one.

If I were to be here as a lady, their conversation would be clipped and tight. They wouldn't include me in their jokes and secrets. And most of all, they'd be quick to shut down their vulgar comments. Little did most gentlemen know, I'd grown up around miners who often forgot I was there—my tolerance for vulgarity was higher than the average lady's.

But seeing how Antonio elbowed me in my stomach, talking about what he'd like to do to the "pretty queen's mouth," no one was going to correct their language around me.

As off-putting as some—most—of their comments should be, I couldn't hold back my laughter. I'd had these thoughts, maybe said lighter versions of some of these things to other women while playing cards, but I'd never been openly brazen. Such vulgarity was beaten out of me years ago by Mistress Beatrice. I had an ingrained instinct to avoid such words nowadays. That it could be nullified with a card game and a little liquor was perhaps telling of my character. I didn't care to admit it, but a title or a genteel façade did not erase a person's nature. I quite liked their conversation despite the warmth creeping up my neck and cheeks at their more *colorful* details. But perhaps my blush had to do with the rum I'd been drinking.

If only I could add to their conversation without looking like a fool. But worry over potential embarrassment stopped me. That and the glint of their swords and pistols in the light from the flames. One wrong move, and the weapons the sailors always seemed to carry could end up against my throat. That was how polite society had always made it seem like privateers acted. I didn't know much about weapons, but I did grow up around men. I could hold my own if needed. But I should like to learn more first. If it came to that.

"How about ya, lad?" Antonio elbowed me again. "Ya ever laid with a lass?"

Not with a *woman.* "Umm, well…"

William stared at me from across the barrel, one corner of his lips upturned. "Yes, John. Have ya laid with a *woman?*" I narrowed my eyes at him. The way he had said *woman.*

"Do not worry, we can teach you all the ways to please one," Jacques added.

"And how to keep your mind occupied so ya don't explode in seconds," Antonio added, eliciting roars of laughter.

My gaze stayed on William. Even with the rum, and in the stuffy crew's quarters cloistered in the warmth of candlelight, chills washed over me. He at last broke eye contact and laughed. "Mac will be wondering where ya be. Let us go before I earn ya a lashing." He rose from the table amongst protests from the other two. "Don't worry about it, Clark. Ya'll miss naught. Antonio and Jacques don't know nothin' on how to please a woman. Any tips from them would make a lass run in the opposite direction."

I followed after William, heart pounding, feet stumbling.

"Damn it all to hell, ya're piss drunk. Mac'll be blaming me for that." He slapped me on my shoulders. "C'mon. I'll make sure ya make it back to the captain's cabin without fallin' overboard." I nodded. "Careful on the ladder."

After we reached the next level, he gave me a big smile. "Ya seemed like ya enjoyed yourself."

I tiptoed cautiously over the slippery deck planks, wary. "I did." Despite myself.

"I hadn't seen much of ya since the tavern in Limerick. And when I saw you staring out blankly this morn', thought ya'd gone mad." He elbowed me in the side.

"I did," I repeated.

He laughed. I'd forgotten what a good sound his laugh was, how infectious. I joined in before I stubbed my boot on an uneven floorboard, falling on my arse.

And then we both laughed harder.

"Christ, Clark." He offered me a warm hand, helped me to my feet, and steered me to the door to Lock's cabin. "I remember my first trip on the *Bluebell*. I felt so alone, isolated... yet could never get a moment's peace to myself."

I scoffed. "I hear that."

"Well, I guess what I'm saying is, if ya need someone to talk to, I've got two perfectly good ears." His smile was wide and bright, even in the dim corridor.

I met his eye, unafraid of him realizing I was a woman at that moment. Perhaps polite society had been wrong about privateers. I wanted to grasp the friendship he'd extended. I nodded. "Thank you. Truly."

Opening the door to the cabin, the uneven wood of the doorframe stuck, so I jammed my shoulder into it, falling into the cabin with gusto. Lock, long legs extended in front of him, reading, hopped up from *my* bed, his book plopping down on a pillow. I scrutinized the cover and giggled to myself. He was reading *Don Quixote.*

He strode over and squatted beside me before offering a hand. "Here, let me—"

I pushed his hand away. "I am perfectly capable of getting up myself."

He smirked. "Verra well, then." I rose and brushed dirt off my breeches. "Christ, I hate to sound like my da, but ye smell like a distillery." He folded his arms across his chest. "Where were ye? I thought I warned ye—"

"Oh, shut it. You're not my *da,* so I very well can do what I please." I stumbled over to the dining table and grabbed a bottle and sniffed it. My nose crinkled at the potent smell. "I am perfectly fine."

His gaze narrowed, and he scrubbed his hands over his face. "This time. But ye may no' be so lucky the next time. So, there'll be no next time."

I scoffed. "If you think you can keep me holed up in here like some kind of prisoner—" I inched in close to him and poked him in the chest. "Oh, you've got another thing coming, you pirate savage!"

He peered down at the finger I jammed into his chest and arched a brow. "If I'd kent I'd go my whole life being called a Scottish savage to a pirate savage by the stuck-up English, I'd no' have worked so hard studying Latin and French with my tutors."

I barked a dry laugh. My body bobbed back and forth, swaying more than the damned ship. "You do so enjoy the sound of your own voice, don't you?"

He inched in closer to me, but I refused to step back. I planted my feet wide apart and peered up at him. From this angle, his jaw was sharp and chiseled, and hair had already grown back in a shadow around his full lips. The bloody alcohol made my whole body feel flushed.

His head tilted ever so slightly toward me, bringing us that much closer. "Well, I can say I do prefer my voice to the incessant English droning of a lass who fancies herself a princess." He put his hand on his chest, blinking his eyes fast. *"Bloody pirate savage."* He said the words in a feminine voice with a poor attempt at an English accent.

"Was that supposed to be me?" I gritted my teeth.

"I thought it was rather obvious." His chest puffed out further. My hands balled into fists as he shook his head. "Go to bed, lass, before ye make a fool of yourself. You're drunk."

"And I do not fancy myself a princess. You don't even know me. Oh, I ought to—"

"What? Impale me wi' your tiny, wee fists?" He laughed. "Bed. Now."

"For the record, I have an excellent left hook, and I know exactly where to kick to disable a man." I tripped over my feet but caught myself on the bed. "All you men hold your pricks on a crystal pedestal, but they're sensitive little things, aren't they?"

Red rose to his cheeks. "I've never heard a lady talk like ye before. Ye spend one night with sailors and your sense of propriety is forgone. What about your reputation?"

"Reputation? I believe that was lost, along with any semblance of hygiene, when this ship set sail." I rose back to my feet. The room spun in a blurry circle. "New rule. I do what I want when I—"

"When ye what, Red?"

I slapped my hand over my mouth and ran to the privy to empty the contents of my stomach into the chamber pot. His raucous laughter rumbled from the other side of the door.

Pirate savage!

7

For the last couple of days, I'd kept myself locked away in the cabin. Turned out I wasn't so brave when sober. But it quickly grew tiresome.

So, I'd ventured out again to the main deck.

Lock caught sight of me and waved me over. He stood at the helm with William at his side. "There ye are, Red."

William arched a brow. "Red, is it?" He grinned widely. "We missed ya at cards last night."

I smiled back. "I've barely recovered from the last round."

Lock ran his hands through his waves. "Aye, and ye canna throw your duties to the wayside again. 'Twould be best to avoid cards again."

I placed my hands on my hips. "Ahh, yes. My 'verra important' duties of reading the logs." Lock met my gaze, and we stared at each other in silence.

William raised his hands in surrender, watching us. "I'm gonna grab something to eat."

Triumph swelled in my chest when Lock looked away first. He

licked his lips. "Well, while you're here, before ye get to readin', I wanted to let ye know that William and I mapped out some stops we think the *Glory* will sail to first once she makes it across the Atlantic. English ports are the most likely, and maybe allies. And I decided on a plan. I'll have ye stay here while William and I go to—"

"You bastard!" I stomped my foot.

"And what have I done this time to offend ye? It's been three days since ye last called me a pirate savage, seemed we were aboot due."

I shook my head. "You made plans *for* me?"

"Aye, ye're still wanting a letter from the commodore for your husband's proof of death, no?" His brows drew together.

"Yes. You know I need it. My life, my livelihood, depends on it." I clenched my jaw.

He waved his hand in front of him. "Then I dinna ken the problem."

"You made plans that affect me, my entire life, *without* me!" I growled from behind my teeth. "Did it cross your thick skull, at least once, that I might have anything to say or to add?" I squeezed the hem of my shift in my hands. "But no, instead, you have me doin' mindless busy work readin' captain's logs." I nodded at his grimace. "Oh yes, I know all about your conniving plan, thinkin' you could keep me occupied with utter nonsense. I won't claim to be a grand philosopher, but I am smart. I can be of use." I planted my heels into the deck. "And when it comes to my life, I *will* have a say."

His face was paler than usual, lips in a thin line, as he stood in stunned silence. I panted, heated, despite the freezing wind snapping around us. I turned around, stomping away, headed back to the captain's quarters.

I sank down into the chair at the navigation table and rubbed my hands down my face and throat, sighing.

"Dammit," I shouted to the empty room. I hated that I needed Commodore Cobbe for John's proof of death, and I hated that I needed the damned Scotsman even more.

He wanted his vengeance, and I understood. I really did. But could I trust him to allow me time to get the letter from Cobbe that I needed? The man was brash. If it came to it, could he contain himself?

I *needed* to know his plan before he went off, cannons blazing. If he thought I was going to stay locked up and out of the loop, oh, he had another thing coming.

I tapped my fingers on the desk. I should take control completely and come up with a plan myself for when we caught up with Cobbe. I couldn't very well leave my life in Lock's hands.

But what reason would I, a random widow, have to come with Lock to meet the commodore? Lock, a wanted man? He'd surely recognize Lock if their history was as long and messy as Lock had said. And if Cobbe had continued hunting him years after Culloden, going so far as killing his wife and child... To be sure, the commodore *would* recognize him.

And I couldn't tell Cobbe I wanted Lock there for protection, because why would an English woman fear an honorable commodore? Unless she had seen him murder a woman in Limerick. I shivered. He would find that suspect. There was always the option to go without Lock, abandoning his help, when we met up with the *Glory*, but truth be told, I didn't want to after seeing what Cobbe had done. His ruthless killin' would haunt my dreams until I died. I couldn't be alone with that man.

"Red." I snapped my gaze to Lock. I hadn't even heard him come in. He peered at the ground for a moment before he returned his eyes to my face, widened his stance, and placed his hands on his hips. "You're right. I should have consulted ye when we began planning. It was an oversight. I'm sorry. We shall begin making plans in the morning." His chest deflated. "Together."

I took a shaky inhale, my face sore between my eyebrows from keeping 'em furrowed for so long, and nodded. "Thank you."

He paced over to my side of the navigation table and leaned against it. "Additionally, it appears that we dinna need the logs to be read anymore. Instead, I'd like ye to help me wi' keepin' the inventory stores up to date." I arched a brow and pursed my lips. "It is *actually* important. The water supplies and all could be the difference between life and death for the crew."

I sat up straighter and adjusted my shift. "And don't forget about the whisky rations. We'll have to ensure we have an adequate supply so the captain's mood doesn't sour."

He smiled. His glorious, wide smile that made his green eyes sparkle. "Aye. Verra important."

8

K eeping inventory had been an olive branch.

And for the first time in years, I felt useful. Although, recording inventory was as bland as reading about weather patterns and well-being checks of past crews. The ramblings of the mad men hunting a secret island with treasure may have been more entertaining than counting and counting and counting again.

But people relied on accurate stores of food and water, and I wanted to do a good job of it. Plus, it meant spending time somewhere other than the cabin, albeit down in the dark hull.

I'd spent all morning there, the work making the day rush by. But back in my hidey-hole of a cabin, I spent the last couple hours making calculations. Squinting at the small numbers on the ledger left my eyes worn out and tired. I blinked a few times, weary, and I was seeing double. As I rubbed my eyes with my palms, a knock came at the door.

My muscles tensed. The only people who regularly came were Lock and William, and neither tended to knock. I exhaled. "Who is it?"

"It's me. William," he shouted through the door.

"Well, come in. What are you waiting for?" I rose and strode toward the door. He entered, shutting it behind him. "You never knock."

"I didn't see where Mac was, so I thought he was in here." He paced to the dining table and picked up various bottles, swirling some, uncorking and sniffing others before he settled on one and poured himself a mug.

"So what if he was in here? You still never knock." I shot out my hand, and he gave me a wry smile before handing me the cup and pouring yet another for himself.

"To be safe, in case ya two were…" He rubbed his lips together.

"What would you think we were doing in here?"

He chuckled under his breath, shaking his head, before he looked away and took a big gulp of his drink. "Never mind, *Red*." My face slackened, my mouth agape. "Right, well, I came in here because it's gettin' rough up top. A storm is brewing, and the ship will be rocking tonight."

My eyes flicked to the wall of windows. Iron-gray clouds loomed in the distance, and a slash of bright-white lightning sliced through them. I wrapped my waistcoat tighter around me, my nausea doubling after regarding the scenery. "A storm?"

"Don't worry. They can be rough, but the *Bluebell* is strong. She don't take no guff from a storm. She's a good ship." He took another sip from his cup, sitting so casually whilst my heart wanted to leap from my chest.

"Shouldn't we prepare or be doing somethin'?" I rose, running my hand over my hat, patting my chest and sides, and paced the room.

"We've hampered down all we could to keep things from flying. Now we wait." He scratched his chin. "Unfortunately, it'll slow our progress and push us off course, most like."

"Off course?" I stopped pacing. "So, we won't be following behind the *Glory?*"

He shrugged. "The *Glory* left a half day earlier than us, but they're larger and slower. If we hit the storm, they'll probably be hit too. We'll all be blown the same direction."

Well, at least I'd not have to worry about losing track of Cobbe. Though Lock and I still hadn't come up with a plan on how I'd get the letter from him, and how he'd get his revenge, I didn't want to lose him in the middle of the bloody Atlantic.

The ship jolted suddenly, a loud groaning sound rolling through the timbers. I toppled against the dining table.

"What was that?" I shouted without meaning to.

Williams's eyes widened, and he slammed back the rest of his drink. "Just a large wave and a loose cannon rolling on the gun deck. I best go double check everything is tied down right." Rising, he crossed to me and placed a hand on my shoulder. "We'll fare all right. Don't worry. But do make sure you blow out all the lit candles and unmounted lanterns except for one you keep close to you. Fire is the biggest danger on a ship, and all it takes it one candle falling over in a storm."

"W-what happens if there's a fire?" Gripping the edge of the table, I held my breath as I waited for a response.

"Well, the perk of sleepin' here is there's a jolly boat right above ya on the main deck. Jump in before the ship burns. Ya can release the davit crane from inside the boat. Just be careful if ya do it from there. It free falls." He clicked his tongue.

I blanched and watched him leave before I ran to the wall of windows. The waves were crashing around us higher than I'd ever seen them. I braced myself as the ship's stern rose high, high, and higher before smacking back down. The water basin slid across the table it sat on.

I ran and began blowing out each candle around me. The sky was dark, but it wasn't yet night, so I could mostly see, but the cabin immediately filled with shadows.

I sank down on the bed just as a loud rumble of thunder roared, followed by a bright bolt of lightning. I jumped back up, shaken. It was just thunder. As if the sky had heard my thoughts, rain started pelting against the windows.

I sat back down, holding the covers between my clenched, white-knuckled fingers. I tried not to peer out the windows, because watching the ship rise and drop from my angle caused my stomach to swirl even more with nausea.

I'd need to keep myself distracted. I scrubbed my face, hands, and nails clean. Even managed to comb through my hair's knotted curls before retying it and replacing my hat. Despite the breeches, I looked more like myself again.

Once sufficiently clean, I sighed, searching for something else to do. I'd already snooped through everything, and there'd be no way I could focus on reading something in these shadows—even Lock's *Don Quixote*.

I gave up and bit my thumbnail and started humming a song my brothers used to sing to me when I was a bairn. Good. Singing was good. Soon I started singing the shanty from the tavern in Limerick. *"What do you do with your mate full on rum? Ain't got his senses come mornin' sun!"*

Another rumble of thunder followed by a flash of lightning illuminated the cabin. *"Leave him..."* Something heavy rolled across the deck above me as the ship swayed. *"Leave him in the sun 'til he blister."*

I fell into a pile on the floor and tucked my knees tight to my chest and kept singing as howling winds shook the windows and the tumultuous waters rocked the ship to and fro. I'd always thought of the *Bluebell* as decently sized, but in the ocean in the middle of a storm, it was far too small for my comfort. We could be swallowed whole by an enormous wave, never to be seen again, like we never existed.

The entire cabin was freezing, and without any lanterns, darkness was quickly overtaking the remaining light. I swallowed and found a tinderbox to light one lantern. I'd hold it close to me—I needed light. My hands trembled, cold and stiff, and I fumbled a few times before the lantern was ablaze.

I sat back on the ground in a little ball, clutching the lantern tightly despite the heat of the glass and brass burning the pads of my fingers, refusing to let the damned thing go and have it possibly fall over.

Oh God, I was going to die. There was no way a ship could withstand a storm like this. I'd gone so far, only to die in a bloody storm in the middle of the Atlantic. My breathing turned erratic. If the cold waters didn't get me, a shark or starvation would. I had no idea where I was. Was there land nearby I could swim to?

No. I mustn't think like that. I focused on the song again.

"What do you do with your mate full—" Lightning lit up the whole cabin for a few seconds as my trunk started to slide across the wooden planks, having never been buckled down like most of the furniture in here. I jerked, bringing the lantern even closer to me, my hands searing. *"K-kiss his wife and bed his sister."*

"Christ, Red." Lock rushed over to where I huddled on the floor.

I didn't look at him, frozen in place, afraid to do anything but sing the damned song between pants. *"Ain't got his senses come mornin' sun."*

"Red. Your fingers." He tried to pry the lantern from my hands, but I couldn't let it go. "Red... Emme!"

The sound of my real name snapped me out of my trance. I looked at him, a cloud of air coming from my open mouth, as he grabbed the lantern from my hands, searing pain pricking my fingers.

He placed it on the ground beside him. "Ye're shivering."

I shook my head too fast, too many times. "No. No... Y-you can't leave the lantern there, it'll tip over and spill a trail of oil, and it'll catch fire and burn the whole ship, and—"

"Dinna worrit." He grabbed the lantern and attached it to a mount on a beam, securing it in place. "There."

I nodded. My fingers were numb and tingly from the cold or the flames, I didn't know. A large shiver rolled through me.

"Ye're freezing. Climb into bed." He offered me a hand. I took it, and he curled his fingers around mine, calluses rubbing against my skin. His hand seemed to engulf mine. It was warm, steady, and eased some of my trembling. Tugging, he helped me up to my feet.

He didn't let go as I walked in a daze to the bed. Once I sat on the edge, he released my hand. I bent down, limbs jerking, to remove my boots. My numb hands, shaking with fear, couldn't grab the edge of the cuff to pull them down. After a few failed attempts, Lock came before me and sank to his knees. My eyes widened when I realized what he was doing as he hooked his thumb over the cuff of my boot and slid it off before moving to the next foot. His warm palm embraced my calf as he tugged my right boot down, the stubborn cuff getting stuck at my ankle for a moment. Once free, he tossed the boot aside, one hand still holding my calf.

Kneeling before me, my leg in his hand, he peered up with that intense green gaze of his. "There ye go, Red."

Our eyes locked, my heart pounding fast before another roar of thunder rattled the windows behind him. I swore his thumb grazed up and down my leg before he gently released me and stood.

He swallowed, his Adam's apple bobbing, and inched closer. "Ye'll be wanting this off?" He gestured to my hat.

"Please," I whispered before he tugged it off my head, setting it down on a displaced trunk behind him. Turning back to me, he seemed even closer than before, body heat emanating from him, encompassing me like a warm blanket, soothing my nerves.

His eyes swam over my face, hand extending to my hair. "May

I?" He licked his lips. "I ken ye usually sleep with it down."

I nodded, unsure I could trust my voice. Twisting around, his fingers brushed against the back of my head as he worked on the leather tie holding my hair together. My hair slackened once released, and he ran his hands through it. My blood rushed in my ears as he gently spread my hair around my shoulders.

He cleared his throat. "There." His voice was thick, his accent stronger. I faced him again. His cheeks were flushed as he nodded toward the bed. "Climb in, Red."

"My coat." My voice was hoarse. "The buttons are—"

"O' course." His Scottish *R* rolled deeper than usual. He gave a small half smile and stepped impossibly closer. My head was in the crook of his neck as his hands fumbled with the buttons of my coat—his normal agility when I'd watched him tie intricate ropes on the main deck seemingly lost. His warm breaths created steam and pressed on my cheeks and hair. I peered up from under my lashes, my breathing shallow.

His hand brushed down my front as he followed the row of buttons until the last one was released. "There."

I exhaled through my mouth and rose from the bed. He immediately came around behind me, warm hands resting on my shoulders, the tips of his fingers grazing the bare skin of my neck for a moment, and slid my coat off. He didn't immediately leave; instead, he hovered behind me, his breaths in my ear. My stomach filled with its own crashing waves, and I let my eyes fall shut.

He said something in Gaelic, and Lord, if I didn't want to know how to speak the language right then. He moved away, and I opened my eyes, swallowing the moment his heat left my back. He turned down the bedcovers for me.

I smiled and climbed in, teeth chattering, and leaned against the back of the headboard, pulling my knees to my chest. Another round of loud thunder roared, and I jumped.

He watched me for a second, pupils large, and bent to his trunk, opening it. He took out a billowing pool of plaid fabric before returning with it to my side. "Lean forward." I obliged, and he wrapped the tartan around me. His gentle care for me made me feel... and I been so tenderly cared for ever in my life?

The thick wool warmed me to my bones. I wrapped it tighter around my shoulders. His face was unreadable as I looked up. When more bolts lit up the cabin, I hauled the covers to my chin.

He peered out the wall of windows. "I should go and let ye rest. Check on things." He nodded to himself and paced to the door.

Without thinking, I shouted, "Wait." He froze on the spot, looking over his shoulder. "Please." Lord, I sounded so pathetic, scared of a storm like a bairn. "Will you sit with me?" I licked my lips and tapped the space next to me on the bed. "At least until I fall asleep."

For a heartbeat, he said nothing—I thought he was going to refuse.

My cheeks heated. The intimacy I'd felt between us just a moment ago was only a spurred sense of duty on his part. "I'm sorry. You must have many important things to—"

"I trust my crew. They ken well what to do." He strode back to the bed on the empty side and sat down, the bed sinking with his weight. Removing his boots, he tossed them aside and stretched his legs out in front of him on top of the covers.

"Thank you." Head hung low, avoiding his eyes and face. I traced the pattern of his blue, black, and red plaid with a finger. "This is embarrassing. Afraid of a storm."

"Dinna fash yourself." He huffed a quiet laugh. "My first storm on a ship was on the *Diamant*. Thought I was a tough Highlander hero, and after a wee bit of swaying and some lightning bolts, I pissed myself like a bairn."

"You didn't." I withheld a laugh at his admission and snapped my eyes to his face, searching for any sign of deceit.

"Aye." He smiled. "I swear it. Normally I'd never admit such things to a lass such as yourself, but I canna, in good conscience, let ye think this is anything to be embarrassed about." He shook his head. "My ego and head were bigger than all fifteen stones of me. Never understood what Sophie saw in me back then. I wasna a man, just a verra large lad."

"Sophie? Your wife?" He nodded. I stretched my legs out and rolled toward him. I thought I saw what she saw in him, despite my feeble attempts at quelling those thoughts. "A beautiful name." I stared off at the sole lantern on the post, watching the flame flicker. "And your son, what was his name?"

He laced his fingers together and put them behind his head. "Alexander."

Alexander. Xander Lock. A pang shot through my chest. "That's lovely."

"Aye," he said, sounding tired.

"It has been a long night." I closed my eyes and tightened his plaid around me, enveloping me in its warmth and his masculine scent.

"Aye."

I woke to another crash of lightning. Peeling my eyelids open, dim, clouded light filtered through the wall of windows. It was still raining, but the clouds were lighter in the distance and the ship's rocking had dulled a tad. Thank the Lord, we made it through the night.

Mumblings in Gaelic and a loud sigh from behind me made me still.

Christ, there was definitely warmth at my back. I rolled over to find the large Scotsman fast asleep atop the covers, in the same place he was before, like tiredness had overcome him and he had fallen asleep on the spot. His black eyelashes fanned on his cheeks as his chest rose and fell. The top of his shift had tugged down a bit, allowing me to catch a glimpse of the top of the curves of the rounded muscles of his chest and a peppering of hair. I exhaled.

He was beautiful.

John had been handsome in his own right. But a kind of quiet handsomeness, one you didn't see right away unless you looked closer to catch the warmth in his eyes and the small smiles he gave sparingly.

Not like Lock. He could never go by without grabbing attention—not with the way he looked or his personality. He was brash and a brute, through and through. Passion embodied.

I sighed. John and I, of course, had done our nuptial duty to consummate the marriage, but beyond a homecoming romp between his military tours, we'd never been particularly amorous—not from lack of trying on my part. I always wondered if he went to brothels or had a mistress on the other end of the earth. Perhaps that was why he stayed away so often and denied my advances. I did always feel like he cared for me, maybe loved me, but never in the way that I'd imagined love could truly be. Never cared for me the way I felt cared for last night. Sometimes, I wondered if he married me to save me from my childhood fate and nothing more. I'd always believed that I could only rely on myself, and this whole voyage to access my jointure was just further proof of it, but in a way, he did provide for me. He'd left everything to me that was his. He hadn't completely abandoned me.

And now here I was, a widow.

I hadn't really thought about what I'd do after I obtained proof of death and claimed my rightful due. I'd dressed as a man and was sailing across the ocean. The wildest, most adventurous, most idiotic thing I'd ever done. I'd even found something useful to do with the inventory. Could I really return to my life as a vapid, London genteel woman, with no real friends or life to speak of when this was all through?

Lock spoke more words in Gaelic before he rolled over toward me. His warm, steady breaths did nothing to calm the new buzz zipping through me as I regarded him, thinking of what my newfound freedom could bring—what I could *do* now that I was a widow. I yearned to reach out and touch him, run my fingers down his chest and through the black waves on his head, finally find out if it was as thick and soft as it looked.

How easy would it be to do exactly that—to touch him? Would he push my hand away? Kiss me? I could do it right now, erase any line between us. Find another way to occupy my time other than by picking a fight with him. Satiate the growing need in my body. I extended my hand toward him and paused midair.

Did I dare close the distance?

Another hammering of thunder made him jolt, eyes snapping open. He took a deep breath, eyes on my face. "Oh Christ, Red. I fell asleep. I didna mean to stay here." He tilted his head, my hand still hovering. "Why are you looking at me like that? Those giant blue orbs ye call eyes are even wider than usual." He gave me his lopsided smile and raised his hands in surrender. "I ken, I ken. I'm a pirate savage for no' leavin' your bed. But I will say, my back hasna felt this good in ages." He sat up and swung his feet to the floor.

I cleared my throat and dropped my hand. If he had noticed it, he didn't say. "So, you agree. It is *my* bed."

He looked over his shoulder and pinned me with a stare before shaking his head. He grabbed his boots and slid them on. "Looks like the storm is calming a wee bit. I'll meet with William and we will try to pinpoint our current location. See if that might change Cobbe's next stop." He rose and arched a brow. "Once we figure that out, you and I can continue our conspirin'. We will close in on the commodore sooner than later, and we must be ready for when we do."

T he storm roiled for a few more days, but not as ferociously as the first night. But the storm I'd thought was brewing between Lock and me had completely dissipated. If I thought he'd been avoiding me before... well, he hadn't even returned to the cabin the last couple of nights.

And it was right after I decided he could share my bed, so long as he stayed on his side. His groaning while he stretched out on the cot two sizes too small for him was uncalled for. There was no reason two adults couldn't share a large bed. The other night had proved as such. After wars and life at sea, surely, he had a number of lingering injuries and a soft bed would be best for his health.

And that was the *only* reason I was going to suggest it, to be sure.

My stomach clenched. God's teeth. What was I thinking? And what was I *doing*? I'd lost my focus. I was here for one reason: obtain proof of John's death. For the first time in my life, I wouldn't have to worry over money, and I wouldn't have to have a man around to access it. I could be independent. Utterly, completely independent.

John had ensured a future for me, even though he was gone.

In the end, he was reliable.

My lips trembled. I'd been so focused on his abandonment that I hadn't realized he hadn't abandoned me completely. I was ungrateful. And now I was in the middle of the bloody Atlantic on a ship full of strange men.

The sting of loneliness pierced my chest.

I'd felt alone before this, but it lingered here, especially at night when I'd hear the crew playing music, their feet stomping on the planks above me to the tune, and generally enjoying one another's company. Perhaps I was even a little homesick, despite enjoying not wearing stays. Lock hadn't forbidden me from joining, but the innate, everlasting fear that loomed over every woman prevented me from joining in.

Out of a need for the familiar, I paced to my trunk and rummaged through the contents, finding my buried wedding ring. The gold band was cold in my hand, and I clutched it in my palm, close to my heart, before lying back down.

I mustn't forget why I was here.

The door clicked opened, and my missing cabin mate paced in.

"Still sleeping at this time, Red?" Lock sat on the edge of my bed and slid off his boots. "We think we've landed pretty far north. The storm is nearly gone. Once the winds die down, we will re-route. I'm sure the *Glory* will have been pushed north too. Hell, she could verra well be in the foggy horizon afore us, and we just dinna ken it yet. But I wanted to wash up a wee bit. Ye dinna mind?"

I didn't reply, instead staring at the plank ceiling above me, pointedly ignoring him with my ring pinched between my fingers—solid and sturdy—grounding me back to a time of leisure and ease.

I thought he regarded me for a moment, but I didn't dare face him before he muttered something in Gaelic and paced to the water basin. With his back to me, I at last turned to him. He slipped off his yellowing shift, revealing all the curves and planes of his back. He'd never taken his shirt off around me when I was awake. My mouth dried.

From the looking glass, his eyes landed on my face. I swore he gave a wolfish smile as he splashed water over himself and took the soap, coating his skin with it, across the expanse of his chest, down his abdomen, a wake of cream lathering after his hand. To be that soap. He took a towel and began rinsing it off, making slow work of the task. I was boiling molten iron ore, knowing he'd smell of the soap and his clean, masculine scent of whisky and mahogany.

He turned around, his torso twisting in a most *interesting* way, as he grabbed a cloth to dry his face, a determined set to his jaw. "I've been thinking. About the other night. I've tried to be..."

He trailed off, and I gulped. Well, this was a change of events. "Thinking 'bout how your blue eyes were so wide when I woke up. And your ivory cheeks, so pink like..." He bit his bottom lip.

His gaze met mine, and I ran my fingers down my warm neck, dragging them across my collarbone. He stalked in my direction like a lion looking at his dinner. Like the Highland charge racing into battle. I could practically hear the bagpipes, but perhaps that was my heart's sound. I pinched the now warm metal ring tight between the fingers of my other hand.

He stopped mid-stride, regarding the ring. He licked his lips. "Thinkin' about your husband?"

I nodded despite the fact my mouth was agape, and I couldn't tear my gaze off his mounds of stomach muscles. I cleared my throat. "Well, more thinking about... how lonely it's been on the ship." I blinked a few times. "I suppose, more so how I've always felt alone."

And dammit, I couldn't keep myself together. I shook my head before looking away. A sob I couldn't hide escaped. I covered my eyes with my hands as both sadness and embarrassment heated my cheeks.

"Och, no. I dinna mean to make ye cry, Red." He closed the distance to the bed.

I rolled away from his view toward the wall. "I'm n-not crying."

He said nothing, but I heard his heavy sigh before a warm, large hand encompassed my shoulder. "Dinna lie, lass. Look at me." I stayed put, refusing to turn or even acknowledge that I heard him. "Emme... please, look at me."

Something in his voice spurred me to twist toward him, my cheeks damp. "Don't worry yourself. I'm fine."

His gaze was warm, his voice soft and low. "You're clearly not. And that's perfectly all right."

My limbs tingled, going numb. "I-I..." I took an audible breath. "I'm scared. For my future. For ship life. Of the commodore. Of these circumstances." I flexed my fingers around my ring. "I hate that I can't really spend time on deck with the others. I'm all alone in a literal sea of the unknown." My voice cracked. "And dammit, I *do* miss him, my husband. But not actually him, I don't think. I miss who he should have been."

He sank down on the edge of the bed, my body slipping toward him because of his heavy weight. "You're no' entirely alone." His cheeks pinked. "I mean... well, what I mean to say, I'm here for ye. To talk if ye need. I ken this all canna be easy."

I sat up, brushing my loose curls off my face. "No, it isn't. I just wish it was all back to normal." My breathing quivered as tears fell anew.

"Ye're so ready to return to London high society?" His brow arched, eyes wide in what appeared to be genuine curiosity.

I swiped tears from my cheeks. "No. Yes. I don't know. But I have nothing and no one left."

He nodded. "Aye. I ken the feeling."

I closed my eyes tight for a moment. "Yes, I'm sure you do."

"After I lost everything, I found the *Bluebell*. A new home. A new family. Ye'll need to figure out what ye'll want to do when this is all over." His gaze seemed to scour my face. He leaned closer to me and I to him, his bare chest a warm invitation for my hands. Did I want to accept it? "We have perhaps more in common than we ever thought." His smile was warm, but small.

"We're just two coaches, crossing paths on a bumpy road, with a passing wave hello, aren't we?" I looked at his lips, arching closer.

"I'd like to think we're more than crossing paths." He blinked a few times, lips slightly parted. "I mean, we've become impossibly entwined in this situation..." He smirked. "And whilst ye think me a pirate savage, I thought we'd gained some friendliness if not, perhaps..." His gaze dropped, like he was too timid to say the next words.

Our faces were mere inches apart. "If not...?" My voice was breathy.

He peered up from under his brows, eyes landing on my mouth. "If not—" A bizarre blaring horn rang through the ship. Lock inclined his head toward the ceiling.

I froze. "Was that a—"

"A conch shell." He hopped to his feet.

"Didn't you say that means we're under attack?" My heart leapt against my ribcage.

"Aye." He slipped on his shift, and slammed the door open, stopping to tug on his boots, hopping one foot in at a time.

Shite. I jumped up and donned my own boots. I'd need a weapon. I peered around and ran to the water basin to snatch the straight-edge razor. It would have to do. He was already out the door, so I rushed to follow after him, bumping into his back as he stopped in the hallway.

His gaze narrowed when he faced me. "What are ye doing? Get back in the cabin."

"The conch shell. Every man must—"

"Every *man*. Aye." He stepped toward me, looming in all his ferocity; a warrior ready to fight. "Go stay in the cabin until I come fetch ye."

My mouth opened. "Until you fetch me? Like I'm a dog?"

He growled. "I dinna have time for this. That could verra well be the good commodore attacking us."

I planted my feet on the spot, fingers gripping the blade's handle. "Even more reason I should come. If it's him, I can get what I need."

He seemed to tremble with barely contained adrenaline. "As long as he doesna kill ye first." His accent was thicker again, like it'd been the night of the storm.

"You're too brash. If you kill him before I can get—" I yelped as he lifted me up over his shoulder and carried me back to the cabin.

"Put me down, you bloody pirate savage!" I kicked against his chest and pounded my fists into his back as I screamed. My protests were in vain, and I was surely hurting myself more than him. "I have half a mind to use this razor on you!"

With surprising gentleness, he lowered me to the bed before he pinned me with a stare. "For once in your life, listen, and stay here. Better yet, hide under the bed and dinna come out for anyone but me."

Lock stormed off before he slammed the door, and there was a jingle of iron outside the door.

Oh, Lord help him if he... Teeth bared, I bolted up to my feet to yank the handle. Locked. I pounded on the door with a sharp scream.

The bloody arse locked me in! I would have his bollocks for this.

10

Swords clinked together. Danger lurked at every swing and miss. Lock's face was fierce, filled with sheer warrior determination, as he slashed his way through the main deck. Men attacked from every angle, trying their best to disable the largest threat on board.

But to no avail. Even amongst some of the larger crewmen of the *Bluebell*, he was a superior fighter and would stop and correct their stances or mention what they'd done wrong.

Ever since the conch shell's warning, they'd decided to train, preparing for unknown dangers.

Turned out the ship we thought was attacking was an innocent trade ship. A false alarm. He had locked me in his cabin for a bloody misunderstanding!

I'd given Lock the silent treatment since. Which he told me was 'a nice change.'

I growled, thinking about it the next morning whilst I perched at the stern of the ship, avoiding Lock and his stupid rules. I was seated on a bench with my legs spread out in front of me. I'd already finished updating the ledger for the grand-arse-who-shan't-be-named.

The men on the main deck sparred with various knives and swords, the sight just visible from my cozy little spot. The clinking of swords caught my attention every now and then. Lock's voice carried on the breeze as he taught the men to fight.

My Highlander cabinmate exemplified exactly why their fighting skills were respected and feared. A wild and brute force. But despite the best swordsmanship, when the English brought advanced weaponry, even the best with a broad sword couldn't have stopped them. To my surprise, Jacques was an excellent swordsman, quick and nimble, and his footwork was like watching a practiced dance. He seemed to be the only one who could come close to besting Lock. The Scotsman was quick, his deadly strikes pure strength. Using a saber and a shorter, dagger like sword, he sparred with three or four men at a time. But smelly ol' Jacques pranced around him in dizzying circles. Who would've thought?

Lock grabbed a ladle of water as William took his place, sparring with other crew members, eager to show off his skills, but I couldn't keep my focus on them because I had, after wandering aimlessly and becoming bored, grabbed yet another captain's log from a prize ship to read. This one caught my eye because the worn cowhide had to be at least fifty years old—and when I opened it in the cabin while Lock and William pored over maps of the North Sea, I knew I couldn't stop reading it, but didn't dare continue reading it in front of them.

The fresh air and sun were refreshing, the sky was finally clear, but it was freezing this far north. My nose and ears had to be redder than my hair from the cold. But I was content and fell into my reading, despite my fuming anger at Lock.

This particular log was by a Spanish captain of a galleon ship who described his time in Tortuga as a buccaneer. Besides the far-too-detailed accounts of slaughtering animals, the handling of their innards, collecting grease, and drying meats, his accounts were rather—*intriguing.*

Apparently, debauchery ran rampant in *Ile de la Tortue.* These were the stories and lifestyle I expected to hear when joining the *Bluebell.* And while I was relieved, this hadn't become my reality... I was a tad ashamed of how much I enjoyed reading about it.

Clinking and shouts drew my eye again. A wave of heat rolled through me, my toes curling in my boots. Lock had returned, having shed his coat and shift despite the cold. The muscles along his chest and torso glistened with a sheen of sweat that caught the light in between his strong movements. My mouth watered. I closed my eyes.

Image branded into my memory, I returned to my log. The buccaneer's detailing of his love affair with a French prostitute named Sabine had garnered a great deal of my interest. While John and I had a dim love life... This was so much more than I'd imagined possible—things I'd never even heard of, let alone tried.

A buzz of warmth zipped through me as I became utterly enthralled by his *very* detailed account of kissing her, her... Well, taking her *purse* with his mouth. By the descriptions of her trembling legs and arched back as he made her cry in pleasure *louder than a woman in labor*, it sounded like I'd enjoy it.

I peered back up at Lock, his arms flexing as he swung a sword. I snapped my gaze back down to the book, fingers clenching the journal until my knuckles blanched. When was the last time John and I were intimate? I was wracking my brain, but I couldn't remember. The image from last night of Lock's bare chest and abdomen, our faces nearly touching, flashed through my mind. What was he going to say? *I thought we'd gained some friendliness if not perhaps...* If not what? I groaned. God, I wanted to know the end of that sentence.

As the captain depicted sucking on a mound between her nether lips, my skin flushed, and heat pooled low in my belly even though this was the third time I'd read the entry. As he recounted, he said he took his tongue and swirled it around—

"There ye are, Red."

"Jesus Christ!" I tumbled off the make-shift bench and fell on my stomach onto the deck.

"Oh, Christ. Ye all right, Emme?" Lock knelt so his face was eye level with me. "Dinna mean to scare ye." He offered me a hand to help me up, but I hesitated. He peered over his shoulder, eyeing the crewmen some distance away. "Emme..."

His hand was both a metaphorical and literal peace offering. After a pause, I took it. Seated right side up on the deck, I smoothed my hair and replaced my fallen hat.

He surveyed the ship around me. His shift was back on, but no coat. The linen had become translucent and stuck to his sweat-dampened skin in the most intriguing way. "What are ye doing over here, anyway?"

"Nothing!" My voice was high. "I mean, I'm reading. The

captain's logs." Snatching the journal from the ground, I was quick to slam it shut and toss it on the bench behind me.

Lock shook his head, still in his crouched position. "I brought ye food to our cabin."

Rising, I brushed off my breeches and shift. "That's it? No apology?"

He shifted his weight as he stared at me. "I said I was sorry last night. How many damned apologies do ye want, woman?"

I shook my head. Here we went, once again. "I have made a decision. In addition to me going wherever I damn please, you shall teach me to shoot. As useless as men are, I can concede that broad swords are quite heavy and with you lot and your ogre-sized bodies, it wouldn't make sense for me to learn sword fighting. So guns it is."

He tilted his head. "And how would ye ken how heavy a broad sword is?" I shrugged. "Is that why there are large gash marks on the door in my cabin that look suspiciously like a wild redhead with poor accuracy hacked at it with a sword half her weight?"

"My accuracy would have been better if it was a lighter sword!" I folded my arms across my chest. "Nonetheless, I still think guns are the way to go. Should you wish to start training now?"

He rubbed his palms together and peered down at the deck, ignoring my question.

"What?" I narrowed my eyes when he didn't reply, instead baring his teeth in a seemingly nervous grimace. "What?" I shouted this time.

"Well, it's just that..." As if he was deciding what to say, he leaned his head from side to side. "Well, I dinna think ye need to learn."

Anger burned through me. "I don't need to learn? As in, because I don't have a cock, I shouldn't be taught to defend myself? Or are you afraid I'll use the bloody pistol on you?"

"Calm down, Emme." He raised his hands in surrender. "As I told ye last night after letting ye out of the cabin... If ye were to be wounded or somethin', it wouldna feel right."

I glared. "And what if I'm hurt because I don't know *how* to fight?"

He rubbed the back of his neck as he gave me a fleeting glance. "Ye wouldna ever have to fight." His words were firm. "I'd hide ye somewhere next time. Maybe in the hull. You're small enough to fit in—"

"Hide me?" Pressing in close to him, I straightened my spine. He took a step back. Point one for me in our verbal sparring. "Oh, this must be a jest."

"Emme..." He eyed me like I was a wounded animal that could be primed to attack at any moment.

Which I very well might. "Holy hell. How can a man be so dense? You said you'd never lock me in the cabin again. I believe I explicitly threatened some of your favorite body parts if you did!"

"And I won't *lock* ye anywhere... just hide you." He shrugged. "I thought it was a good compromise."

I ground my teeth together. "You think that's a compromise?" Pinching the bridge of my nose, I shut my eyes for a moment.

"Red."

I snapped my eyes open. "Do not *Red* me!" I poked him in the chest. "No! I won't stand for it." I folded my arms over my chest.

His eyes were hooded, as if angry at my lack of compliance. He inched closer until his chest pressed against my crossed arms. "I could always drag ye down to the brig and lock ye in next time. You dinna weigh verra much."

"Oh, I'd bet you'd enjoy that." I leaned away, dropping my head back so I could see his face from my shorter height.

"I quite enjoyed it yesterday." His face flushed as he smirked. "Never mind that I took a little extra time to come back for ye. Had myself free of ye for a *whole* hour."

I knew he'd kept me in there longer than necessary! "Overpowering a small woman like me? Is that what you think of when you pleasure yourself?"

"I think ye'd like to know what I think of." He gritted the words from behind his teeth as he pushed his crossed arms further into me. The back of my knees hit the bench behind me. "For fuck's sake, woman. You're tryin' my patience. And while we're at it with rules, no more cards with William. Ye've a foul mouth already. Canna return to proper society sounding like ye do."

I growled. "That'll be a no. You are not my husband or father, and even if you were, it'd still be a no. I'll play cards with whoever I wish."

The heat from his chest seeped into my arms. His pupils dilated as he glared. "Did ye talk to your husband like this? Have ye ever thought he left for war after war because he wanted to get away from ye? Or was his hand sore from permanently lashing ye?"

"How dare you? He never hit me. He was forward thinking." I

jutted my chin toward him. "Not a pirate savage like you."

He narrowed his eyes. "That's a damn shame."

I was aghast and froze for a heartbeat. "Bastard." I slapped my hand across his face with a loud crack, my hand tingling with pricks of burning pain.

Lock's mouth dropped open, and he placed his hand on his cheek. His nostrils flared. "You—"

I raised my hand to slap him again, but he caught my wrist in midair, holding it in place. He tugged my wrist and brought me that much closer to him. We were both silent, both of us panting hard from the argument. I wasn't sure if he wanted to throttle me or kiss me.

Did I want him to kiss me?

Last night, yes. Right now, no. I stomped the heel of my boot on his toes. He jumped back, bouncing on one foot. "The sooner I can get off this ship won't be soon enough!"

"On that, we can at least agree." His brows knitted together. "I want my ship back, along with my peace and quiet."

"Peace and quiet? Don't you mean your lonely, empty life? You're chasing a man across the world for revenge. I hate to break it to you, but killing him won't fill the empty hole in your heart. It won't bring them back!" The moment I said the words, I slapped my hand over my mouth, and his face turned ashen.

His hands trembled by his sides. "Ye dinna think I dinna ken that killing Cobbe won't erase the past? I know that." He stared off behind me. "Sophie died because of me." His words were spoken so low, it took me a minute to decipher them. "They tormented her.

Cobbe and his men. He'd been keeping tabs on me after Culloden. He wanted to see me hanged. Apparently, he went round to Sophie many times after I was sent to the colonies. Trying to slither his way into her bed to discover my location." He scoffed. "I dinna ken what exactly transpired between Sophie and Cobbe, but once the *Diamant* released me, he was hell-bent on finding me. It ended with him incessantly calling on her to find my whereabouts. What—how my son was involved... did he mean to kill them?" His voice was rough, and I wanted to wrap my arms around him. "Does it matter what he intended? I let her down once by leaving her in the first place, allowing that man the opportunity to... I willna let her down again. I *will* kill him." He twisted away from me, one hand running through his waves. "Do ye no' see that I canna let him harm ye as well? That if we had been attacked, and it had been him, I..."

I took a deep, shaky breath. "I do. But I won't stand by and let everything happen around me, to me, for me. I must take charge of my own life. I'm not a lady. I didn't grow up with wealth. I'm a miner's daughter. A miner who'd drink so much he'd forget my brothers and I needed necessities like food." He turned back to me, eyes wide. "For so long I've thought I was a victim of my circumstances. That everyone who was supposed to take care of me had abandoned me. But now I know I shouldn't have relied on others in the first place. Which means I won't sit in a cabin locked away, and I'll learn how to defend myself. Because I won't abandon myself, unlike every other person in my life."

He nodded and his eyes searched my face. "Fine. I'll teach ye to shoot. But only because I often wonder if Sophie knew how to fight, would my family still be alive?"

His words pierced my heart. I stepped forward and squeezed his hands. "Thank you, Lock. It is all I can ask."

"Gents."

I dropped Lock's hands and hopped back from him at hearing William's voice. I bent away from William's squinting eyes and picked up my secret captain's log.

William shook his head. "I've been looking for you two. We've spotted an island." He gave us a pointed stare. "There's a marooned ship on it waving a white flag."

I gasped. "A marooned ship?"

"Christ." Lock ran his hand through his hair. "How far?"

"Half hour, mayhap." William lifted his hat off his head and scratched his scalp. "There's ice in the water. I've spotters on each side of the ship. We should try to sail as close as we can and row the rest of the way in the jolly boat."

Apparently, the ship had succumbed to the fate of the weather. I placed my hand on my chest. Had we narrowly missed the worst of the storm? Our own fate could have been much different.

"Flag?" Lock stood straighter, hands on his hips, still close to me from our conversation moments ago. I wanted to linger on the impassioned moment, our newly shared understanding, and the burning desire to soothe him of all his past pain—but, alas, ship life brought us back to reality. I wasn't sure if I should be grateful for that or not.

William bared his teeth. "English. Looks to be a trade, though." He cursed in Gaelic. "Could be a decoy for an ambush."

"Aye, mayhap. But they look short of a good deal of crewmen for the size of the vessel, and the ship looks nigh destroyed." William looked past Lock's shoulder at me.

Lock nodded, lips in a thin line. "What do ye think?"

William shrugged. "I say we take our chances. Offer help in exchange for whatever is left of their cargo to sell."

"Aye." Lock's gaze was alert as he scanned the horizon. "We'll take our best men then, heavily armed. Prepare for the worst."

"And hope for the best." William saluted. "Aye, aye, Capt'n Mac."

Lock peered over his shoulder. "And I suppose ye'll be wantin' to come?"

I pulled my shoulder blades together. "Naturally."

"Aye. I'll ready the crew." Lock stalked away, talking to himself loud enough for me to hear him say, "What did I get myself into?"

William pinned me with a stare. "Do ya wanna tell me what that was all about?"

I stopped breathing. "What do you mean?" I surveyed William's face as he arched a brow, finding no ill intention. Good Lord, how I wanted to confide in him, tell him everything and examine my confusing emotions about Lock. "I... Lock and I. Well, we... I." I couldn't divulge my secret because it could mean trouble for me and Lock.

"Clark, ya can tell me anything. I won't spill your secrets." I tilted my head in disbelief. "Truly." He paced closer and leaned toward my ear. "If I couldn't keep secrets, then everyone on board would know that ya're really a lass."

I wrapped my arms around myself. "I-I—"

"Relax." He waved his hand. "I won't tell. I figured it out long ago."

"How?" My brows furrowed. I'd been so careful.

He laughed his warm, boisterous laugh. "I was pretty sure ever since Limerick when ya'd be drinking and some of your moustache and beard smeared away as the ale dribbled down your chin." His eyes sparkled. "But I thought perhaps ya wanted to appear older to become a crewmember. But I quickly realized the truth when Mac suddenly started spending more time than ever holed up in his cabin with ya."

I exhaled, muscles relaxing. "It'll be nice to be myself around someone else and have someone to complain to about my cabin mate." I extended my hand to him. "Very well, I should properly introduce myself then. I'm Emme Clark."

He offered me a small smile and shook my hand. "Nice to *finally* meet you, Emme. I look forward to talking with you. I can imagine your list of complaints about the Scotsman is long." He offered me his arm, and I hooked my elbow around his. "Mac may have the face of an angel, but he sure knows how to be a giant pain in the arse if he chooses."

Face of an angel? Odd thing to say about another man.

I peered down at our crossed elbows as we walked across the main deck. "Won't the crew think it odd that you're escorting a cabin boy like a lady?"

William shrugged. "A lot of men here do odd things while on the ship. Some turn to a life of privateerin' to have the freedom to live an alternative lifestyle, free from the burdens of society." He stopped and eyed me. "If ya know what I mean."

I crinkled my brows. I didn't know what he meant, but I understood the appeal. "There is a certain freedom here, isn't there? Even in my silly costume, I feel more like myself than I have in ages."

"Aye, there is." He dropped my arm and climbed to the deck below. "Now, ya must ready yourself to go ashore."

The island the ship marooned on was one of several utterly beautiful isles. All hills and mountains covered in deep, brilliant green moss and grass.

Not dissimilar to the color of Lock's eyes.

The ship's hull was all but ripped completely away when it had crashed on the island's rocky cliffs. It had been a fairly large ship, but only five men stood on the shore.

Lock stood in front of the men, glaring, chest puffed, one hand on the hilt of his sword, the other on the handle of his flintlock. "Is this all who remain of ye, then?"

One man, his clothes in rags, three teeth missing from his yellow grin, nodded. "Aye, Capt'n."

I placed my trembling fingers against my lips. "The rest are all dead?"

A man beside the one who answered shook his head. He focused one eye on me, but the other rolled to the side. "Nay."

Lock's fingers tightened around his weapons. "No?"

"No," the first sailor replied. "Another ship came by this morn'."

Lock shot his gaze between the men. "Then why are ye still here?"

"It was a naval ship." The man stuck his tongue through the gap created by his three missing teeth. "Their commodore called it the *Glory*. He was tryin' to press us into service, that he was. Saids, 'serve or be marooned.' I had the mind to think other ships 'twould be caught in the same storm and sail by. I ain't signin' up in the middle o' a war, I tells ye."

Lock nodded toward William and me, and the three of us huddled together a few paces away.

I raised the front of my hat and rubbed my brow. "I know we're in a war, but are we so short of men that His Majesty's Royal Navy must abandon those unwilling to fight? What happened to the respectability of my countrymen?"

Apparently, we hadn't walked far enough away because the partially toothless sailor stood on his tip-toes. "We dinnit think 'twas for naval service. The commodore said we'd be workin' on a remote isle off of Nova Scotia."

That piqued my interest. "Nova Scotia? That *is* an English colony now." Odd to use men for something there with the war going on with the French.

Lock puffed air out between his lips. "Yet another thing the English took from the Scottish."

I faced the men again. "You could've worked on the ship until you arrived and booked passage back to England when you arrived?"

The sailor scratched his nose, flakes of skin floating from it.

"From the sounds o' it, we dinnit think 'twould be Nova Scotia proper. Innit right, Orrick?"

Orrick focused his good eye on me. "Nay, I overheard some of them sailors talkin' when I was behind those rocks"—he pointed down the shore—"pissin'. They dinnit know I was there. They saids somethin' about a special project they was keepin' secret from the Crown. I ain't gonna be hanged for no treason."

My eyebrows furrowed. So, Cobbe had a secret project he was recruiting men for. A project that wasn't authorized by the Crown. Something that was worth killing his sister-in-law over—and if she was to be believed, perhaps worth killing his very own brother. What was this man up to?

And how in the world could I get proof of John's death from him and come out unscathed?

"All this tryin' to pinpoint where they might land has been useless. We head toward Novia Scotia, then? And hope we run into *Glory*?" William's gaze snapped between Lock and me.

Orrick clicked his tongue. "If yer chasin' the *Glory,* ye needn't go tha' far. She's headed to Reykjavik. The Danish 'ave remained neutral, they ain't worrying 'bout causin' no war there."

"Iceland? That's but a two- or three-day sail." Lock's lips split in a smile. "And luck is on our side—we have a Danish letter of marque. We could go right up to the *Glory* without fear o' meeting the ends of the barrels of an entire ship's guns." He inched down and whispered in my ear. "You could easily get your letter certifying your husband's death."

I raised my eyebrows. "And you could get your revenge without fear of getting hanged for treason."

He exhaled deeply, chest thrusting with the action. "Aye. If we can lead him away from his ship and crew. *After* ye get what you need, Red."

I nodded, heart pumping. This was what I'd been waiting for, and it was but a day or so away from finally happening. "Then we head to Iceland?"

Lock nodded, his gaze set on something far away. I could almost watch him think, as if observing the wheels turn inside of a clock. "Iceland is a braw place as ever to hoodwink him and eventually lead him to his death."

I shuddered.

"I'll get planning," Lock exclaimed as he took large strides to the rowboats to head to the ship.

"No." I planted my foot on the sandy bank and crossed my arms. Lock froze, his brows scrunching together. "*We'll* get planning."

12

"All right. There ye go. Now use the ramrod to tamp down the powder and ball." Lock pointed to a detachable rod on the underside of the barrel.

I fumbled with the flintlock pistol and nearly spilled out some of the black powder, but Lock caught the tip of the barrel before the grains poured onto the navigation table, his fingers wrapped around my hand. I winced. "Bloody hell, I'm sorry."

He didn't let go of my hand as he smiled. "Dinna fash. Ye'll practice so much it'll become muscle memory." The calluses on his fingers grazed against the top of my hand, and goosebumps erupted down my neck and arm before he let me go. "Try again."

I sighed. "I can't believe soldiers can load a gun four times in a minute. I can't do it once in two. And when will we get to the actual shooting?"

His green gaze landed on my face, eyes sparkling in the flickering lantern light, and he smirked. "Patience, Red. Kenning how to shoot will do ye no service if ye canna load it to begin with." I grumbled with a frown. He laughed and grasped my chin, steering my gaze to him. "Ye'll get it. Try again. And we'll go to the main deck and shoot a few times before we lose all daylight."

I peered out the wall of windows; the purple hues of twilight lingered in the distance. "To be sure, it does get dark early this far north."

"Aye." He gave a wide grin. "But wait until ye see the night sky and the Aurora Borealis. I could see them from time to time in Scotland, but not as bright as they are here." His gaze seemed distant. "So vibrant that the Vikings thought the Northern Lights were a rainbow sky bridge connecting us to the gods."

My mouth opened as I blinked. "Brilliant."

He inclined his head toward the gun. "Aye. So get on wi' it. Dinna want to miss them." I groaned, tired, having wholly been unaware of what work shooting a gun entailed. "And if ye get yourself comfortable enough, ye should carry it with ye. I willna tell ye to stay in here." He gripped his hands together. "I've learned my lesson. But there are five new, unknown men on board."

The blood drained from my face, and I nodded on an exhale. "Reet."

He placed his hand atop of mine and squeezed. "Nothin' a miner's daughter couldna handle, I'd suspect."

I fought a smile, shaking my head. "I shouldn't have ever told you."

"Ye shoulda told me sooner. I wouldna have been so rude in the beginning. Think I like ye more, *princess.* " He laughed, and I glared despite the word now sounding like more of an endearment than an insult.

"And here I thought you didn't like me at *all*." I grabbed the gun and poured in more shooting grains from the powder horn.

"Well, now that I ken ye aren't from London, ye've grown on me." He handed me the ramrod.

I arched a brow. "And why do you think I didn't grow up as a chit from London?" tampered down the powder and cloth covered ball.

He placed his hand on mine, again guiding my fingers, but I didn't think his touch helped me any, not when I was all too aware of every inch of skin his fingers touched instead of where he guided me on the pistol. "Your accent. It slips out every once in a while. Like just a moment ago. The way ye said right. Or when you're mad at me. Besides, I ken there are no mines in London. I do know a thing or two about England."

"Newcastle," I said by way of answering while trying to control my breathing. It was very warm in the cabin, despite the icy northern air.

He let go of my hand as I cocked the gun. "Aye? Well, that pleases me verra much. I've always hated Londoners. Verra elitist, ye ken? Sayin' we Scots dinna how to talk and the like."

As much as I'd tried to fit into London high society, to be treated like one of their own, his approval somehow pleased me more than I'd have thought. I raised my chin a tad higher. "Some Londoners have said the same of my fellow peers from Newcastle. That they can't understand a word we say."

"Aye, doesna surprise me. A lot of Scots moved there to become pitmen. Thought aboot it myself for when my indentured servitude would be over, before the *Diamant* and fate had other ideas." He pinned me with a stare. "I imagine there's quite a mixin' of the two accents. And perhaps why ye can understand me better than most English can."

"And who says I can understand you? I just smile and nod. I don't catch a word." I gave him a grin with a wink and handed him the loaded gun.

There was a gleam in his eye as he inspected the flintlock, and he gave a nod of approval. "You're ready to shoot. And this evening we'll plan what we want to do tomorrow when we land in Reykjavik."

My cheeks warmed.

I cleared my throat and formed my hands into a steeple on the table. "About Reykjavik. I have an idea, but we'll need William's help if he's so inclined."

Lock tilted his head, meeting my eye. "He might find out you're a lass, Red."

I shrugged. "Apparently he's known since Limerick."

"Christ." He smirked. "O' course he did, the sly devil."

Minutes later, we were on the stern of the ship away from prying eyes, waiting for William—I think Lock had been relieved to bring him into our plans, if Lock's furrowed brows finally relaxing were any indication. Perhaps he needed someone to talk to as much as I did.

William sauntered toward us with finesse as his eyes locked on us. "Ya've requested my presence?"

"The *lass* has a plan." Lock arched a brow.

William eyed me, his fingers cupping his chin before his gaze landed on the guns we both had holstered around our waists. "Should I be worried?"

"Probably. Who knows what scheme the mad woman has concocted?" Lock grinned. "The guns are for practice, but if she's already tellin' us what to do, why no' teach her how to shoot so she can stage a full-on *coup* and mutiny?"

I rolled my eyes. "Do you want Cobbe or not?"

He folded his arms across his chest. "Do tell us your grand scheme, Red."

I paced, pushing an escaped strand of hair back under my hat. "Well, I don't want to meet the murderous man alone, but it'd be odd for me, an English woman, to be scared of the commodore of His Majesty's Royal Navy. And, to be sure, he'd recognize you, Lock. He'd be immediately suspicious if we were together—unless we had a reason to be together."

Lock planted his hands on his hips. "I dinna ken if I want to even ask."

Tapping my pointer finger over my lips, I shrugged. "If you had a personal investment in obtaining my husband's proof of death, since I couldn't remarry until I had a letter to show the Church, it might be more believable if we told him we were betrothed. We would meet with him to write the letter together and then you could lure him away alone."

Lock's whole body seemed to stiffen, his eyes squinting. "You want to pretend to be betrothed?"

Waving my hand around, my mouth agape, I shrugged again. "It seems like a good solution."

He nodded. "But should the crew see me accompanying a lass around Iceland whose hair is as bright as my cabin boy's—could raise some suspicions."

"And how would we ensure the commodore even comes to meet with ya?" William leaned against a mast.

I shook my head with a smirk. "I bloody well can't think of everything."

A wry smile splayed across Lock's lips. "Fake betrothal? If ye wanted a reason to get close to me, ye didna need to make such an elaborate scheme."

I elbowed him in his side. "Well, are we shootin' or what? We're losing daylight."

William set an overturned bucket on the railing, tying the handle to the ship so we wouldn't shoot it into the water. Lock and I unholstered our guns, the weight of mine heavy in my hand, but still not as heavy as that damned broadsword.

"Plant your feet wider and square your hips. If ye dinna have a solid base, the kick back will knock ye on your arse." Lock modeled the pose, and I adjusted my stance, mirroring him. "No, no." He handed William his gun and walked behind me and placed his hands on my hips, angling me, before tapping on the front of my thighs. "Wider."

I exhaled through my mouth, trying to concentrate. I needed to shed my coat. Shooting apparently worked up a sweat. Even though I hadn't actually fired yet.

William, leaning against the mast again, arched a brow. "Mac, perhaps I should instruct Emme for a bit. I don't think she's focusing on anything you're *saying.*" I shot him a glare as he took a sip of whisky from Lock's wine skin.

"Nay. She can do this." His head was beside mine, the warmth of his breath on my cheek. "All right, line your eye down the line of the barrel, ready your finger by the trigger. Right before ye squeeze it, exhale, and dig your heels into the deck." He pressed behind me, our bodies flush against each other. He angled his head to peer at me, our faces close. "I'll stand right behind ye." I nodded, breathy. "In case ye fall, o' course." His voice was thick.

I nodded again, too fast. "Of course."

"Jesus," William muttered while sipping on more liquor. "I'll leave ya two alone. I'm gonna go find meself a cask of that Indian Pale Ale from the trade ship."

"Ready?" Lock asked me, ignoring William. "Just dinna shoot a hole in the side o' the ship and sink us." I snapped my gaze to his, my heart beating fast. "Jesting. Ye can do it, Emme."

I was ready, and I *could* do it. My finger grazing the trigger, I pressed down through my heels as hard as I could, and lined my eye down the barrel. Aiming on the exhale, I squeezed the trigger. A quick spark illuminated before a boom, and the gun hammered back into my shoulder with searing pain.

I flew backwards into Lock, my feet physically leaving the ground. "Shite. Fuck. Christ."

He wrapped his arms around me, hauling me upright. He laughed, the deep sound rumbling his chest.

I turned around and smacked him. "It isn't funny. That bloody hurt."

He brought his fist to his lips. "Sorry. I dinna mean t-to laugh." He said the words between poorly contained chuckles. "But ye shoulda seen your face." I smacked his chest again, as hard as I could. He grabbed where I hit. "Och. That wee hand of yours does more damage than one would think."

I placed my hands on my hips. "Oh please, I couldn't hurt you even with a blacksmith's hammer, you ogre."

He arched a brow, lips split in a sideways smile. "Ogre, is it now?" He stepped closer and leaned in. "I dinna ken if tha' is an upgrade from pirate savage."

Our faces were a breath apart. He licked his full bottom lip, and I followed the gesture with my eyes. If I could shoot a gun, I could also be more brazen. I *wanted* him to close the distance between us.

Lord. I wanted to kiss him. And I would tell him so, done with fighting my instincts. Fighting my true nature. I wasn't a lady—so why did I keep pretending I was? "I want to—"

"Ye dinna look at the bucket yet, Red." He nodded behind me. "You're a braw shot." Twisting toward the bucket, I examined the damage. There was now a perfect hole in the middle. A swell of pride filled my chest. "Ye'll be a better shot than me if ye keep that up. C'mon, let us find some ale afore William drinks it all."

I'd permitted Lock to share half the bed with me the night before. Because he'd need his full strength and energy for today, and for absolutely no other reason.

Not because of the way his body felt pressed against mine when we were shooting, nor how I wanted him to kiss me after.

Well, fine. I had *some* ulterior motives. Every time Lock came near me, it was like my entire body was made of burning embers, and he knew exactly how to stoke them. And despite myself, Christ, I wanted that man to stoke them.

I barely slept, knowing he was beside me, a half-foot apart, and knowing our plan to pretend to be betrothed. My imagination had gone a tad mad picturing what we might have done to... authenticate our betrothal.

From the sound of his irregular breathing, he didn't sleep well either. The sky was still dark, but I suspected it was later than it looked; sunrise came later here. The rainbow stripes that had illuminated the night sky were fading away.

I exhaled and extended my limbs, hands at my sides above the covers. I'd slept under the duvet and him atop of it again. But as he breathed deeply in the wee hours of the morning, I thought he at last had fallen asleep, completely unaware of my burning need.

My yearning for *him.*

Goodness gracious. This feeling was nothing more than being close to a man in a way I never had before. Nothing more. It was best to hide these feelings deep inside me and never let them see the light of day. I was so close to having my financial independence, my freedom. I mustn't ruin it all over such foolish, carnal desires.

One-sided carnal desires, to be sure.

Lock was a privateer who sailed the seven seas from port to port and with that face of his and that body, he probably never left one unsatiated. He didn't need me to fulfill *his* needs. And why would he want me? I'd been a thorn in his side since day one and any semblance of anything more over the last few weeks was surely due to the fact that he needed me for his plan. Nothing more.

I huffed, trying to close my eyes to get at least a little sleep, but my hand brushed his. I gasped. I didn't move. Our pinky fingers touched so lightly, I wasn't entirely sure we'd made contact. His breathing changed and his body tensed as he swiped his pinky across mine. I shut my eyes tight, feeling that touch roll through my whole body, my breath shaky. Did he mean to—

He hooked his pinky around mine, slowly inching his fingers over, his thumb caressing the back of my hand. His breaths, now ragged, finally gave me some indication that he might want me as much as I wanted him.

I rolled toward him, and he followed suit, angling himself in my direction. Our fingers entwined. His green gaze was darker than usual as he scoured my face with such an intense stare. It felt like he was physically touching me. My lips parted, and his eyes dropped to them. I clenched the blanket in my free hand and arched toward him.

He slipped his hand around the back of my head, fingers digging into my hair. "Christ, these red curls."

His brogue was thicker than usual, rumbling his chest, and it sent chills down my spine. He moved his hand from my hair down to my face, cupping my cheek. Our gazes locked. I licked my lips as he leaned forward, our breaths mingling.

And then a knock sounded at the damned door. Lock's face turned into a pained expression. He took a deep breath, squeezing my fingers before he let go of both my hand and my face. As he rose from the bed, I laid back against the pillow, puffing a burst of air through my lips and making a curl fly.

I would bloody kill whoever was at the door.

William entered. "Good morn', Mac, Emme." His gaze landed on me for a minute, and heat rose to my neck and cheeks as he smirked. "Long night?"

Lock shot him a glare. "Aye, couldna sleep."

William's lips trembled like he was holding back a laugh. "All of our schemin' for today gets the blood rushin.'"

That it did. I slid out from under the covers. William's gaze dropped to my breeches, and he tilted his head like he was surprised they were still on.

He rubbed his lips together. "The port is in our spyglass. Too far to tell if the marooned sailors were correct. But we should know in an hour or so if the *Glory* is in the port."

Lock nodded. "Verra well. We shall need to prepare to land. Prepare the crew. I'll be up in a minute." William dipped the brim of his hat before leaving Lock and me alone once more.

Lock's eyes landed on me, watching me slide on my boots. His face was unreadable as he tapped his fingers on his thighs. "I-I must..."

I gave a heavy sigh. "Of course. Go. I'll be right behind you. Should reapply my soot."

"Right." He sucked in his bottom lip and brushed the curl away from his forehead. "I—" He paused before he smiled. "I'll see ye up top, if ye're ready, *my betrothed.*"

Reykjavik, green and misty, was very similar to the small isle where we'd found the marooned ship. Here, however, small stone buildings with moss and grass-covered roofs, primitive compared to anything found in London, sat nestled at the base of sharp snowcapped mountains and cliffs of porous, volcanic rock.

It was beautiful, but I didn't think I could live in such an underdeveloped place.

I stayed close to Lock at the helm, who'd been shouting orders. Sails were being pushed and pulled in all directions, and a boom nearly swept me off my feet into the icy waters of Faxe Bay.

"There she is." Lock pointed toward the port as he steered the ship. There, across the smoky bay, was the giant Man o' War, the *HMS Glory,* bobbing up and down.

My heart beat in my ears. This was it. The reason I was wearing these damned breeches. I would finally obtain John's proof of death, and I'd return to London and claim what was lawfully mine.

A niggling feeling pressed into the pit of my stomach. I peered back at Lock, his jaw shadowed with stubble, having left the cabin unshaven. Devastatingly handsome. Perchance I would enjoy my day as his fake betrothed. Maybe too much.

He returned my stare, brows furrowed. "Having second thoughts about today? I can go by myself—"

"No. I was just thinking how close I am to finally getting what I need." I toed the deck with my boot, shoulders sagging.

"Right. It must be such a relief." Eyes faraway, he pushed his cheek out with his tongue. "Ye've already secured your passage back to London, and soon enough, ye'll be on your way. No more dealin' wi' pirate savages, eh?" He arched a brow, but his gaze was missing its usual spark. "After we drop ye in Jamaica, then we really be, as ye said, two coaches crossing paths on a bumpy road."

I twisted my lips to the side. "And I'm sure you'll be glad to be rid of me. To have your peace and quiet again." My stomach clenched, waiting for him to deny it.

He broke our eye contact. "I'm sure ye're excited to re-enter society again and wear a dress."

Was I excited to return to society? I'd never fit in, nor particularly enjoyed it. "I could go the rest of my life without ever wearing stays again, but it would be nice to put on a dress and feel pretty."

He gave me a smile, a full wide grin. "Even with all that soot on your face and wearing breeches, ye've always looked bonnie."

My stomach bounced like it was filled with exploding black powder. He'd never made any indication he'd ever thought me pretty. Mistress Beatrice had told me that despite my hair, I'd been a rare beauty, and therefore a man with a scorned or scandalized family might look past my breeding. John had never made me feel particularly beautiful, though.

Lock beckoned me closer, an illicit thrill shooting through my entire body as he bent down to my ear. "Should we enact our plan now? I feel it 'tis as good o' time as ever?"

I sighed, lips pressing together in a tight line. "I can't think of why not."

He cleared his throat, eyeing me. "William! Cabin boy! Come here."

William and I both faced him.

"When we land, go to the brothel and fetch me a lass for tonight." Lock's voice was overly loud, and he gave me a pointed stare. "I'm particularly in the mood for a fiery redhead with a temper."

I bit my tongue to keep from giving him some choice words. He smirked.

"Isn't this neckline cut a little too low?" I yanked and tugged at the bodice in a vain attempt to bring it higher.

William shrugged with a laugh. "Nay. The is crew 'sposed to think ya're a whore."

I sniffed the cornflower blue ruffled sleeve, overbearing flowery perfume accosting my nose. "Well, it certainly smells like a French whore."

He stopped walking and scratched his chin. "I believe the woman I bought it off of was Danish."

I shook my head. "It's like I went from one ridiculous costume to another."

William ran his gaze from my head to my toes. "Ya'll fare a'right. That color blue is rather strikin' on ya."

I angled my face in either direction in the looking glass to make sure I didn't miss any soot and pinched my cheeks for some color. "Remind me again why I have to dress as a whore?"

"One, ya needed a dress. The second part of the plan ain't gonna work with ya in lad's clothin'. Because why would a woman betrothed to the captain need to sneak around the ship like a man? But specifically a whore, because if any crew from the *Bluebell* tha' are drinkin' in the tavern downstairs should see ya and Lock, they won't think twice, thinkin' I've already procured him a lady for the evening. He's not one to go to a local brothel, so it would be awfully suspicious if he was there with someone who has hair as red as his cabin boy. But this way, we've already set it in their minds, and we'll have backup nearby should things turn sour with the commodore."

I turned back toward him as I gnawed on my cheek. "Would the crew really take so badly to a woman on board? Would they terrorize someone there under Lock's protection? Women are privateers too. What if a woman were to stay on the *Bluebell* full time?"

He met my eye, squinting. "Most, no. They're good men. But I can't vouch for all of 'em. We're always recruiting. Even now we've five new crew members from the marooned ship. As for those women who privateer, many do dress as men. But most would respect a woman there with a certain role. Like the captain's daughter or..." He raised his brows.

I frowned. "Hmph."

He tilted his head from side to side. "A gown wouldn't exactly be practical on a ship anyway, would it?"

I shrugged. "No. But perhaps a nice riding habit. Tailored waistcoat, no pannier, durable skirt, and most importantly—no stays."

"Thought a lot about it, have ya?" His eyes widened.

"No, I just... I was just curious. I'm so close to obtaining John's proof of death and Lock will soon have his revenge, and then the *Bluebell* will take me to Jamaica, and I'll return home." My gaze turned unfocused, feeling conflicted. "Am I supposed to pretend like this never happened?"

He clasped his hand on my shoulder. "Have ya said any of this to Mac?"

"Say what, exactly?" I shook my head. "That after one decent shooting lesson, I want to forgo my estate and become a privateer? He's no doubt ready to be rid of me."

He planted one hand on a hip, brow high. "Would it be to *just* privateer, though?"

I scoffed. "Please. What else would it be?" His head dipped to the side. "I know what you're implying. And no." His eyebrows raised. "What? I should tell him I want *him* instead of my jointure? To forget this hapless journey?" I began to pace our small, rented room in the inn. "Or better yet, we continue the plan, and claim my jointure together in London? He's a wanted man." I stopped and planted my feet wide, hand over one hip. "Besides, that'd mean he'd have to want me, too."

William rolled his eyes. "Ya're anything but dense, Emme. Can ya not see—"

"I see he might have an attraction to me. That the journey is long and lonely, as he's said so himself. But he's had ample opportunity. And…" I exhaled loudly. "He's chasing a man across the world for revenge on behalf of his late wife. I'm nothing more than a means to an end at this point. This isn't what he wants, nor what we planned. I'll be headed back to London once we stop in Jamaica."

He shook his head. "Aye. But things rarely happen the way ya expect 'em, do they? Sometimes ya don't know what ya want until it's right in front of ya."

I wished that were true. But did I want to stay on a ship for the rest of my life? Did I want Xander Lock?

Shoulders sagging, I sighed. "Well, we should be gettin' along with the next part of the plan before my breasts topple out of the top of my bodice."

William laughed in that infectious way of his before shooting me with a pointed stare. "I, for one, cannot wait until Mac sees ya in that dress."

I groaned. "You should mean to say, when he sees me dressed as a whore."

"Semantics."

14

It'd been so long since I'd worn a dress, I nearly forgot what an inconvenience they could be. My exaggerated hips bumped the walls of the narrow staircase. I descended them slowly, so as to not slip in the heeled boots, down to the tavern from the rented room we'd used to pull off the cabin boy-to-whore switch.

Once at the bottom step, I blew out air through my lips and searched the rudimentary tavern. Wooden log walls and basic communal tables and benches amongst roiling hearths totaled the place. A far cry from the ornately decorated salons of Paris I had once frequented with Mistress Beatrice, or even a tearoom in London. In a dim corner, the Scotsman sat at one of the sole private tables— his size hard to miss, his striking face even more so. With most of his back toward me, I had the opportunity to ogle him without him knowing.

A few leers and whistles broke the moment. I blinked a few times, peering around me. I'd nearly forgotten what it was to be a woman amongst men in the last few weeks.

Lock turned and froze the moment his gaze landed on me, his

mouth ajar. After a heartbeat, one that hammered in my ears, he hopped to his feet as if remembering that's what he was supposed to do.

I paced to the table as his eyes swept over me before returning to my face. "Captain Lock, I presume?"

He pulled out a chair beside his, fumbling a bit. Out of character for him. A few crewmen from the *Bluebell* gave us sidelong glances. I cleared my throat and dug my wide-eyed stare into his face—I was supposed to be a whore, not a lady.

He stood straighter, understanding me. "Aye. My quartermaster said ye were verra expensive. I expect ye the whole night. Sit." He spoke loudly for the benefit of everyone around us.

I sank into the chair. He'd chosen a table where he could see all the inn's entrances, one far away from prying eyes and ears, too. A place where we'd see Commodore Cobbe coming.

He sat down and tugged my chair closer to his, placing an arm around me to rest atop my chair's backrest. I arched a brow. "I did pay ye good money, wench." I wanted to roll my eyes, but I batted my eyelashes instead. He bent down and brushed my hair from my ear. "William just left with the letter. I suspect we have an hour or so until the good commodore will arrive." His breath tickled my ear and neck.

I placed my hands on my skirt, smoothing it. "And the wax seal—you're sure he'll believe it was an official one from the governor here?"

Arm still wrapped around my shoulders and chair, he toyed with one of my curls on the side of my head. Every one of my muscles tensed. "Aye. With a Danish marque, we seal letters with their wax seals often. I doubt he'd ken the difference between ours and a royal one."

He began wrapping the curl around his finger. I clenched my hands on my skirt. "And the letter? You wrote what we had discussed?" My voice sounded shaky, but I wasn't scared of what was to happen with Cobbe.

He nuzzled his face in my neck and hair. "Lass, relax. Ye're supposed to be a whore, and ye look scandalized by my every touch." My eyes shut. The feeling of his lips brushing my neck and ear as he talked sent goosebumps down my arms. I wasn't scandalized. I was worried about losing all semblance of control. "And yes. I wrote the letter exactly as we discussed. 'The governor would like Commodore Cobbe of *HMS Glory* to meet a beneficiary of the Danish Crown at the Smoky Bay Tavern.' I also added that he'd consider it a personal favor, and if he didn't acquiesce, his actions would reflect the whole of His Majesty's Royal Navy."

I opened my eyes, mouth suddenly dry. "He won't think that it's an ambush?"

He leaned away again to take a sip of ale. "Nay. The Danish are desperate for trade. It'll sound like a stuffy nobleman thinking he's more important than he is." He pulled his arm from behind my seat and placed his hand atop my clenched one sitting on my skirt. "And Christ, Red. It looks like ye paid me to seduce ye, not the other way around. Time to play the part. And moreover, once the commodore is here, he'll have to believe we are truly betrothed and can't keep our hands off each other and are in a rush to get married and need your letter certifying your husband's death to do so."

I nodded and took a deep breath. He replaced his arm on the back of my chair. This was what I had been wanting to do for some time now; why not indulge a little? "You're right."

Biting my lip, I placed my hand on his tan breeches, his large thigh beneath my fingertips. I splayed my fingers wide, his warmth radiating into my palm. What would it be like to be on the receiving end of those powerful legs of his? I kept my hand planted on the spot, afraid to be more daring by caressing or anythin' of the like. From under my eyelashes, I met his gaze. His green eyes shone shades darker than usual, his pupils large. Heat welled low in my belly. Christ, of course I had to be wearing stays again when I finally got to touch him like this. Did they have to keep it so warm in here?

He trailed his hand from the backrest to my neck and to my shoulder, grazing, the touch light, sensual, his fingers making relaxed circles over my sleeve. He continued the swirling on my shoulder, and every so often his fingertips ran over my uncovered collarbone. A chill rolling down that side of my body made me squeeze his thigh.

We should be focusing, going over what we'd say, verifying our story. Instead, we were allowing ourselves to indulge.

I wanted more. I rubbed my hand up and down his thigh, feeling vines of long, interwoven muscles, his thighs no doubt made of as many intricate muscles as his back. My lips parted on an exhale.

I didn't want this little ruse to end once we left the tavern—I wanted to haul him upstairs and claim what I'd been yearning for.

But I couldn't, because this was all pretend.

Our eyes locked, and he didn't drag his stare away as he more brazenly grazed his fingers across my collarbone and down the column of my neck.

I shut my eyes, arching into his fingers, as a breathy sigh escaped my lips. I gripped his thigh, my thumb caressing up and down on the inner seam of his breeches.

"Christ, Red." He rolled the R in my nickname. With his free hand, he clamped down on my hand on his thigh.

I snapped my eyes open. Did he mean to shove my hand away or spur me on further?

The intensity of the fire burning in his eyes didn't look fake.

For the briefest moment, I thought he started to drag my hand closer to him, but then he stilled.

"Kiss me." His eyes were wide.

My heart doubled in pace. "Wh-what?"

"Cobbe is here." The hand that had been leisurely caressing my shoulder wrapped around the back of my head and into my hair. "Kiss me."

I inclined my head toward him, his own bending down to me. His warm breath pressed on my face before he brought his lips against mine. Our lips caressed, tender and hesitant at first, but his hand tightened in my hair, and I arched my body nearer, and our kiss deepened.

Oh God, his kiss. It didn't feel pretend.

"Aw, and here are the lovebirds. As promised, no ambush here, your whole battalion in wait outside." William's voice cut through the moment and we broke apart. "And clearly, as I explained, they're quite ready to wed. The governor will take it as a personal favor if you could procure for Mrs. Clark a letter certifying her late husband's death so they can begin their joyous nuptials."

As we broke away, Lock kept his eyes on me, grasping my hand and bringing it to his lips to kiss. His expression held a million unreadable emotions. And damn if I didn't want to understand at least one of them. At last, he broke eye contact and faced the approaching men.

What the devil had William said? A whole English battalion accompanied Cobbe outside. It would be impossible for Lock to continue with his mission.

I kept my gaze on my lap to gather myself before I regarded the men before me. William waved his hand toward our table, steering the commodore to us. I stopped breathing.

There he was.

Commodore Cobbe. The man I had chased across the world. Well, half the world, to be fair. His blue uniform was as pristine as it had been in Limerick, but no hat this time. His brown hair was pulled back into a long ponytail. Odd that in his station he didn't wear a wig. When he had come to me to deliver the news about John, I hadn't really paid him any attention, not realizing he would play such an integral part in my life. Had his face been so cold and pallid then and escaped my notice in my fog of grief?

His gaze landed on me, and I stiffened, the image of his sister-in-law mouthing *help me* flashing in my mind. Lock squeezed my hand.

A sharp pain shot through my chest. If I felt like this after seeing him kill a random woman on the street, how in the hell did Lock sit here, keeping his face unbearably calm? I squeezed his hand in return.

If he didn't kill the man, Lord, I wanted to kill Cobbe for him.

But he couldn't kill him here. It would be an assured suicide mission.

William looked at me. "Commodore, may I introduce Mrs. John Clark and Alex—"

"Alexander Grant MacLachlan," the commodore finished in his cold voice. His gaze narrowed in Lock's direction. He laughed while shaking his head. The sound sent chills down the length of my spine—chills very unlike the ones Lock had given me moments ago.

I tried to keep my eyes from widening. I'd figured Xander was short for Alexander, but hadn't put it all together. Alexander Grant MacLachlan. A true Highlander name.

Lock's grip tightened on my hand, his trembling a bit, his whole body taut and leaning on the edge of his seat. "Lieutenant…" Lock's voice was eerily calm compared to the storm that must have been brewing inside him. "I'm sorry, *Commodore* Cobbe now, isn't it?"

Time to try out my acting skills.

"My love." I cleared my throat as Lock turned his eyes on me. I cupped his cheek. "You didn't tell me you knew the man who could expedite our marriage."

He placed his hand over mine, the shadow of hair on his face scratching my fingertips. "Aye. 'Tis why we had to go to the governor himself and call in a favor. I dinna think he'd write a letter certifying John's death if he had kent who was asking."

"Good Lord." Cobbe's eyes lingered on Lock's. "After all this time, I still cannot understand a word you say. May I?" He inclined his head to the empty chair and sat without waiting for a response. "I suppose once a Highlander savage, always a Highlander savage."

Lock laughed, licking his lips. "Red here prefers to call me a pirate savage." His eyes flicked to me, a small smile on his face. "Isna right, *mo ghaol?*"

I brushed away the hair from my face and smiled widely. "Only when you anger me so, my love."

"I do believe it is illegal to teach Gaelic." Cobbe's nostrils flared before he at last regarded me. "I suppose congratulations are in order. A wedding. How marvelous." He arched a brow. "And to an Englishwoman? I never thought I'd see the day, Alexander."

I smiled, like a lady was supposed to, like the men expected. "Ah, yes, my Englishness. A fact he loves to remind me of daily."

Lock nuzzled his face in my ear and hair. "Dinna be sour, ye ken I love everything about ye, despite your Englishness." I smiled. Lock was still himself, even under this guise. He glared at the commodore. "And as we're in a Danish territory, teaching Gaelic isna outlawed."

Cobbe sniffed again, like it was a nervous tic, before placing his eyes on me again. "I'm sorry. Who did you say your late husband was?"

I licked my lips and exhaled. "John Clark."

Cobbe's gaze flicked up to the ceiling for a moment, like he was trying to remember who he was. He snapped his fingers. "Yes. Yes. I remember him very well. Well, I must have been standing in your drawing room but two months ago to deliver the news, and here you are, in Iceland, to be wed again." He narrowed his eyes. "And in such haste."

"What are ye impylin', commodore, about my betrothed? I'll no' entertain allegations against my future wife's virtue." Lock's voice was cold and held an unspoken threat.

The commodore's nostrils flared again. "I suppose you've received a large jointure, Mrs. Clark? I do believe Captain Clark was one of the Baron of Rye's younger sons."

Right on cue, Lock replied, "That's neither here nor there."

Cobbe laughed. "I've hunted you for a decade, and here you are beckoning me. I searched Scotland for years after the whole debacle with that French *corsair*. What was it called?"

"The *Diamant*." Lock's mouth was tight. The tension between the two was almost unbearable.

"Yes. The *Diamond.*" Cobbe nodded. "And the frigate in the port, sailing under a Danish flag, the *Bluebell,* captained by a Xander Lock. I don't know why I'd never put it together. I always assumed you'd return to Scotland."

"Ah. Yes." Lock raised his mug in the air. "Ye've done your research on the ships here."

Cobbe sniffed and nodded. "I am a commodore. It is my job to know all of the nefarious vessels in the sea."

My pretend betrothed scratched the back of his head with his free hand. "Privateering under a Danish marque. Perfectly legal. In fact, the *Bluebell* and its crew are an extension of the Danish military."

"I understand quite well, if not for your accent, what you're saying. I can't drag you away here as a wanted man from the Crown. And denial of your request could pose consequences." Cobbe tapped the table before glancing my way. "John Clark. He had a brilliant mind. Not much of a fighter, preferring logistics and tactical warfare. I remember he had an aptitude for explosives. But good Lord, he could barely load his musket. I was surprised when he didn't accept the position of commodore, but it went to my late brother after John refused it."

I stiffened. He'd been groomed to eventually be an admiral. A commodore would have been a natural progression, but he'd said they always passed him up, and so he remained a captain for years, forced to always leave, when as a commodore he would have had stability at home. He could have been stationed somewhere on land instead of on a ship, and I would have been able to follow, create a new home. My brows furrowed as I blinked.

Cobbe inclined his head. "You didn't know? He did prefer to read and strategize. Find new ways to use cannons. I supposed as commodore, he'd have been removed from the action. But in the end, his lack of fighting skills did him in."

And Cobbe did in his own brother so he could become commodore to have his secret island project in Nova Scotia. What was he doing there that made it worth killing his own family?

I pursed my lips. "He did enjoy ship life." Lock rubbed his thumb on the back of my hand.

"And fate has brought us three together, intertwined. Needing a letter certifying his death so you two may marry. Fate has her laughs, doesn't she?" Cobbe laughed as if to emphasize his point.

I tapped my free hand on the table. Lord, we just needed to finish this already. But Lock wouldn't be able to move forward with his part of the plan here. As if reading my thoughts, several privates slammed open the door to the tavern, peering over at our table.

I gave a tight-lipped smile. "Yes. It is a small world that seems to grow smaller every day. Now, since you failed to do your due diligence and register my husband's death with the Naval Board, would you be so kind as to write a letter verifying it so we may all move on with our lives?"

"So that you and Alexander may marry as soon as possible?" His cold voice warmed to a degree with his curiosity.

Lock leaned in and kissed my cheek, his breath tickling my neck, making my toes curl. "Aye."

I nodded. "Yes, and then you can be on your way to Nova Scotia." Cobbe jerked, and the heat blood drained from my face at my admission. We weren't supposed to know about his secret project. I licked my lips. "I mean, I suppose geographically that would be the most natural next stop for you. It being an English colony now. I had read in a daily that we'd recently acquired it." Lock's grip tightened around my hand as if to keep me from talking.

Cobbe narrowed his eyes before glancing between the two of us. "You know, we should let bygones be bygones. We're all British now, after all. I will write your letter."

I took in a sharp breath. Oh, thank the Lord, I hadn't just dismantled our whole plan.

"And as a wedding gift to you, Mrs. Clark, the widow of a high-ranking naval officer, I'll stop hunting your soon-to-be husband. But you must wed before the *Glory* sets sail tomorrow." He smiled, but there was no light to it.

"W-what?" Could they hear my heartbeat?

"If you're so eager to marry that you needed to call in a favor from the governor and search for me, surely you both would prefer a wedding sooner than later? But you must marry before we leave, otherwise, as soon as the *Bluebell* sets sail and is no longer in Danish waters, I will finish what I started and return Alexander to England." He did his sniffing tic thing again, giving me a pointed stare. "And of course, as his betrothed, you'll want to have him free... unless you're not really betrothed and you're here under duress, and Alexander only wants access to your jointure. As an Englishwoman, it would be my duty to protect you, and under that scenario, I am sure the local Danish authorities would undoubtedly support me in capturing Alexander on their soil."

"Ye bastard." Lock began to stand, but I yanked him back down.

My hands trembled. "I am not here under duress. And I do not appreciate the threat you've hung over my betrothed's head." I exhaled, words falling from my mouth before I had a chance to think through what I was saying. "I agree to your terms."

Did it matter what I agreed to? Lock would kill the man. We just needed to get through the meeting, and get this damned letter from him. We couldn't take him off the street when he left here like Lock had originally planned, but maybe we could still lure him away.

The corner of Cobbe's lips pulled up. "Lovely. I'll even offer the *Glory's* chaplain." He peered up at William. "Could you return to my ship and inform them I'll be needing the chaplain to return with you? And whilst we wait, I'll write the letter."

My heart leapt into my throat, a new idea forming in my mind. "We have a room. You can write the letter there. I have a quill and parch—"

"No need." He opened his coat and retrieved a quill and inkwell.

I peered at Lock. His eyes were wide. "Surely, ye'd be more comfortable—"

Cobbe scribbled on a piece of paper. "No, I'm already nearly done." A few more scratches, and he passed the paper over.

Everything I'd gone through had been for this damn letter in front of me.

Cobbe peered back up at William, who'd been silently watching the whole thing whilst leaning against a wooden post. "Why haven't you left yet? The chaplain. Go."

William didn't so much as move.

My mouth was agape, and Lock looked as unsure as I, with his Adam's apple bobbing. He caught his bottom lip under his teeth. "Ye dinna intend my bride to marry on the spot? She'll want to ready herself. If ye mean it as a present, then allow her the chance to prepare."

Cobbe's gaze returned to me. "Very well. You'll have until dawn to marry, and the *Glory* will leave soon after." His eyes snapped to Lock's. "Otherwise, I'll wait outside the Bay of Smoke for however long it takes. So, unless you're planning on living in Iceland, you'll be getting yourself a new wife before the sun rises. If you already have a room, we can have the ceremony here in the tavern."

"Nay." Lock slammed his fist on the table. "We're already marrying on your terms. We will at least marry where we want to. On the *Bluebell*. She's our home. Ye're welcome to bring your chaplain aboard at dawn."

He must have some kind of plan. Lure him to our ship and grab him and drag him away from witnesses?

"On your ship?" Flaring his nostrils once more, he smiled. "Very well, as you wish. I don't want to deny a blushing bride her day." His eyes dipped to my low bodice, distaste filling his features. "Even if it is her second marriage. But I will have my cannons at the ready should you try something nefarious." He gave an odd smile, like he got some kind of perverse pleasure over our marriage. "I do love a wedding."

The second the door shut after the commodore, I exhaled loudly. I picked up the cream-colored parchment declaring John's death with Cobbe's signature sprawled across the bottom. He must have stamped it with a seal before he left the *Glory* after asking William what the favor was for.

This tiny piece of paper carried the total sum of my existence.

My breath was ragged as I exhaled. "What is your plan?"

Lock let go of my hand and cursed in Gaelic. "Christ, Emme. I have no plan. We can lure him from the main deck of the *Bluebell*, but I'm sure he'll have orders in place to fire if they don't see him."

I looked him in the eye. "Why would he even offer to do this?"

He shook his head. "I dinna ken. Assert his will over my life? To trick me and lie in wait for me to land at the next English port? Who knows with that man?"

I carved my teeth into my bottom lip. "Say his word is true… You'd be free from the man and his incessant hunt."

Scrubbing his eyes with his fingers, he nodded again. "There's an appeal to the idea—eleven years after the fact, most wouldn't recognize me in Scotland. I could return home, see my family. He's the only one who'd remember. It's personal between him and I." He snapped his gaze to mine. "But none of that will matter once I kill him. Just have to figure out how to get around the *Glory*."

"But I spoke about Nova Scotia. He'll know we were asking about him. It'd be suspect if we didn't agree to his terms." I ran my hand through my hair. "H-he'd claim I was here under duress and capture you on the spot."

I didn't want to add to Lock's list of reasons to be hanged. Although, I did have what I came for now. I could always sneak away from them both. But could I leave Lock at the mercy of the commodore? No. Additionally, from Cobbe's perspective, I should want this for Lock. It'd look extra odd after mentioning Nova Scotia... because if I didn't know more about him, why wouldn't I, an Englishwoman, walk right up to a naval ship to talk to a plain commodore when I saw his ship, without bringing in a wanted man to the mix? Fiancé or not.

"I'd never force ye into wedding me." His eyes scanned my face.

I shook my head. "*You're* not forcing me into anything. The damned commo—"

"I would like to see my family again, but I willna force ye, directly or otherwise. But..." He turned his whole body toward me and grasped both my hands, his eyes hooded by his pinched brows. "If ye wish to stay on the *Bluebell*, ye *must* wed me." That he was even entertaining the idea made me gasp. "Even if we managed to slip past the *Glory*, they'd know for sure a lady was on board, and one with money, dressed as a cabin boy or not. It'd be too dangerous for my crew and me. But I ken ye booked passage from the Indies, and I canna leave ye stranded." He reached into his pocket and tossed a large coin purse on the table. "This should be enough to get passage from here and then some. And if ye decide to stay on the *Bluebell*, then this should be enough for a wedding dress." He rose.

My blood rushed in my ears. "Lock—"

"Ye have until dawn to decide, but if you're on the *Bluebell*, we'll be having a wedding." He exhaled loudly and stalked out the door.

I clenched the edge of the table.

William, still leaning against the beam, folded his arms and arched a brow.

"You've been awfully quiet."

He lifted his hat and scratched his head. "Just thinking that if ya're gonna be Capt'n's wife, we didn't need to make you look like a whore. Could've picked the pretty lavender dress. We won't need to protect your identity now. They'll leave you well enough alone."

My mouth dropped open. "Captain's wife? I may very well take the money and skip town."

His head tilted to the side as he gave me a pointed expression. "Lass, please."

My face pinched tight. "You know you can be quite annoying when you want to be?"

After a chuckle, he jutted his head toward the door. "Ya know I'm right. C'mon, let us get some fresh air. I haven't had time to enjoy Iceland yet."

I rose and linked arms with him, patrons gawking, and I realized I was still dressed as a whore. After a quick hop upstairs to gather my things and my coat to cover myself, we walked back outside, my eyes adjusting to the bright afternoon that was a sharp contrast to the tavern's dim lighting.

His chest heaved with a big gulp of air. "Oh, blessed dry land. I could kiss this fish gut covered dirt with my bare lips." William's energy was infectious, and despite the looming decisions ahead of me, I laughed. "Well, as soon as the land stops moving from under my legs. I'd gone from the *Bluebell* to the inn with ya back to the *Glory*. Need my land legs still."

"Aye, dry land. Feels like it's been ages, doesn't it? Especially after the damned storm." I took a deep breath of chilled air—still salty, but dirt and grass and earth mixed in with it.

"Oh, where Mac had to calm ya and stay with ya all night. To be sure, horrible." He rolled his shoulders and stretched his neck in each direction. "Now let us see if we can find you a nice dress shop. Maybe a gown was never picked up, or it was made in the wrong size. I refuse to let you marry looking like a whore. Ya'll be needin' some rouge."

William marched away, but I grasped his lower arm, stopping him. "Hold on a second. I haven't decided if I will marry him. Maybe I should ask around, see if there *are* any passenger ships back to London."

His eyes lingered on my face, his breathing forming clouds in front of him. "And what's back in London for you?"

"Everything! My-my..." My townhouse, my dead husband's

money, my friends who were… nice enough. My face must have crumpled in defeat because William's expression changed from playful to sympathetic, eyebrows creeping back down his face.

"Oh, my sweet." He rubbed his forehead. "Fine. Let us go back to the inn. I'd kill for a hot meal and a bath, anyway. You can pretend to drink over your options."

The icy air and steam from my breath disappeared the moment we re-entered the inn. I'd been so focused on Cobbe I hadn't noticed that, despite its rudimentary interior, the roiling hearths invited all kinds of folk inside—fishermen, wealthy merchants, aristocrats, sailors… he place was bustling.

William's gaze lingered on a handsome man with striking blue eyes a few tables over. I examined them before realization struck me. No wonder he'd never made any of the advances I'd been warned about once he figured out I was a woman. Very well then.

After hot meals and ale, William paid for a hot bath and headed upstairs—shortly followed by the man he'd been making eyes with. Well, technically Lock paid for the bath—an exorbitant amount, may I add—and I continued drinking in the common room by myself. We'd switched from ale to table wine. It was rather astringent, but by my second glass, I no longer noticed.

I stared into the burgundy liquid and weighed my options. Marry Lock and live at sea until… well, I didn't know. Stay here and find passage to, I supposed, London. Looking up, I found several leering men with their attention on me. Or I could stay here and find myself a husband or actually become a whore; with this dress, I already looked the part. After the last of my wine was swallowed in one hearty gulp, I refilled my empty cup with the carafe.

William returned, sinking down on the wooden bench next to me, an easy, relaxed smile on his face. "Bad news. Local dressmakers ain't got nothin' on hand. All of it must be ordered well in advance, as the fabrics must be shipped here. This place is in the middle of nowhere."

It took a minute for his words to register as I savored another large swig. "Oh, well, if I marry, it shall be in this dress bought off a whore. Seems fitting. Growing up a miner's daughter with a father who often gambled and drank away most of our money, I was lucky to have a dress not marred with holes and grime. This dress is perfectly suitable."

"A miner's daughter?" His raised eyebrows nearly disappeared into his hairline. "No wonder ya're able to keep your face passive amidst vulgar talk and general unruliness."

A warm laugh bubbled from my chest. "I had to have my own vulgar talk and unruliness beaten from me—for 'an uncouth lass with no talents who can't speak right' wouldn't have married well."

"Your father paid for tutors?"

Another laugh burst from me, the booze warming my stomach. "Bloody hell, no. The crotchety old lady who took me in after Papa died did. She was a proud, strict old woman, but she did reet by me."

"I can hear it. Slipping in. The more wine ya drink, the more your prim and proper words evade you. I'm glad. I was worried Mac would find a stick up your arse later tonight." He winked and sipped his wine.

"Yes. And a proper lady shan't drink too much… and I think I'm

well on the way to being drunk." If the old bat could see me now...
She'd have wrung my neck the moment I put on breeches.

"Well, we have time. Enjoy your last hours of widowhood,
Emme." He raised his glass.

I clinked mine to his. "I've still made no choices."

"That's because there are no other good choices. Only one right
answer. Take the easy route. Marry him, bed him, see where life
takes you that isn't this"—he waved his hand in front of my face—
"stuffy, genteel disguise. Ya may have been dressed as a lad since
I've known you, but this woman with her nose permanently turned
upward ain't you either. Be yourself, I don't judge."

I squeezed the top of his hand. "And you know you can be
yourself around me too?"

His eyes widened, and maybe even a hint of fear for the briefest
of moments flashed through them, but as his gaze searched my face,
he must have found whatever he was looking for, and he sighed with
a nod. "So... what say you?"

His words echoed in my mind. Unease at my inner truth cut
through some of the wine haze.

Who was I? My choices had always been dictated by the men
of my life. My father, my brothers, my husband. All of them had
left me, and I was alone. Now that John was gone... What was my
purpose?

Wouldn't marrying Lock mean another man would run my
life until he too eventually parted from me in some way? But if I
could find a passenger boat, what if I couldn't sneak off in time
or got caught trying? And if I outright refused to marry him, what

would Cobbe do to me if he detained me under the pretense I'd been kidnapped? My stomach clenched. The Danish would surely relinquish me to him under the circumstances.

Oh God, and what would become of Lock under that pretense? I couldn't do that to him.

The last month on the *Bluebell* had been trying, but also the most I'd done in my life by myself. Entirely on my own. I didn't know if I could go back to being *just* a wife. It felt good to be useful.

Now that they'd know I was a woman, would that change? Would Lock push me into the traditional roles of a wife like I'd prepared for my entire life?

Ship life offered me a freedom I hadn't realized until now. At the beginning I'd thought myself trapped and confined on the *Bluebell,* but I'd since gained a sense of purpose.

Would it be so bad? I'd been dreaming of independence, but married people led separate lives all the time. I had what I wanted: John's proof of death and access to my jointure. My original plan didn't need to change; we could marry and I could still keep my passage from Jamaica to London. We wouldn't have to change much—but of course I couldn't ever remarry. I'd lose my chance to perhaps find someone who wouldn't leave, who was actually reliable. Someone I could depend on.

Someone who actually loved me.

My chest heaved as I took a deep breath. The reality was, the unknown dangers and challenges of *not* marrying Lock at dawn greatly overwhelmed the weak reasons I had to deny him.

I had my decision then.

Mayhap there could be more to this than pure convenience.

Christ. I twisted a curl around my finger. I wasn't afraid of going through with the marriage. I rubbed my palms over my face. I was afraid that I *wanted* to go through with it.

I wanted to claim what I'd been yearning for. I wanted to claim Alexander Grant MacLachlan.

And I had no idea where he stood—did he even like me? Want me? I'd be giving up my chance to find someone who did, only to remarry someone who might very well, once again, abandon me. But Lord, if I didn't want to take the risk. I chugged the remainder of my wine.

"I must marry him. It is the most obvious solution." In vain, I tried to calm my breathing, but it was too shallow and erratic to control.

"Don't panic. Everyone is nervous on their wedding day." William refilled my cup until purple dripped down the sides and pushed it toward me.

With greedy appreciation, I gave a nod of thanks and wrapped my hands around the cup and drank. And drank. The burgundy liquid burned down my throat, and my lungs demanded air, but I didn't put the glass down until I emptied it and slammed it on the table with a thud.

After exiting the inn, William halted in the middle of the street. From my vantage point, the *Glory* floated front and center in the harbor. Could I somehow set the whole damned thing on fire?

He grasped my shoulders, forcing me to focus on him in my drunken haze.

"You know where we must go, then?" His eyes dipped to my cornflower gown, and I groaned. "That dress doesn't reveal much if you keep wearing that coat. Perhaps they'll have others. Something suitable to wear for your wedding."

I hiccupped as he dragged me forward. "If I'd known I'd be stuck wearing dresses bought from a brothel—*hiccup*—I'd have figured a way to sneak some of my own aboard."

William stopped walking again. "Pull your overly proud little head from your arse, Emme!" My mouth dropped open. "You're a privateer's wife now; survival and doing what you must do is your future."

Oy. I eyed my hands, roughened from sea life, my nails brittle stubs. Suppose I should get used to this. My life of luxury was behind me. I'd grown up poor and in rags. It wasn't so hard. As long as we had everything we *needed*, we'd be fine.

We. As in Lock and I. The thought was almost enough to sober me. *Almost.*

I punched my fist in the air in front of me, like a battle cry, as I charged forward and shouted, "To the whorehouse!"

The brothel was much different from what I anticipated. It was one of the few stone buildings amongst all the rural wooden structures. The inside was clean. Elegant with navy blue wallpaper covered in gold swirls and a large crystal chandelier with taper candles emitting sparkling rainbow light across the colorful woven rugs. It was more of a men's club with fancy hors d'œuvres and apéritifs. Men played cards, and hazy smoke floated in the air, mingling with flowery French parfum. I'd been brought numerous gowns to buy off some of the women, but none worthy of a wedding.

Not that it should matter. And it didn't. One of these dresses would be perfectly suitable. It was a marriage of convenience. Right?

I even said so as the women fussed over me, going so far as to ransack various closets. I received clicks of indignation as a reply. So, bringing the elegant crystal glass to my lips, I sipped on claret as William nibbled on dried fish and some Icelandic version of caviar.

We bided our time, having until dawn to return. I should like to celebrate my last night of being a widow.

Several women had taken it upon themselves to make me presentable. One combed my hair and tugged it this way and that in an intricate design, weaving flowers through it. Another kept bringing down various dresses and hovering them beside me to decide which would be the one. And I indulged it. When was the last time I'd been waited upon like this? When would it ever happen again?

It probably didn't hurt that William took the whole pouch of coins and handed it to one of the prostitutes, stating what we needed in return. After seeing the hefty amount, they'd been trying to entice William to go upstairs for additional coin—to no avail, of course. I smiled behind my cup every time one tried.

"And what is going on 'ere?" A woman on the floor above gripped the banister and peered down at the parlor below. Her black hair was pulled taut in an elegant bun. Even from afar, her undeniable beauty, despite the lines of time, was evident.

"Madame Toussaint." The woman doing my hair jumped up, backing away from me.

Another lass dropped the gown she was holding on the stairwell. "We... we—"

"Are being treated exactly as we requested. And paying handsomely; I expect this is not a problem?" William rose and raised his glass in the air toward the stern woman.

"And *what* is it you exactly wanted?" A black brow arched high on her forehead.

William nodded toward me. "To prepare a bride for her wedding."

Madame Toussaint said nothing for a long, tense minute. "A wedding?" Her gaze landed on me, silent for a long pause. "Well, we cannot 'ave her marry looking like that."

Hours later, the brothel was a bustle, and I'd been bathed, parts of me splayed and scrubbed to a new layer of skin, nails cleaned and manicured, oils and balms rubbed all over my bare body. No shyness or prudence allowed here, it seemed. A woman painted my face. I declined the white powder, despite having peered into a looking glass and finding my skin had tanned deeply since sailing. Like it was when I was a little lass playing outside of mine entrances all day. She lined my eyes with kohl and painted pink on my cheeks and lips.

A hushed silence fell over the entire room when a voice announced, "I've found you the dress."

I gazed up to the balcony where Madame Toussaint displayed a light gray satin gown.

Thick silver embroidery hit the candlelight, and the silver transformed into shimmering pinks and blues. I stopped breathing. It was beautiful. She descended the staircase, holding it with care.

Despite not wanting to make a fuss over this contrived wedding, despite not wanting to care what I looked like when I wed Lock, despite *myself,* vanity won.

I rose and, as if in a trance, stumbled my way to her and traced my fingertips over the skirt. Pearl colored beads were sewn in amongst the intricate swirling silver-threaded embroidery. "It's... it's perfect."

Toussaint dug her stare into mine. Fooled earlier by her cold, tough exterior, I missed the warmth and passion hidden in the depths of her eyes. "It was my wedding dress."

I snapped my hand away. "I can't accept this. Thank you, but—"

"Nonsense, I 'eld on to it for far too long. Waiting for the perfect person. When I set my eyes on you, I felt something, something that calls out to me." She passed the gown into my hands. "You must wear this when you wed. He—my 'usband—was the great love of my life. It'll suit you well."

The world spun around me, and this time, it had nothing to do with all the alcohol I'd consumed. "T-Thank you." I nodded.

She gave me a warm smile. "Now, let us see 'ow it fits!"

At the top of the gangway, I halted and took a deep breath, peering at the twilight sky. The colorful streaks of the aurora had disappeared, and the starlight was fizzing out as the purple hue of dawn lit the horizon.

With my eyes shut, I pushed air out between my lips before sucking more in. In and out. In and out. A slight breeze swirled the tendrils of hair around my face, but not enough to muck up the beautiful braided arrangement one of the girls had arranged.

"Emme, let us make haste—they'll think ya've declined his offer if we wait any longer."

At Williams's words from behind me, I peeled my eyelids open and climbed the last steps onto the *Bluebell*. Whistles and whoops accosted me. Several crew members on the main deck, preparing to disembark in an hour, paused to gawk at me.

"Wow, Clark, ya lookin' quite different," one said.

"Pretty, pretty," called another before making kissing noises. I didn't think it was supposed to be a compliment.

"Maybe once Capt'n is sick of ya, ya can come to my hammock," a third said, eyebrows raised.

Heat rolled down my face, down my neck. My skin was probably as red as my hair. I wanted to run back down the gangway.

William leaned in behind me, close to my ear. "It's a test. To allow a lass on board—some fear women are bad luck, others don't want to share their food with someone who won't pull their own weight. And ya've deceived 'em."

I nodded, exhaling the steamy air.

Pinching my shoulder blades together, I raised my chin. "Yes, gawk at me. I have breasts, and I bleed once a month." Many of them looked away. "Yet, despite my lack of bollocks, I've been more of a man than any of you lot." Perhaps not entirely true as I'd hidden in a cabin most of my time on board, but I'd needed to say something to erase the scowls off their faces.

There was a heavy silence, and then an eruption of laughter. My shoulders relaxed and men were quick to offer me a hand as I traversed through the main deck—whether it was an attempt at chivalry because they now knew I was a woman or because I was still a little tipsy and swaying, I didn't know.

William covered his smile with his fist. "Go down to your quarters. I'll find ya when we're ready. Eat somethin' to sop up the booze. Ya're stumbling like a babe learnin' to walk on leading strings."

After a meal and water, I was somewhat more levelheaded, and nerves rose anew.

A knock at my door snapped me from my thoughts. "Emme." William entered. "They're ready for you. I volunteered to escort you."

It felt like my voice was stuck in my throat, so I nodded and gave what I hoped was an appreciative smile. He offered his arm, and I took it, rising.

He smiled. "Christ, you look beautiful." His cheeks illuminated in the orange hue of lantern light. "Mac won't know what to do with you."

"Thank you." Although the dress was wonderful, I felt silly wearing such a superfluous gown for a ruse of a wedding.

"Cobbe and some heavily armed men are waitin' on the main deck. Ya should see the smug smile on the commodore's face. Enjoys puppeteering people's lives, it seems." He led me through the corridor around rigging and beams.

My fate was sealed then. I couldn't go running now. "I'll see his sadistic smile soon enough." I sighed. "He couldn't leave well enough alone. He gets some perverse enjoyment about controlling Lock."

"And pressing men into service. The man has control issues." His lips twisted to the side.

"Apparently, for some secret project on a remote island. What would be so important a dedicated soldier would deceive the Crown?" My brow wrinkled, pressure pushing in the pit of my stomach.

Something was amiss.

"Well, never you mind with that righ' now." He smiled widely, his teeth bright against his skin. "Wait until ya see the main deck. They've found some decorations."

William's words spurred me from my musings on Cobbe to remind me of the task at hand. I would soon be married.

To Lock.

Again, words evaded me as I exhaled. I grasped his arm more firmly. The gown weighed heavy against me with all its embroidery and beadwork as I pushed forward.

He continued chatting, but his words were muffled as we traversed through the ship, the landscape bobbing up and down at each port window. My ears rang, and my limbs tingled as they moved on their own, floating like I wasn't in my own body, like this was happening to someone else.

But it *was* happening to me.

I froze.

William faced me, a beam of rising sunlight coming through a port window hitting his face. "Are ya ready?"

My breathing was shallow, and I nodded several times too quickly. I suspected I didn't look at all ready. "I need... I need a minute." I rotated away from him. My skirt's heavy fabric swooshed, and the beads clicked together with the movement.

Oh, dear God above, please send me a sign. Give me something, anything, to show me this was the right choice. I panted in the nearest corner. Had I doomed myself to a life of unhappiness?

Lock. Poor Lock. He wanted to avenge the death of the love of his life, and here I was, interrupting his plans. I was sure he was wishing right now he had never agreed to this whole debacle.

Could there be a way out of this?

No, there wasn't. Cobbe was waiting somewhere above my

head on the main deck.

My hands trembled, and I exhaled, trying to steady my limbs. Facing William once more, I frowned. "I'm ready, but I must speak to Lock first. Please, fetch him for me?" I couldn't keep my unsteadiness out of my voice as I begged him.

Thuds on the stairwell and a large hovering body behind me were my only warning before his deep baritone rumbled my ears, my chest, my entire being. "Emme?"

I swallowed and faced him, but the air was knocked from me. His black hair was combed and swept across his head, but that damned curl still splayed across his forehead. He'd shaven recently, but there was already a shadow of growth returning. However, the most striking part, the thing that was making it difficult to breathe, was his outfit. I had once wondered what he'd look like in full Highlander garb, and now I had my answer—striking.

My eyes widened, and I remained silent as I took him in. A dark blue and hunter green kilt hung on his hips and draped into a sash across his chest and over a matching blue coat, held in place by a shoulder brooch—a bronzed family crest of some sort, with three crowns and a knight's helmet. His white shirt had a ruffled neckline and sleeves that popped out from under the jacket. In the front of his kilt, the outfit was completed with a leather sporran. Everything about his clothing drew attention to his features—his chiseled jaw was sharper, his cheekbones higher, and his eyes greener.

My exquisite wedding gown no longer felt silly or superfluous.

He peered down at himself and smoothed his sash. "I didna ken if ye'd like a kilt, but it's tradition, so…" He rubbed his hand over the back of his head.

My breath hitched. "You look very handsome, Lock. Truly."

"Please call me Alexander, or even Alex. After all, I'll be your husband after this. But in front of the crew, always Xander or Lock." I licked my lips and nodded. "And ye..." He inched nearer but halted, seeming to catch himself. "Ye look divine."

"Thank you." Brushing a stray hair from my eyes, I regarded him. "I... are we making the right choice?" I thought I had my sign as soon as I saw him, the question feeling suddenly unneeded.

Lock—Alexander—gave me a small half smile. "A little late to question that, Red. Cobbe is on the main deck with what seems like a whole garrison waiting."

"I'm a very strong swimmer. I could jump out that window if need be. I'm sure I could make it to land if I don't freeze to death first." He chuckled, and I stared at him for a long moment. "I know this isn't what you want. I understand we're in this mess because I spoke about his secret project, and I can't help but think I'm dooming you to a life you don't want."

I needed something from him, something to spur me forward down that aisle.

No doubt sensing my unease, he closed the distance between us and clasped our hands together. "Emme, this isna what I planned, but I never told ye this isna what I want."

"You don't have to. Why would you want to tie yourself to an impetuous Englishwoman?" I tried to yank my hands away from his, but he tightened his grip, holding them in place. "I need some reason to walk down the aisle."

Rubbing his thumbs over the back of my hands, he sighed. "Impetuous, tha' ye are." He smiled. "And, aye, the Englishness is unfortunate. But I am here willingly. I have an opportunity to no longer be chased by the man who haunts my dreams."

"But—"

He clicked his tongue and gave me a stern look. "Red, ye've said your piece. Now it is my turn." He squeezed my hands as reassurance. "I didna set out to wed ye. Bed ye, maybe... I willna lie tha' I didn't want to ken what it'd feel like to run my hands through your wild fiery hair that never seems to settle while I... I, well, I am a man so a thought or two crossed my mind.

"However, I didna think I'd wed again, but this is the best solution. And truth be told, I'm no' so upset that it 'tis." He chewed his lip for a moment. "Ye dressed as a man to join a ship's crew, sailin' across the ocean to unknown dangers. All because ye wanted to take control of your own life. Ye didna give up." He unlinked one of his hands from mine to wave it down the length of me. "Christ, look at ye. Ye could have married righ' away and found a new life in London if ye hadna been so daring to board a privateering ship. Ye woulda been fine." His exhale was deep, heaving his whole chest. "I guess what I'm saying is, for the first time in a decade, I've been waking up excited for the day, my thoughts upon ye. To the point I lose reason, I think of you. Even if it was just to wonder how far I could push ye before you called me a pirate savage."

We both laughed for a moment. But then the only sound between us was our heavy breathing.

Good Lord, I wanted this man.

Walking down the aisle, the floating, cut-of-body experience returned.

But I was quickly snapped back into reality like being hit by a strike of lightning the moment my gaze landed on Commodore Cobbe in his full Royal Navy garb, several privates behind him.

I could not wait until Lock—Alexander—would at last be able to claim his vengeance on the man.

Next to the commodore was a man wearing black robes and a white kerchief around his neck holding a Bible. The chaplain.

My hands trembled. I'd married John in a church under vastly different circumstances. I'd been excited for a new life, but I didn't have this feeling, like a thousand fireflies full of energy flying in my stomach. When my sight landed on Alexander, standing in front of the chaplain, looking like a warrior ready to fight for Scotland, I wanted to reach out to him, cup his face, and promise myself to him. Wanted to fall into his green gaze and lose myself completely. My knees were weak. I wasn't sure I could make it the rest of the way, but his face, his eyes, full of warmth, were like a magnet.

I was a moth, and he was the brightest flame. Inexplicably drawn to him. His fire threatened to consume me, but Lord if I wasn't already burning.

I didn't even notice at first that a wooden archway with realistic carved flowers stood behind the men.

Reaching Alexander, we held hands, facing each other under the arch. The ship bobbed in its berth. I understood now why Reykjavik meant "bay of smoke." The golden, early morning light shone through smoky-like fog. One of the crewmates, who usually played light-hearted drinking reels, had transformed into an orchestra-worthy violinist. It was surprisingly beautiful and, like my gown, this wedding no longer felt like a ruse. A thick lump formed in my throat.

The chaplain said the generic lines; we repeated each word. The whole ceremony passed in a haze. I wasn't sure what I was vowing, but I would have promised Lock anything if it meant I got to keep him.

Even as he said, "Will you, Xander Lock, take Emme Clark, to be your wife, to have..."

Whether from the lack of sleep or booze, my vision was as foggy as London's sky. Until Alexander stared into my eyes, slid a ring on my finger and said, "I will." His voice was sound, sure.

Then the chaplain asked me the same question he asked my soon-to-be-husband, but I could just make out the words over the thudding of my heart in my ears. I met Alexander's gaze and lost myself in his eyes. For a moment, it was just the two of us, and a real smile found its way to my face as warmth built in my chest. "I will."

And I would.

"I now pronounce you husband and wife. You may kiss your bride."

Alexander took a step near me and wrapped one hand around my waist to tug me closer to him. He licked his lips and chuckled, a slight tinge of pink on his cheeks. It wouldn't be our first kiss, but this would be under entirely different circumstances. I angled my head back as he bent his, and our lips brushed. Each traverse of his lips on mine sent a ripple of heat down my body as his hand tightened on my waist, and I arched my body nearer his, our kiss deepening. Cheers erupted around us, pulling us from the moment.

We looked upon the crew as the chaplain said, "I'd like to introduce you to Captain and Mistress Lock."

A pparently Lock—Alexander—had spent most of the evening planning everything. Had he been so sure of my decision?

We had a delicious feast of seafood prepared by the ship's cook and a variety of spirits we usually lacked.

It was odd, sitting next to my *husband.* My body hummed at the very idea—when I was able to sit, that was. I believed I'd danced with every crew member at least twice—well, every member except my husband. In their defense, I was the only woman on board. I'd been reeled and jigged and spun and tossed about the main deck for hours now. Even though I hadn't slept, I had enough adrenaline to spur me forward.

Catching my breath, I peered down at my ring finger and up to my husband sitting beside me on my right. The ring was a simple metal band, but I didn't want anything else. I'd had that life of luxury—and I was learning that maybe it wasn't what I had hoped it would be.

"It was all I could find." I was about to ask what he meant, but his gaze was on my finger. "I wanted to get ye somethin' more, but most smiths were closed for the night and—"

"It's perfect. Truly. I've no need for anything elaborate." I offered a smile and met his eyes—it was a little awkward between us, especially considering hours before we'd been perfectly able to play man and whore.

He fiddled with his sleeve. "Well, elaborate looks good on ye, if your gown is any indication. Have I told ye how beautiful you are?"

My cheeks warmed, and I stared down at the beady-eyed, shelled creature on my plate for a minute before returning my eyes to his. "I believe divine was your exact word earlier. But I'll take both."

His lips hinted at a smile. "You deserve both." He slid his hand across the space between us until his thumb grazed my pinky. For a moment, his hand flickered as if he'd meant to grab mine, but he rested his palm back down on the wooden table, allowing me to consider his touch a coincidence.

I bit my lip and placed my hand on top of his, entwining our fingers. Leaning to the shell of his ear, I whispered, "You can touch me, Alexander."

He raised his gaze to mine, our faces close enough to kiss, and searched my eyes. "I suppose it would be odd if I didna."

"Aye." I squeezed his hand, the air lighter between us.

He rotated our clasped hands. "Your hand is so tiny in mine, Red." He paused, drawing circles on my hand with his thumb. "'Spose I could get used to this." The smile he offered me was full, genuine, and it sparkled in his eyes. My stomach fluttered as he lifted our entwined hands and kissed the back of mine.

The commodore and his cronies marched towards us, a smug

smile upon his face. His stare landed on Alexander before flicking to me. "I do believe congratulations to the happy newly wedded couple are in order. A deal is a deal. We are set to leave today. As promised, I'll cease hunting you."

Alexander's grip tightened on my hand, and I squeezed him back. My teeth were set on edge. What was this man playing at? More importantly, could we take him at his word?

Cobbe's thin lips curled upward as he made his sniffing tic. "Do ensure the wedding contract is legal and binding."

Legal and binding meaning consummated. I was surprised he didn't ask to sit in the room at this point.

As he stalked away, Alex didn't release his tight grip on my hand until they completely disembarked. William nodded from across the deck.

His hand relaxed with an exhale.

"Do you think he has something in play? This seems too easy."

After a dry bark, he shook his head. "Nay. We will send out some long boats to scout before we set sail on the *Bluebell*. But I suspect he willna lay in wait. Something that completely destroyed my life for the last decade has been but another notch in a long list of his indiscretions. What is the death of a Highlander woman to the likes of him?" He tucked his bottom lip under his teeth.

I squeezed his hand again. "We'll find him again. With a new plan. You'll have your time with him."

His chest heaved before he rolled his shoulders. "This is not talk for a celebration. Now, drink, eat, be merry. These hogs willna leave us a crumb or drop for tomorrow. Enjoy it now. It is all for ye, after all."

My chest filled with warmth.

I'd long since learned what transpired on a wedding night. But here I was, blushing and as awkward as I was on my first one as we wound around the ship. With every step we took, I was more and more aware of the feel of Alexander's hand in mine. His warmth. His calluses. His large fingers engulfing mine.

I shouldn't be nervous; we'd technically spent many nights together. But I was lying to myself. This time *was* different.

Twisting the key to the cabin in the dark, he creaked open the door and waved an arm before the entrance. The room was illuminated by dozens upon dozens of candles and lanterns, and there was champagne waiting for us. "After ye, *wife*."

A hysterical laugh nearly bubbled from my chest. *Wife*.

Entering the cabin, there were more spirits and another spread of food laid out on the navigation table. The large bed had been made with fresh linens.

He rushed past me. "Can I offer ye a drink? There's champagne, wine, even found a new bottle of Scottish whisky in port. Though the spiced wine is tradition." He was talking fast; perhaps he had his own set of nerves to combat. I didn't reply as I continued to scan the room. Someone had even gone so far as to put fresh, powder-pink flowers that deepened to a rich purple around their centers in vases. "But nothin' about this wedding has been traditional, so have whatever it is ye fancy."

I registered his words at last as he hovered on his toes some distance away from me. His shyness endeared him to me. Here he was unsure, not the powerful captain ordering his crew around.

I stepped closer. "Oh, umm, I'll have whatever you're having."

He stood in place, his eyes roving over me, dipping to my bodice's plunging neckline. As if catching himself, he snapped them back up to my face. "Aye. How about some whisky?" He turned his back to me as he uncorked the bottle with a *pop* and poured two glasses.

My skirt swished on the floorboards as I walked behind him, placing a hand on his shoulder, his muscles stiffening at my touch. "You don't have to look away." He faced me, both cups in his hands, his eyes wide. "After all…" I waved my hand down my body. "The makeup, the hair, the dress... this is all for you."

I echoed his words about the feast. Would it be too much to hope he could grow to love me? We were both perhaps trying to please one another. Our new spouses. He nodded and passed me a cup. Our fingers brushed when he handed it to me, my hand tingling everywhere his skin met mine.

Sitting at the foot of the bed, I sipped the amber liquid. Alexander leaned against the table, working on his own drink. It was silent, but not uncomfortable.

I finished my drink and looked up at him from under my eyelashes. He was peering into his cup, seemingly lost in thought. If only I knew how he felt. But maybe he was as nervous as I. We needed to relax. I rose and popped the champagne.

The sound caught his attention, and he rushed over. "Here,

allow me."

I shook my head and smiled. "No, sit, I've got it."

We both reached for the same empty champagne coupe glass, knocking it over, sending it to the floor where it shattered. I gasped as he *hmph*ed, and our eyes met. A giggle bubbled from my chest, slowly, one at a time, until it turned into full-fledged laughter. Lock's baritone chuckle quickly followed.

I swiped at an escaped tear as I reined in my laughter. "We don't need glasses, anyway." I took the champagne and swigged straight from the bottle before offering it to him.

"We're really muckin' this up, aren't we?" He swallowed a hefty amount before white fizzy foam coated his upper lip. Without thinking, I brushed it away with my thumb. He froze at the contact, his stare zeroed in on my face.

I sucked the champagne off my finger without breaking eye contact. "Aye. I suppose we should be undressing each other with reckless abandon."

"Reckless abandon?" He took another draw on the champagne bottle before returning it to me and sitting on the edge of the bed. "Is that how it was on your first wedding night?"

His question elicited more laughter from me. "Heavens, no. John spent four hours showing me the insides of various clocks before we even went upstairs to the bedchamber. He fancied himself more horologist than navy captain fighting for the Crown." Holding the bottle, I walked around the shattered glass to stand in front of him. "And then when we were there, our first interaction was more like a business transaction. We weren't exactly—"

I cut off my words abruptly—I was talking about being intimate with my dead husband to my new husband. My face blanched.

"I willna ever tell ye to no' speak of him. He was a part of your life. Here"—he gestured to and fro between us—"ye can share anythin' ye wish."

My chest heaved with a heavy sigh. "I didn't expect to be in this circumstance." Smoothing my skirt, I avoided his gaze. "I've never... Well, John was the only person I've been to bed with."

When it was silent for a moment, I gathered the courage to look at my new husband, hoping he'd say something.

His expression was distant, the shadows from the candlelight flickering over his handsome face. He chewed on his lip for a moment. "We dinna... well, I'd never press ye into anythin'." From under furrowed brows, he peered at me. "If we dinna consummate, ye could have an annulment. I dinna want a wife who doesna like me. I'd understand ye no' wanting to be tied to a man wanted by the Crown. That you might want to go back to your fancy life—"

I placed my fingers over his lips. Truth was, he was right. This very well could end here. I hadn't even considered the idea, because I had wanted this moment so damn badly. Wanted him. Not just physically, but... more.

And apparently, I needed to show him that.

I dragged my fingers down his mouth, his bottom lip pulling with the movement before I slid my hand to cup his face, stubble scratching my fingers. My body burned. My skin flamed. My stomach warmed.

Lifting my skirts, I climbed on top of his lap, straddling his legs as I ran my hands through his thick waves, his head leaning back. "Alexander, I want you."

He mumbled something in Gaelic that I suspect would be incoherent to me, even if I spoke the language. "Thank fucking Christ."

He crashed his mouth against me, and the world stopped turning with that kiss. His mouth ravaged mine like he was a starving sailor marooned on an island, and I was his first meal. But he pulled back, cutting the kiss short, a question in his eyes. I nodded, but he didn't move, instead letting me take control, to move at my own pace.

Still sitting on top of him, I slid his waistcoat off his shoulders, his mouth breathing into the crook of my neck.

"Ye're tremblin'." He squeezed my hand. "We dinna have to do anythin' tonight."

Every muscle in my body vibrated with anticipation. "It's not out of fear, Alexander." I bent to kiss his neck over his pulse. "It's out of need."

His eyes shut at my words. When they reopened, they were hooded. I removed the brooch holding his plaid sash in place and tugged on the side closest to me to undo it. He anchored his hand on my waist, his warm breath pressing into my neck. Winding my arms around his hips, I unlatched his sporran and tossed it aside. His thighs tensed between mine. I leaned back to admire him, now that he was left to only his kilt and shirt.

The tips of my fingers touched the bare skin and hair peeking out of the top of his shirt. My stomach tightened, warmth coiling low. I rolled my hand down his chest, his stomach, grazing every mound of muscle hidden beneath his shirt. I yanked the edge of his shirt free from his kilt. With a newfound courage, I ran my hands under his shirt to get an even better feel of his stomach and chest.

He grunted, the sound emanating from deep in his chest. Wrapping a hand around my waist, he jolted me closer to him, the hard length of him pressing against my thigh. I lifted the hem of his shirt, and he raised his arms for me to tug it off. He was now bare from his hips up.

I explored his body with my hands, caressing him everywhere. He allowed me to peruse him at my will. I swirled my thumb over a nipple, and he grunted again. He leaned forward to nuzzle my neck, his hand clenching my hair.

I knew he was passion embodied. A man who vowed loyalty to his family even beyond death. And those facts were perhaps my first undoing when it came to him. But good Lord, the fact he felt like this underneath my hands... I was utterly done for.

He was holding himself back. His hands twitched, as if aching to touch me as he grazed his lips, not fully connecting, down my throat. He kept himself steady at a distance, perhaps permitting me time to make myself comfortable, permitting me control.

But I wanted him to lose control as much as I had. I rose, climbing off his lap, and turned my back to him. He answered my unasked demand, rising and sweeping my hair over my shoulder on one side. His breath tickled my exposed ear as he began to work on the top button. His knuckles grazed my back as he made his way down the row.

He fiddled a bit with the last one at the small of my back. "It's stuck." One hand palmed my lower back as the other worked the button. "Sorry. Almost got it. There." His palm didn't leave my back immediately; he swiped his thumb on my skin above my shift. "Your skin is verra soft."

His touch shot chills up my spine, and goosebumps crept down my arms. My hands ached to reach out to him. I faced him again, dropping the gown, letting it pool at my feet. My stays and shift were the only things left on me.

I pushed him back onto the foot of the bed. Placing myself between his parted legs, I inclined my head and dropped my gaze to the ties of my stays. "If you'd be so kind."

He gave a small half smile, peering up, gaze hooded. "I'd be verra much obliged." Without breaking eye contact, he tugged one side of the bow before moving to the other side and undoing the knot completely. He hooked his fingers on the lacing and spread the tie before raising the stays over my arms and head.

I placed my palms on his bare, beautiful chest. I was left in only my shift, and his gaze was appreciative, hungry, and Lord, I'd lost all semblance of control.

Dropping my hands from his chest, I grasped his cheeks and pulled his face to mine. Hunger filled my kiss as our lips met—and his responding kiss told me he felt the same. We were heavy breaths and caresses, devouring each other's skin wherever we could place our lips.

And as if I'd broken the dam, no longer satisfied in giving me the helm of his ship, his touch transformed into a craze before he rose to his feet again. His arms encircled me, and I was lifted into the air until he placed me gently on the bed. As he stood before me at the foot of the bed, I slid my hands under his kilt, massaging his massive, muscular thighs. I reached higher, wrapping my hand around him, and stroked my hand up and down. His head dropped back, and he muttered garbled words.

I should have felt embarrassed at my heady need for him... But instead, all I felt was him, here in this moment, the heat of our bodies mingling with the flames of the candles, his thickness heavy in my hand.

This marriage might work—I wanted him, wanted this moment, to feel closer to him as our bodies joined. The sense of shame I expected over being with a new man so soon after John's death, about my raw desire instead of propriety and duty expected of me as a wife... well, it never came. I shouldn't have been so uninhibited, but I was.

Ready for more, I fumbled with his kilt, trying to remove it. I was tempted to drag it down him, but he captured my hands, and dutifully undid his kilt for me, his gaze on me, taking a slow time of it. I didn't remove my eyes from his deft fingers until, at last, the garment dropped to the floor in a puddle of plaid. He was completely bare to me. His massive body, in all its muscled glory, was a work of art. I swallowed the nerves building in my throat and leaned back, perching on my elbows, chest arched toward him. His eyes swam over me despite still being fully covered by my shift. A small smile graced his full lips, and it made me ache in deep places, yearning.

Stalking forward, he nudged himself to stand between my knees, and lifted the hem of my shift up my legs to my thighs. Although simple linen, my senses were heightened to the point I felt every inch of the material slide up. He brushed his fingers across my cheeks, down my neck, before bending to claim my lips.

Kissing was an art he made slow, agonizing work of. I reciprocated, as starved for this as he was, but he cut it off and peppered kisses down my throat. A breathy moan escaped my lips, and my head lolled back, every part of me hyper aware of where he touched.

He lowered his lips to my chest, to the swell of my breasts. Through the material, he brushed his fingers over my peaked nipples and cupped my breasts. I pushed myself into his palm. His breathing was as shallow as mine. Bending down, he took a hardened nipple into his mouth through the light linen. Between the wet warmth of his mouth and the rough fabric rubbing against me, I was driven mad. I placed my hands on his shoulders, simultaneously pulling him closer and clenching my fingers into his skin.

Releasing his hold on me, he leaned back to assess me, his stare scouring my face with unabashed desire.

He toyed his fingers with the tie over the shift's keyhole on my bosom. "May I?"

"Oh God, please." My voice was nothing but raspy breaths.

He tugged one side of the bow, loosening it, and chuckled. "I'm glad we're in agreement." A yank on the other side released the bow, and the neckline billowed. He pushed one side off my shoulder before repeating the action on the other side, and it fell to my waist. Any sense of embarrassment I thought I'd feel was burned up by the flames heating my body, aching for all of him. He palmed my chest, shooting a shock of pleasure low in my belly.

I scooted back and lay down on the bed, and he crawled over me while he rubbed his hand up my legs under the dress, puddling it around my hips, before his thumb swiped between my thighs. A burning hot sensation made me yip out loud. His chest rumbled, and he nuzzled my neck, showering me with his lips in the sensitive spots over my neck, my breasts, everywhere.

Our slow dance transformed into heady, desperate need. I was out of control as instinct drove me. I caressed his silky head and length with urgency before he tugged down my dress. I lifted my hips to let him peel it off me completely. He smoothed his hands over the swell of my backside. My knees arched on the bed, my thighs pressing against his waist as he settled himself in a comfortable position against me.

For a moment, neither of us did anything, and then he bent his head down to kiss me. A questioning kiss, a last chance for me to stop this. But there was no way I could stop now. I clasped my hand around him and guided him toward my entrance, and he slid in with ease. The moment we connected fully, I released a relieved sigh, his body soothing an aching need.

He thrusted in, and I squealed—in shock and pleasure—and he grunted. Our bodies quickly found a rhythm. I wrapped my arms around his neck, kissing and sucking his ear. Running my hands down his back to his arse, I relished the feel of him as his muscles flexed under my fingertips.

He roughly pulled my hair to further expose my throat to his mouth. The slight stinging tingles of my scalp added to my pleasure, to the excitement, and I clenched myself around his hard erection. He moaned, and I clenched him again. He cupped my breasts and sucked on each nipple, swirling his tongue around before taking a quick nip with his teeth. Burning pleasure sent mini shockwaves through me.

I dug my nails into his buttocks, tugging him closer. He picked up his pace and thrust harder, faster. I was at the brink of pleasure, and when I thought I could take no more, he swiped his thumb over the spot between my thighs again, and I cried out. My body clenched tight around him as waves of pleasure pulsated through my body, and he thrust at a near painful force. His own groans of pleasure came as he slowed to a stop until he released all of his warm seed inside me.

We were panting, a sheen of sweat coating both of us as we stayed connected. He twitched inside of me, his sagging body crushing me, but I didn't want to leave this position, this bed, this room. The smell of our passion lingered, mixing with the melting candles and the echoes of our vows to each other. Our gazes met, and we kissed, soft and satiated.

"I dinna want to move from this position." He ran his nose along my jaw as if he read my thoughts.

"And I don't want you to." I captured his cheeks and pulled his lips to mine, sweeping my tongue over his before licking down his ear and throat.

"If ye keep doin' that, I willna," he replied, a brilliant full smile on his face.

"Mmm. Promise?" I arched my back, my nipples rubbing

against his chest, as I continued kissing him.

A small laugh mingled with his groan, and I felt him hardening inside me once more. With lightning speed, he flipped us so he was on his back and I was on top of him. I rocked my hips back and forth over him. His fingers found the sensitive spot between my legs, and I was already on edge.

Coils of lightning stirred through my body. "Holy... if you keep doing that to me, I may never let you leave this room."

"Promise?" he asked.

I never got a chance to answer because he squeezed my nipple with one hand as his other brought me to fruition. I shattered with a loud cry before he flipped us back over, and he propelled himself into his own release.

I watched the muscles of his bare backside flex as he padded over to pour us each some wine. God, I could look at him all day. When he turned back, I was accosted by his front side. Every mound of muscle in his stomach demanded to be explored, and his manhood swung against his thighs as he stalked back to me.

My mouth dried. After three times of joining one another, I should be satiated, but Lord, I somehow wanted more.

"Ye keep lookin' at me like that, we'll never sleep." He climbed into bed next to me before he handed me a glass. "And while that'd normally not be a problem, neither of us have slept in two days. I canna already be failing my wife by not ensuring her basic needs are met." He placed a kiss on one corner of my lips, then my ear.

I gulped a large amount and sank my body against his. "I've many needs. Right now, sleep is not one of them."

"Wife, ye undo me." He traced his fingers down my side. I'd noticed, when next to me, he'd kept a hand on me at all times. "Will I never tire of ye?"

I finished my wine and laughed. "I hope not."

"Is this how it is with ye? Did John have to leave because otherwise he was never able to leave your bed?" His hands perused my body while he drank, like it was natural, like we laid in bed nude together all the time. "Ye'll be bad for my productivity."

I laughed. "No. It was never like this with him. This..." I paused, unsure what to say. I met his green gaze. "This, we're, well. T-that was..." My cheeks warmed. "It's never been like that before. For me."

He finished his wine and took mine and his empty cup, placing them on the floor beside the bed. "Nor I." He grazed his lips down my jaw. "That was..." He kissed me deeply, as if trying to portray every emotion he felt with his lips. "But now we must sleep."

Leaning back, he patted the spot next to him. I curled up beside him, his warmth already safe and familiar. "Goodnight, wife."

In a moment, his chest rose and fell. I was tired and well-satiated, but I couldn't sleep.

I had been so worried about him yesterday, being bound to another loveless marriage, and now I was worried about the opposite.

I had another husband. Another man in my life who could let me down, abandon me.

My fear all this time was about losing my jointure. Was it

possible I didn't want to lose him even more?

18

A knock sounded at the door, and I clenched the duvet between my fingers, tugging it over me just before William walked in. Drapes were yanked open, and bright sunlight accosted me, forcing my eyes shut. I peeled open one eye and used my hand to block the light.

"The scouts have returned," William announced. "There is work to be done, Capt'n."

A glare pasted itself on my husband's face. "Message received."

An illicit thrill shot through me. *My husband*—odd, exciting... terrifying.

I didn't unclench my fingers from the sheets until the door clicked shut. With a heavy sigh, I looked up at Alexander and flicked my eyes away from him the moment I took in his bare chest. My cheeks heated as memories of the night before washed over me. Echoes of his touch lingered on my flushed, sore skin. His scent clung to both my body and the sheets that wrapped around me.

He squeezed my hand. "Good morning, Emme." His voice was stilted; perhaps he was a tad shy himself this morning. "Suppose we should dress."

I smiled, regarding our entwined fingers. "Indeed."

In the morning light, and mayhap in sobriety, a touch of awkwardness returned as we fumbled out of bed, covering bare parts of ourselves we laid raw to each other mere hours ago. His back muscles rippled as he perched on the edge of the bed and slid on his breeches. A flash of how it felt to have my hands rub down his thighs stirred flutters in my stomach.

"I think I'll miss the kilt." I bit my lip to prevent any further words from spilling out.

"Oh, aye?" He peered over his shoulder at me, eyes glittering with... I didn't know what, but I'd sure like to learn what it meant when my husband looked at me like that.

Heat coursed through me, and not just my cheeks this time. "Yes." To hell with shyness, this man was my husband. I rose from the bed and sashayed to my discarded nightdress on the ground, taking a particularly long time to slip it on over my head. His gaze was on me when I finished, and I smiled, leaning against the table. "Seems easier."

"Easier?" He stood and stalked across the wooden floorboards to me, every step as intentional as my own. My back dug into the table behind me when he placed a hand around each hip, gripping the wood. "Easier for what?" The golden skin of his chest and sinewy arms were enticing enough to urge my words forward.

"For access." I licked my lips.

He hummed into my neck, grazing my jaw with his nose. "I was hopin' ye'd say somethin' like that. When ye saw me naked just now, your face was so red I thought maybe I'd made up last night in my head. The color so crimson it nigh matched your hair." I'd no time to reply because he sucked my bottom lip in his mouth before he finished saying his last word.

I melted against him, his hips pinning me to the table, and I wrapped my arms around his neck as our kiss deepened.

His hands ran through my curls, which were no doubt a knotted mess. He removed his lips from mine long enough to say, "Have I ever told ye how much I love your hair?" Resuming his kisses, I'd no opportunity to answer, but as his hips ground into me, I didn't care. He stopped too soon and brushed my lip with his thumb, his stare intense. "Thank ye for last night, Mistress MacLachlan."

I stiffened. Emme MacLachlan. Forever gone was Emme Clark. A simultaneous bolt of fear and elation shot through me. I had no idea where he stood. Was this all convenience? To be sure, there were some obvious signs he liked me, one very large sign currently pressed against my stomach, but as he had said, it was a long, lonely voyage to the Indies. Could he want more?

"I'm sorry." His Scottish brogue was thick, and he backed away a bit, allowing me some distance. "I shouldna push. Everything was..."

I shook my head, snapping out of the uncertain moment.

"No." Inching near him, my hands found a home on his chest. "It was a momentary shock. A surprise. Not shock. Shock sounds as if it was unpleasant and it's not, and—"

"Red." He cupped the backs of my hands on his chest. "I willna..." He shook his head and cleared his throat. "I am here for whatever is to come."

I eyed the floorboards for a long pause before I dared to meet his gaze. "We're in this together?"

His lips curled into a small smile. "For as long as ye'll have me." We were silent for a few beats, taking comfort in our closeness and each other's arms. "Now, dress yourself, wife. If I lost reason when I thought of you before... Well, ye'll need clothes. We need to get to scheming again."

I nodded as he walked away to slip on a shirt before he shuffled papers on the navigation table. On an exhale, I peered at the ceiling, staring for a moment.

Once I looked back down, he was already concentrating on a map, lip tucked under his teeth, his curl falling across his forehead, his sleeves rolled to his elbow, revealing those muscular forearms. Strength and power embodied, yet he'd let me make all the decisions last night.

Now that I had had him, I didn't know if I could let him go if he made me.

"Walkin' a bit of a challenge for ya today, Emme?" William skittered up from behind me.

I rolled my eyes. "Oh, devil take you."

His lips split into a wide grin. "Ya know I jest." One brow perched high, he leaned in. "But tell me, was it everything ya were hopin'?" He fanned himself. "Heaven only knows..."

I giggled and ran my hands over my warm face. "You're a

meddlesome, incorrigible man."

"Aye." He winked. "Where ya headed?"

On a groan, I frowned. "Back to the whorehouse. Can't wear this blue dress and my wedding gown everywhere."

"Don't sound so excited." He linked his arm around mine. "I'll escort ya. So long as we can have one more hot meal before we depart today." As we descended the gangway, he paused and arched his brow. "Perhaps they have a riding habit ya could buy off 'em."

"You remembered?" I smiled widely about what I'd dreamed staying on a privateering ship would look like.

"When ya declared your undying love for Mac?" He chuckled. "Aye, I remember."

I elbowed him in the ribs. "You're irksome, you know? There were no declarations of love." I huffed out air. "This marriage was pure convenience."

He rubbed the back of his neck. "Convenience? What do ya call last night, then?"

My chest was tight, and I unlinked our arms to wrap my arms around myself. My gaze landed on a particularly barnacle-covered dock pole, foamy waves lapping against it. "More convenience, to be sure, on his part. Easier to bed your new wife than pay for a whore."

William clasped my chin and steered my gaze to his. "Ya ain't serious?"

I yanked my chin from his hand lest he see the tears threatening to fall. "Yes."

"Goodness, ya can be daft, lass." He folded his arms over his chest. "If ya haven't noticed, he's as mad about ya as ya're him, ya're—"

I shook my head and continued walking down the dock as seagulls cawed before me, fighting over something on the ground a few paces away. "If you're here just to insult me, I will go by myself."

His boots thwacking on the wooden planks were my only sign before a hand on my shoulder stopped me. "Emme, I'm not here to insult ya. Just knock some sense in ya. I care for ya both. Don't ya think I want you to be happy?"

I pursed my lips, swallowing, and remained silent. He was wrong. Right?

A groan escaped me as we paced through the last of the dock to try land. "Fine. I'll indulge you. Why would you think what transpired between us meant *anything* to him? He travels the world—I'm sure he has a lass at every port."

And there had been that letter addressed to a Violet on the navigation table. Was she a lover? If the buccaneer captain and his lusty journal were any indication, captains were prime meat for the amorous ladies in port towns—and all of 'em were rakes, through and through.

William shook his head. "I assure ya, he doesn't. He stays in the ship most stops."

I arched a brow. "Then you'd procure him a whore, like our plan alluded to the other night." My feet planted wide on the dirt. "If it hadn't been me last night, it would have been one of the women I met who helped ready me for the damned wedding."

"Negative." He shoved back the brim of his hat, revealing more of his forehead and his hair. "I don't remember a time he's ever indulged in the local fare. If you recall, that part of the plan had been your idea."

A nagging feeling turned my stomach. What about the commodore? Once Alexander had his revenge, this could all end. He could very well drop me in Jamaica and leave me for good.

And I'd be left all alone again.

But maybe William was right.

I toed my shoe on the ground as I stepped aside, leaving room for the grumbling sailors to cross with their heavy cargo. "You mean to say that last night could very well have meant something... something more to him?"

"Aye, lass." He linked his elbow to mine again, tugging me in the direction of the town. "That's what I've been tryin' to tell ya."

With my free hand, I clutched my chest. He could very well feel the way I felt, which was... hopeful? Excited? What would it be like to allow myself to fall in love with him?

I didn't know, but I couldn't wait to return home to the *Bluebell*, to him, and ask him my questions—and spend another night learning about each other's bodies.

19

When I returned to the *Bluebell*, we were ready to set sail. Some of my curls floated around my face from the icy breeze as I stood on the quarterdeck with William and Alexander. The smoky mist didn't let any daylight shine through.

"And you're sure Cobbe will not lie in wait to ambush us?" I asked, my eyes dipping to the rope in my husband's hands as he tied an intricate knot. Lord knew I'd discovered exactly *how* dexterous and apt those fingers were. My chest and neck warmed in a flush. Could a person be jealous of rope?

William shouted orders to the crew buzzing around the deck. A group of men at the capstan heaved and hoed and it began to rotate, gears clicking, as they raised the anchor.

"The scouts followed them in the longboat for almost a whole day. They found no indication of a plan." Alexander peered at me, my eyes still pinned to his hands, my lips parting slightly. "Did ye want me to teach ye some knots?"

"What?" I snapped my gaze to his. "Oh no, I was... never mind. Don't you think it was all too easy? There must be some kind of trick. Maybe something about the island project."

"Easy?" He arched a brow. "Christ, Emme. We're married now. Not exactly the easy way out."

I flinched, feeling my face blanch. "Right." There was the confirmation I had. "I—I'm tired, I think I shall lay down." I started walking before I finished speaking, my throat constricting. I didn't want him to see my face.

"Dim-witted fool," William said, presumably to my husband, but I was already climbing the steps down to the next deck.

Once I'd slammed shut the door to the captain's cabin, the warmth in my eyes gave way to the tears I'd withheld. I sank down on the ground. My silver ring caught in the light of the lanterns. I twisted it about on my finger and swiped away the tears on my cheeks.

"Why are you crying, Emme Clark?" I asked myself before huffing a dry laugh. "Or rather, Emme MacLachlan."

There was no need for tears; I had everything I'd come for. I had John's proof of death, thereby gaining access to my jointure. And now I'd just have to help Lock with his asinine plan and then we'd stop in Jamaica, and I'd be back to London before I knew it.

Alexander Grant MacLachlan was just a very minor, at best, bump in my journey, and he'd be erased from my memory like shells in the sand during high tide.

I rose to my feet and held my chin high. No, I'd not cry over the man.

Even if he had a muscled body, that he *indeed* knew how to use. Or that he was the embodiment of loyalty to family. No, I would not cry.

My shoulders sagged. The green landscape of Iceland started moving past the wall of windows. Good. That much sooner we'd be on our way, and I'd be away from him. Good riddance, *dear* husband.

The door creaked open, and I stood straighter, arms folded, watching the swaying landscape pass by us.

"Emme."

I pursed my lips and refused to face him, instead focusing on the sharp mountains of Reykjavik.

Warm hands clasped my shoulders from behind. "Red." His lips were at my ear, the name breathy, eliciting goosebumps down that half of my body.

I momentarily shut my eyes before I remembered I hated the man. I shrugged his hands off my shoulders and faced him. "Thank you for last night. I had thought you rather enjoyed yourself, but I see I was mistaken. I hope it wasn't too difficult for you."

I shoved past him and removed my coat, tossing it on the bed, revealing the low-cut cornflower gown, because I hadn't yet tried on any of the others I'd bought that morning—though I wasn't sure if they were any more modest. "I will not ask you to lay with me again. Now, if you'll excuse me, I should like to take a nap."

I perched myself on the edge of the bed and bent over to remove my short boots. When I sat back up, I found his eyes on my bosom. I pushed my cheek out with my tongue and folded my arms around my chest.

"Red." He stalked toward me.

"Do not *Red* me!" He was closing the distance between us, his expression unreadable. I clutched the bed cover in each hand, feelin' suddenly like prey. "You-you—"

"Pirate savage?" He inclined his head as he cupped my cheeks, leaning my head back to meet his gaze.

I narrowed my eyes, his face close. Too close. "Get your hands off me. I'd hate for you to be obligated to—"

"I'm sorry." He slid one hand from my cheek to grasp my hair. "When I said we didn't get off easy, I meant *you* didn't get off easy." He grazed his lips down my neck. "Ye're the one good thing that has come out of this whole fiasco." He kissed my neck at the pulse, and my toes curled in their stockings. "And if ye didna ken that…" Another kiss on my collarbone, and heat coursed through me. "I've already let ye down as a husband." A quick kiss on my lips, and I melted.

He pulled back, eyes scanning my face. "Do ye still want me to take my hands off ye?"

"I…" Did I? I slowly shook my head. "I've had a husband who was never there. The life I had expected, wanted—I didn't get." I swallowed. "And if we are to live separate lives, if we are not to be husband and wife more than on a piece of paper, then spare my heart. Because if we keep…" I licked my lips. "I don't know if, when the time comes, if I could part from you, should we stay on this path." I waved my hand between us.

His breaths were shallow, the hand in my hair clenching. He didn't say anything. My heart pounded so loud I was worried he could hear it, but he still didn't move, and then he dropped his hands from me and twisted away.

Slumping, I exhaled and nodded. "Very well th—"

He paced to the navigation table and pulled off the piece of rope he was practicing knots on earlier, and sank to his knees on the floor. My eyes widened. "I lay myself at your feet, Emme MacLachlan." I sat straighter. "I canna promise ye the world, but I can promise ye all of me. I am yours, fully, if ye'll have me. Say the word."

My lips parted, and I arched toward him. "Yes."

He gave me a lopsided smile. "Come…" His proffered hand hovered in the air between us, and I knew if I accepted it, there'd be no turning back. I'd leave my heart and soul for him to cherish or decimate. And dammit if I didn't want all of him. I curled my fingers around his and lowered to my knees on the floor in front of him.

"We're in this together," he said, my *husband,* his warm hand encompassing mine.

The grin splitting his lips brought a wide smile to my own. A thousand butterflies stirred in my stomach, flying as erratically as the beating of my heart.

He took the rope, and with one hand, tied it around my wrist, and then tied it around his. He spoke a few sentences in Gaelic, the language unfamiliar yet beautiful in my ears. His green eyes were luminous as they met mine. "I vow you the first cut of my meat, the first sip of my wine, from this day it shall only be your name I cry out in the night and into your eyes that I smile each morning; I shall be a shield for your back as you are for mine, nor shall a grievous word be spoken about us, for our marriage is sacred between us and no stranger shall hear my grievance. Above and beyond this, I will cherish and honor you through this life and into the next."

I stopped breathing altogether.

"A traditional Highland wedding vow." He leaned forward and gave me a chaste kiss before pulling away. "'Tis bad luck if the knot comes undone." He slipped it off my wrist, then his, and placed it in my palm. "Keep it like this."

I curled my fingers over the coarse, fraying rope, a knot sitting halfway through it, and pressed it to my heart. "How can you be so sure? That is, why did you even agree to marry me? I thought you tolerated me at best."

"I can be sure because of faith. And what I feel here." He took my hand and placed it on his chest over his heart. It thudded heavily against my palm. Steady, sure. "And dinna ye ken by now why I wanted to marry you? Because if I married ye, then I'd get to keep ye."

I was left speechless. Unguarded. And I wanted to give all of myself to him, too. Every soft corner and sharp, jagged edge. My knees ached from the wood floor, but I reveled in the feeling of my hand upon him. "I think I'm very fortunate to have found you."

With my hand on his chest, I crumpled the front of his shirt in my fingers and pulled him close to me and brought my lips to his. I brushed my lips over his full, soft ones. Sweet, and agonizingly slow at first, before he dropped from his knees to his bottom, and I climbed over him as he leaned back. I deepened our kiss, parting his lips with my tongue before he opened to me, kissing me back with reckless abandon.

And God, his kiss.

I grasped his hair between my fingers, grateful for his sturdy weight beneath me, because if he had kissed me like that while I was still on my knees, I'd have toppled over, having gone weak in them.

He kissed his lips across my collarbone, up my neck, to my ear, and captured my earlobe. The hair on the back of my neck rose from his shallow puffs of air. "Can I still no' touch ye yet?"

"If you *don't* touch me, I'll have your neck." My head dropped back, eyelids fluttering closed.

"I shoulndna ever taught ye how to shoot a gun." He sucked on my throat, tongue tickling over my pulse as he ran his hands up my legs under my petticoat, cupping my rear. "Ye're verra bonnie in a dress, but I do miss how those breeches hugged your round rump."

I laughed, but it turned into a sharp gasp as he smacked my arse, light, playful. "Pirate savage."

He yanked my hips closer and somehow managed to raise us off the floor, my legs hooking around his waist until we tumbled on the bed. He stood at the edge, and unbuttoned each side of his breeches flap before his erection sprang free, and lifted the hem of his shirt over his head, abandoning it somewhere behind him. "Aye. And I plan to plunder me treasure."

"Oh Christ, what have I started?" I laughed, and he laid over me, one large bicep braced on either side of my head.

He bent his head down and sucked my bottom lip into his mouth, the length of him hard and ready against my hip as he freed one breast out of the top of my bodice. I tugged up my layers of skirts, wet heat pooling low, aching for him, ready to claim what was mine.

My husband.

He trailed his tongue across my collarbone to my breast and to the top of my pebbled nipple. He swirled his tongue once, twice, before he nipped. I yelped and dug my nails into his shoulders.

"If you don't take me right now, Alexander, I swear…" My breathing was shallow and erratic, and I sounded needy even to myself.

"Redheads are always fire and dramatics with death threats. As ye wish, Mrs. Maclachlan." He thrust deep into me and my back arched off the bed.

We rocked our hips together in time to the sway of the ship sailing west on the North Sea. The cabin was silent save for the sound of our impassioned breaths mingling and a bell tolling somewhere on the main deck.

He slid his hand between our bodies to the apex between my thighs and swirled his thumb around the sensitive mound, and my entire body jolted with a zap of pleasure, starting from my core to the tips of my tingling nipples.

I garbled some incoherent words, not even sure what I was trying to say, but as our bodies continued to join, seeking pleasure and relishing in the feel of one another, his gaze met mine. His eyes were an intense storm of green, and I felt as though I was on fire under their weight.

"You undo me, husband," I said into his neck as I kissed up the cords of muscles there.

"Say it again," he whispered, his thrusts coming faster.

"What? Husband?" I licked the shell of his ear, and a groan of pleasure escaped him.

"Aye," he rasped as he toyed with his thumb over my sensitive spot again.

"Husband," I said and sucked on his earlobe, sparks of pleasure fizzing through me. "Husband." He hammered himself into me, and my thighs clenched around his waist as pleasure overwhelmed me, and we both cried out at the same time.

He sagged atop me for a moment before rolling off and lying beside me, both of us panting.

He sighed. "I best get back up top before William starts giving me death threats, too." He rotated my way and grasped my hand. "Halifax, Nova Scotia, awaits in a mere fortnight. Dinna fash, we'll find Cobbe again."

He hurried to redress and kissed my cheek before leaving the cabin.

I exhaled. I wasn't worried if we'd find him, but what would happen when we did.

I couldn't sleep for the third night in a row, plagued by images of the night in Limerick. The closer we came to Nova Scotia, the more anxious I'd become. But my husband's warm chest heaving up and down underneath me, my head in the crook of his arm, told me he had no such problems.

To avoid my unnecessary thoughts, I distracted myself by looking at my husband's sleeping face, lashes fanned over his cheeks, while I drew letters and words on his bare chest with my finger.

"Are ye writin' a novel, lass?" His accent was thick, heavy with sleep. Eyes still closed, he stretched and slid his hands behind his head.

"Aye. Writing it on my favorite canvas." I drew his name on his chest.

He sighed. "I've a better canvas for ye, a little lower."

"Hmm…" I smiled into his chest. "And if I use that canvas, what will you do for me in return?"

"Anything. Literally anything ye'd like, wife." His words were an enticing dare. I slid down his bare body, dipping below the silky duvet covering us. He cursed in Gaelic as I made my intentions clear.

A knock on the door stopped me short.

More Gaelic curses. "I'll kill whoever is there."

"It'll be William. I asked him to help me practice loading the flintlock this morning. But he does have impeccably poor timing." I climbed out from under the covers and pulled a shift over my head, quickly followed by a gown, then opened the door.

William sashayed in and took one look at my husband's glare. "Someone take a piss in your gray sludge of a breakfast this morn'?"

"Don't ask." I gave him a tight-lipped smile. "Let us make haste before my husband challenges you to a duel with one of these." I handed one pistol to him and placed one in a holster and tied it to my waist.

"Lass, please." He arched a brow. "I'm a far superior marksman. He'd never do such a foolish thing to challenge me. It'd be a death wish."

Alexander grumbled, and I pushed William out the door. "Come, let me show you who is truly the superior markswoman."

"Keep the priming powder far from any lantern!" Alexander shouted behind us. "Ye nearly lit the whole ship on fire last time."

I shrugged, closing the door, and linked my arm with William's as we traversed through the ship. "He should have told me the primer granules were extra fine, therefore all the more volatile. Blame the tutor, not the pupil."

William bared his teeth in a grimace. "Oy. Send a spark even near primer, and it'll go off like them fancy French fireworks."

"Well, the bloody ship didn't burn." Crisis averted. Once we climbed up to the main deck, I was met with some wide-eyed stares. Mostly curiosity. I was a woman aboard their sacred home and I had deceived them for so long.

"After target practice, I've a special treat for us to share." From inside his waistcoat, he flashed the cork of a bottle in his pocket. "Aquavit. Got it at port. The good stuff."

The harsh air was windy and frigid. My fingers were so cold they were pink and numb, adding to the difficulty of loading the pistols. But once I'd squeezed the trigger so many times that I no longer flew backwards, I was quite proud of myself.

I leaned against the railing and stared out at the endless blue sea as the ship sliced through it. We were on top of the world here, or so it seemed. The options and opportunities were as limitless as the horizon before us. I took a deep breath and icy, briny air filled my lungs. "It is rather exciting, isn't it?"

After the audible popping of a bottle, William perched beside me, taking a swig before handing it to me. "How do you mean?"

"Privateering. Sailing. Traveling the world." My body tingled, my head light. I could have more than I ever dreamed... I sipped on the clear liquor, the spicy clove flavor coating my tongue as it burned down my throat, warming my stomach. I wiped my lips with the back of my hand. "Bloody hell, that burns."

His chuckle was quick. "Aye. But it warms you."

"That it does. No wonder they drink it in ice-covered lands." I passed the bottle back and gripped the rail in my palms.

"So, I take it you and Mac made up?" Leaning my way, he

nudged my shoulder with his. My knees weakened, and I smiled. "If that sappy grin is any indication, that would be a resounding yes."

"I think I might... I mean, I may be..." I was tongue-tied just thinking about him. Was this love? "He isn't as bad as I thought he was..."

You may be able to fool yourself, but ya don't fool me. Ya've burned for the capt'n since the moment ya laid your eyes on him." He passed back the bottle to me.

"Fine. I think he is quite handsome, and I am rather smitten." I took another sip.

William pushed the bottom of the bottle, tipping more liquid into my mouth. "Ya'll be needin' more if I want the truth."

I coughed, some of the liquid burning my nostrils. "Bastard."

"Ya love me." He raised his eyebrow. "Maybe not as much as ya love Mac." I scoffed. His lips quivered, fighting laughter. "For days now, I've been forced to watch ya two make love with your eyes across the damned ship whenever ya're not directly next to each other. Which isn't often. I'd think ya were sewn together at the hip. Can't believe ya even asked me to help ya shoot today."

I sighed, chest warm, and I didn't think it had anything to do with the aquavit. "Well, I am quite content learning about my new spouse. We may very well work out." I clenched the railing, my knuckles turning white. "But every man who was supposed to love me, who I was supposed to be able to rely on, has always abandoned me. And I'm afraid, so damn afraid, of history repeatin' itself. If I allow myself to fall for Alexander, what will I do when the inevitable happens? I don't think I could start over after losing everything a third time."

He placed one hand over mine. "Emme..." I peered up at him, his eyes warm. "You don't need anyone but yourself. Ya're a survivor." He squeezed my hand. "But ya can't let fear stop ya from seeking happiness. Mac is a good man. Let him in."

I blinked and nodded. "You're a good friend, William."

"Lass." He placed a hand back on the railing and pursed his lips. "I'm the best."

I hugged his arm and leaned my head on his shoulder. "And what about the good commodore? Alexander seems to think he can still lure him out on his own and snatch him in Nova Scotia. But the man goes everywhere with a crew of his men."

William tapped his fingers on the rail. "Whatever his secret project is, maybe he will voyage out on his own, away from prying ears and eyes, and we'll have a better opportunity. Once we land, I will do some investigating."

I gnawed on my lip. "I want my husband to get the justice and revenge he craves... but I can't help but worry it'll all go wrong, and what if he is caught? Or worse, killed?"

"If ya care for him, all ya can do is support him and have his back. I need to know that if I swing the sword to help a man, another one of the crew is at my back swinging one for me. That's what it means to have a crew. Support your crew, your family, until the end. Ya can't be livin' in what-ifs. And look at that holey bucket over there, ya *can* support him. I'll make a privateer out of ya yet."

My eyes landed on my shooting target, the overturned bucket riddled with holes. I smiled. "You think I can commission a riding habit in Halifax?"

21

I scoured the horizon from the bank of windows as if I'd see Cobbe's secret island at any second. A day's sail from Halifax. It could very well be nearby.

"Ye've been quiet." Alexander plopped a bruised pear in between his lips. The juice filled the air, still sweet. Most of the fruit from Iceland had already turned. "Ye havena been this quiet since ye gave me the silent treatment for locking ye in the cabin. Dinna tell me I've angered my wife?" He kissed the hair atop the crown of my head.

"No. I'm just lost in my thoughts." He wrapped his arms around me from behind, and I leaned back into his comforting embrace, placing my arms around him. I could lose myself in his arms. The thought made my stomach clench and my muscles tighten.

William's words echoed in my head: *Ya can't let fear stop ya from seeking happiness.* But couldn't I? It was safer. I knew what it was like to have great expectations, and the bitter bite of disappointment after. If I fell for this man, would he catch me?

"Ye ken, ye can tell me anythin'. Ask me anythin'." He squeezed tighter for a moment.

"Is that so?" I twisted so I could see his face.

He planted a kiss on my lips. "Aye."

I tilted my head from side to side and clenched my teeth, bracing myself. "There *is* something I want to know."

"Why do I feel like I'm in trouble?" He stared deep into my eyes as if he could read my thoughts if he looked hard enough.

"Who is Violet?"

He blinked fast. "Violet? How did ye—"

"I saw your letter on the table back in Limerick." I yanked myself from his arms and faced him, hands clenched. "Is she a past lover? Is it over?"

His mouth hung open. I bowed my head just as he erupted in laughter. I snapped my gaze back to him.

"Sorry, Red. I dinna…" He covered his mouth with his fist, trying to stifle more laughs. "It's just your face, and your tiny hands balled into these adorable wee fists."

I lurched forward. "I'm going to pummel you with these adorable wee fists if you don't stop laughing and answer my damned question."

He raised his hands, palms facing me. "I'm sorry. I'm sorry." He rubbed his chest. "Violet is my sister."

My cheeks burned red hot. "I—I thought—"

"I ken what ye thought. Dinna be embarrassed. I havena told ye about my family. Ye dinna ken." He stepped close to me and pulled me into a hug. "I suppose we should learn more about each other."

I leaned back and pressed my lips to his. "I want to learn

everything."

"Careful what ye wish for—we Scots do love to tell a story." He undid the buttons on his breeches and slid them off, his thick thighs mostly hidden by the hem of his shirt, and climbed into bed, patting the spot next to him.

"You're insatiable. I'm still sore from this morning." My toes curled at the memory.

He smirked. "I meant to talk. But I do love the way ye think."

Into the early morning hours, and long after nearly draining his wineskin dry of whisky, we were a fit of giggles and kisses and touches. I'd learned about clan life and Highlander traditions, about his large, extended family.

In the dim candlelight, he bared himself raw to me. And when the conversation became stilted or stalled, awkwardness lingering, we found comfort in each other's tender embraces.

Even now, as a sheen of sweat covered our nude, sated bodies, and we laid side by side facing each other on what seemed like the world's smallest bed with his giant body, as he animatedly described his sisters—he had six of them—he was raw and unguarded. "And Violet, ye ken, she is my twin. We were born early, my ma didna ken if we'd make it. But Violet had taken up much of the womb and was nigh full size. But me… she says I was a wee thing, no longer than her forearm. The midwife said I'd not make it past infancy."

He grinned and handed me the leather wineskin. "My ma says I never listened to what anyone said. I was a fighter since day one."

I laughed and took a swig of whisky. "You, small? I can't believe it. Now, the not listening to anyone and fighting, that seems more like you." The whisky burned sweet smoke down my throat.

"Aye, when I was just a laddy, probably twelve, I'd wake up every morning and say 'today's a braw day for a brawl.' Violet always said I was as stubborn and wild as an unbroken horse." A sideways smile split his lips before I handed him back the wineskin, and he took a sip. "Canna say she was wrong."

I couldn't help but laugh and enjoy his presence in these stolen moments at night in our cabin. "You must miss her very much."

He grazed his finger up and down my arm and looked at the flickering flame of the sole lit candle in our quarters. "Aye. I do. As much as she's a pain in my arse. She went and got herself married to a Grant. But hell, I miss her, all of them." A comfortable silence followed before he asked, "And you? What of your family? Ye dinna talk about them much."

Acrid sourness filled my belly—and not because of the rocking of the boat in the icy waters. "That's because there's not much to say."

"No?" He brushed a strand of hair off my forehead. "Surely ye've a story or two to tell. Like this red hair"—he tugged a curl—"who'd you inherit it from? Your ma or your da?"

His attentive green eyes implored me to spill all my secrets. And God, if I didn't want to when he looked at me like that. "My mother. I'm told I look just like her, that her hair was as red and wild as mine."

"Told?"

The copper tinge of blood filled my mouth as I bit the inside of my cheek. "She died when I was two, in childbed, along with the baby. I have no memories of her."

He squeezed my hand. "I'm sorry, to be a lass without a mother... did your da ever remarry?"

I huffed a dry laugh. "He would have had to put down a bottle long enough to do that." Suddenly cold, I tucked my arms around myself and looked away.

"Red." Grasping my chin, he directed my sight back to him. "Where'd ye go, *mo ghaol?* Dinna run away from me now, lass. I willna judge you nor ask ye to offer me more than you're comfortable sharing."

For a beat, I just stared into his eyes, the flame light reflecting off his pupils. In them, I found truth and understanding. They seemed to tell me that he'd listen to whatever I offered him, and not pry for more.

"He was the town drunk." Acid filled my voice. Anger I'd held back and buried for years seeped into my every word. "Left his children to fend for themselves. Spent nigh every coin he made on more alcohol—that was, when he was sober enough to work in the mines to earn it. Forgot that we needed food or clothes more often than not."

Left to lean on the townsfolk's charity, we'd beg or find odd jobs, often illegal: moving smuggled items and cargo from boats, gambling games in town, even stealing and pickpocketing a time or two. I wanted to laugh at the turn of events. I'd stuck my nose in the air about privateering. London society had fooled me into thinking such affairs were scandalous instead of conducted for basic survival. But I'd done my fair share of illicit work.

Because my damned father, the bloody fool he was, couldn't be bothered to remember to care for his children.

Tears pricked my eyes. "Hell, he often forgot who I was by the end of a bender. Let alone that I needed supper or shoes."

Holey, hand-me-down garments I'd sewed together were my only option. Hunger pangs suppressed by a rotten apple and some ale had often been my only sustenance for days. As if I felt them again now, I mindlessly stroked my stomach.

Alexander grabbed my hand and kissed the back of it before lacing his fingers through mine. "I canna offer you my inherited lands, to be lady of a clan, or even my family. As a wanted man, I am unable to return to Scotland and claim my inheritance. But I can promise ye, so long as you're my wife, ye'll no go hungry or without, even if it means givin' you the shirt off of my back and the food from my verra own plate. But somethin' tells me ye woudna need me to rely on."

A knot swelled in my throat. I took a deep breath and nodded. "Thank you."

And I meant it, despite having already promised myself I would never go without again. That I would not allow myself to return to that helpless place. And I'd proven it over and over again—that I'd do whatever it took to survive. But to have someone on my side for once, someone who would be there when all else failed—it was an astonishing assuagement.

I cleared my throat. "I am grateful for your commitment to me.

To us. Despite having been forced into this marriage, your loyalty is unyielding."

"Forced?" His Scottish R rolled on the word. "I thought we already established I dinna do what I'm told? Tell me about your siblings." He ran his hand down my bare waist until his palm flattened on my hip. His thumb stroked the inside of my hipbone, eliciting a tickling tingle.

My laugh turned into a groan. "Brothers. Both older than me. Pains in my arse like your Violet. I was the youngest."

His thumb stopped stroking. "Was?"

My shoulders drooped. "Aye." I finished the last of the whisky in one gulp. "I'm the only one left... Of my whole family, really." Leaving me utterly alone. "My brother Samuel left for war and never returned. My other brother, Nathaniel, died in a mining accident."

I stared off at the dancing candle flame. "I resent my father— for falling into drinking and gambling after my mother died, for neglecting me my entire life, for forcing my brothers to raise me and leaving me alone when they were gone... Hell, I even resent him for dying."

"What happened after all that then? You met your husband, John?" His eyebrows were raised high.

"No. Before my papa had even died, Mr. Davies, the mine owner, would give me a few pence for my father's attempt to work some days. Near the end, his heart had all but physically stopped, but his mind had been long gone before that. But as I neared ten, the mine was spent. Mr. Davies came to me to tell the mine was closing, and that he could not spare any more charity. He told me, the way he saw it, my papa was already dead, and I had two options: join a convent or go to a whorehouse. I was young, but I had some inclination what women did as whores. I'd seen a coupling in an alley once, didn't fully understand it, but thought the woman hadn't seemed like she hated it. I figured it was my best option; become a parlor maid of a whorehouse until I was of age to do the *other* duties. The idea of the peril I'd have been in never crossed my mind."

I swallowed a lump and barked a dry laugh. "I remember the day perfectly. I was pacing outside of the whorehouse, debating how long until my hunger would force me past the gate. My dress was hole-ridden and smeared with mud. Rags. Finally, as my head turned woozy, I decided it was time to go in. I remember the latch was stuck, and I was struggling to open it. And then a voice called from behind me. 'Girl, you should not like to be wandering in there.' When I turned around, I saw an elegant carriage and the woman inside it, wearing the fanciest clothing I'd ever seen. I said, 'Ye hev a ood wey o' taaken'.'"

Alexander broke out into laughter. "Ye dinna talk like that. Even I couldna understand ye."

I'd never shared so openly about my childhood. It was easier to try to forget, but as I laid myself bare to my new husband, I found my muscles relaxing. I smiled, feeling lighter. "Aye, ye don' knew wha' a wee lass from Newcastle sounds lek?"

He laughed some more and leaned forward, chin perched on his hand. "Well, what happened after she saw ye?"

I scoffed. "Chance was on my side that day. Carriages like that usually stayed near the estates, not frequenting the mines or whorehouses. She'd eventually told me her late husband had invested in a mine and she had been visiting its manager and they'd taken a wrong turn. And when I talked, her eyes widened, and she turned to her footman and asked, 'Good lord, did you understand what the creature said?' Her eyes swept down me and they glimmered in the most unusual way, almost like recognition even though we were complete strangers, and she said, 'She is a pretty little thing, though. Collect her. She looks like she needs a good meal.' Eventually I'd convinced her to take me on as her ward. Though I reckoned she had really never needed any convincing. Every once in a while she'd call me Mary, the name of her late daughter. And, well, eventually she introduced me to John by way of a scheming set up. Which, you know how that ended."

"Ye dinna talk about him much." He captured one of my stray curls and toyed with it between two fingers. "Ye can, ye ken."

I shook my head. "There's not much to say. He gave me a good life, took care of physical necessities. But it wasn't like…" *This,* I almost said.

"Like what?"

"It wasn't a love match." I shrugged.

His eyes wrinkled at the corners like he knew that was not what I was going to say. He leaned in and took my mouth with his. When he leaned back, his eyes were warm and full of emotion. "Emme, I…"

He stopped, shook his head, and laughed. "I'll have ye ken, when ye were shootin' wi' William the other day, I was cleaning up and found a certain captain's log under your pillow." I stiffened, and heat rose from my chest to my cheeks. "Ah, so ye ken the one. There were pages dog-eared." He winked. "I dinna ken all the times ye called me a pirate savage, it 'twas because ye were lusting after a buccaneer captain. I too found particular interest in entry fifty-seven. I figure it's a braw night as ever to try it." He inched down my body.

"What?" I asked, trying to sit up as he crawled lower, his hand pressing me gently on my belly, forcing me back down. "Now?"

"Aye." He looked up at me from under his lashes as he peppered kisses down my torso. "Ye'll tell me if I'm doing it, right?"

My head fell back the moment his lips found their target. Oh, holy hell…

I was reminded of Madame Touissaint, and her insistence that her wedding dress would suit me well. Beyond the physical compatibility, there was a closeness, a trust, between us I couldn't describe. A wordless understanding.

I was scared for what this meant. This feeling.

I knew one thing for certain—Alexander MacLachlan had given me hope for a new life that had otherwise been dismantled.

Hope for a chance at happiness. Hope for a chance of finding a new family. Hope for, I dared to say, love.

Entering the Harbor of Halifax, there were several islands scattered throughout the bay, hidden by the dense mist and fog until we were close. One large island, with a grand fort, displayed four rotting corpses on nooses swaying in the breeze as we sailed by.

Alexander pointed to it. "Cornwallis Island. A warning to all who dare enter. One of the reasons I was eager to secure a Danish marque was due to their neutrality. If had a Spanish or French marque instead... even with papers, they'd hang us here as pirates." A chill rolled through me, and he wrapped his arm around me, tucking me close to him.

As we sliced through the bay toward Halifax, a vast array of ships docked at various wharfs floated in the gently rolling waves. It was a growing port, full of bustling excitement. Log buildings speckled the horizon, mixing with vast evergreen trees as tall as the eye could see. Smoke billowed from chimneys of various establishments and from a couple of large houses, no doubt owned by some rich duke or the sort. In front of one of the several forts stood a wooden pillory where two men were restrained. A few warehouses were even scattered along the boardwalk.

Once docked at a specific wharf—which my husband explained some people called Privateer's Wharf due to its most common use— he paid the dockage and many of us were quick to disembark.

As we climbed onto the dock, I was met with wobbly legs, no longer used to the dry land. But I quickly stopped short. The *Glory* bobbed up and down some hundred paces away. I grasped Alexander's coat sleeve, stopping him. I pointed.

He followed the direction of my finger. "Aye. Do well to remember Nova Scotia is British soil." A warning laced his words.

I regarded our surroundings. "I couldn't forget it if I tried after seeing the rotting bodies. It is quite green here, too."

"Aye. But a different green than Iceland. In a way, the grass and moss of Reykjavik reminded me of Scotland." His voice was thick as his gaze lingered on the landscape.

I slipped my hand into his. "Oh?"

He gave a large sigh, chest heaving. "But it dinna smell the same." He tugged on my hand, and we hiked further down the dock.

"What, pray tell, does Scotland smell like?" I wrinkled my nose.

Stopping again, he eyed the forest in the hills. "Like earth and musk and grass and mist. Like home."

Bringing our clasped hands toward me, I kissed the back of his. "You know we could go there? Now that the one person who'd recognize you or care said he'll not hunt you and has some sort of project keeping him on this side of the world, that is. It's been eleven years. Your indentured servitude would have already been over with. Hell, we could leave today."

His gaze was distant, a ferocious storm brewing in his eyes, before he wrapped his arms around me from behind and placed his chin on my head. "Wouldn't I be letting my family down if I let him live?"

"What do you think they'd want?" I arched my head back to look at him.

He said nothing for a while and dropped his arms. "Let us go. William looks like he's growing more impatient by the second." Sure enough, William was pacing on the shore. "Besides, I want to treat my wife to some hot food and fresh ale."

One thing that never seemed to change very much from place to place were the taverns. All of them, like this one, were filled with sailors in various states of disarray. Tobacco smoke hung in the air mixing with the sweat and grime of too many bodies packed close together. A roiling hearth always welcomed us, as did a hot meal and a pint for sixpence.

When we entered, no one batted an eye. We were merely more sailors looking for a place to unwind. But my steps faltered the moment I caught sight of a Royal Navy uniform.

From the corner of my eye, I met Alexander's gaze. He gave a tight-lipped smile and jutted his head toward some empty spaces at the communal table. He sank down on the bench, and I followed suit. William paced around to the other side, sitting, facing us.

I rubbed the back of my neck and leaned toward my husband's ear. "You think they're from the *Glory*?"

He kissed my cheek. "Some, no doubt, but to be sure, some are stationed here permanently." His low tone tickled my ear.

William leaned across the table. "Aye, some of them are from the *Glory*. I recognize him from Reykjavik." His eyes flicked to a sailor at the far end of the table.

It was the man who'd followed him up the stairs at the inn. The sailor noticed William's gaze and raised his glass, and William reciprocated. I arched a brow.

He shrugged. "Gotta have a man on the inside."

"... and then he said the commodore mentioned some kind of private island. Called it Oak Island." My attention snapped to the sailor closest to me, one with hair the color of straw.

I elbowed my husband in the ribs. "*Och*, what—" I widened my eyes meaningfully, and his gaze landed on the men to my left.

The sailor across from the blond, deep pock marks marring his face, tilted his head. "Oak Island? I been here 'round a year now and don't know about no Oak Island."

"That's what he called it." The blond leaned across the table. "We been on the *Glory* recruitin' all these men for the past two years. Well, every time we come back here, they suddenly ain't back on the ship. I don't think they're even recorded with the Naval Board."

The scarred one lifted a brow. "Could it just be some special project for the Crown? What's them frog eaters call it? Espionage?"

"I dunno. Seemed like the captain would've been savvy to such a scheme, and my mate said the commodore stopped talking when our capt'n approached." The blond scratched his head.

The other one furrowed his brows. "And what happened to your mate?"

"Well, I woke up one morning, and he was gone from his

hammock. I asked 'round, and my lieutenant said he died in his sleep." He snapped his head in either direction, surveying his surroundings, and I kept my face aimed at the tabletop before he leaned across it, closer to his friend. "We landed two days ago. I went to the commissioner here, wanted an address to write to his family, and send my condolences. They ain't got a Thomas Smith of Yorkshire listed. His death was never recorded with the Naval Board."

My breath caught, and I stiffened. Alexander slid his hand across the table and placed it on mine.

"So, what are you saying?" The pock-marked one took a sip of ale.

The blond rubbed his nose. "Alls I'm sayin' is there's something fishy going on, and it ain't got anything to do with actual fish. I think it has something to do with that there Oak Island. You sure you never heard of it?"

The other sailor shook his head. "Nay. But you go exploring enough around here. There's at least a thousand or two little islands."

The blond shrugged and downed his drink. "Anyway, where's the local brothel from here?"

I exhaled before looking at William's and Alexander's faces and leaning in close so only they'd hear me. "Something is going on here. I know it."

William nodded, his eyes distant before they focused on us, and he leaned in. "If this Oak Island exists, that's how we can get to Cobbe. He won't be telling all the men he usually has following him around port. He'd go by himself or with a small group of men. We could lay in wait, watch for him, and see if we can intercept him."

I ran my hand through my hair and peered at Alexander. "What do you think?"

His lips twisted from side to side. "It'd be a good way to capture him. But like the one said, there are thousands of islands around here. We dinna ken how far or close, or who could be waiting around any corner. We'd need to know more. Pinpoint its location a wee bit. What do you think, Emme?"

"There's something here. Something going on, and it's not sittin' right." Nausea pressed against my throat. "But I agree. We need more information."

William shifted his eyes between us. "Even the toughest men get loose-lipped with pillow talk after a night of passion." His gaze landed on the handsome sailor again. "I shall report my findings to ya come morn'."

A'reet then.

"What, will you tell me to stay behind and that I shouldn't shoot anymore?" I folded my arms over my chest.

"I'd say no such thing. I ken well tha' ye hold my bollocks in your reticule." His brows waggled.

I rolled my eyes. "I haven't carried my reticule in months now. I think it still sits in my trunk with John's pocket watch."

He stopped and stepped in front of me, grasping my waist. "Ah, so what ye're saying is, there'd be no room for the likes of my family bagpipes?" To top it off, he winked.

"Lord, there's no livin' with you." I pecked his lips and walked around him. "And you're deflecting."

He grasped my hand as we strolled down the wharf, passing by the ladies of the night, hoping to attract a lonely sailor's attention, the sun dipping below the blue sea horizon. "Nay, I wasna deflectin'. I said I dinna want all your learnin' to go to waste if…"

Our boots thumped on the wooden planks, the water lapping beneath us. "If?"

"If mayhap we dinna go after Cobbe." His grip tightened on my hand, his palm a little sweaty.

"You mean you'd give up all your plans?" I held my breath.

He stopped and pierced me with his gaze. "I mean tha' I've a wife now. I dinna want to keep lookin' back. If I do, how could I ever move forward wi' you?"

I took a sharp inhale, my mouth opening and closing as warmth spread through my chest. "I—"

"Would ye think less o' me?" He wrinkled his brow.

"What? No. Never." I cupped his cheek with my palm and pressed up to my tiptoes, my heart thrashing in my chest. "You'd choose me over… choose a life with me instead of—"

"I'll always choose ye. Ye're my family now." He moved his head toward my hand on his cheek and kissed my palm.

I stilled. Good Lord, I was done for.

He crashed his lips on mine, his fingers lacing through my hair, and every stroke of his lips was like a way to show me how he was feeling, telling me every word he couldn't quite say yet.

And thank the Lord. Because my heart couldn't handle the

alternative.

Because I was absolutely falling in love with Alexander Grant MacLachlan. And he was choosing me.

23

I ran my pointer finger over his bare chest and sighed, resting my head against him. His sturdy heartbeat thumped soothingly under my ear. He played with one of my curls, pulling it straight, releasing it to watch it spring back, only to yank it straight again.

"I could stay like this forever." I splayed my fingers wide, my palm resting on his chiseled chest. A slice of heat burned through me. Even after having him, I wanted him again. Would I ever tire of him?

"Ye can. Just like this. Wi' your beautiful breasts pressed against me, and your bonnie hair wrapped around my hands, between my fingers." His deep brogue made his chest rumble beneath me.

I laughed as I stared out the bank of windows at the bay. The horizon was bobbing up and down as the early light of the rising sun shot streams of light into our cabin, illuminating rainbow flurries of dust floating in the air. "Why are you infatuated with my hair?"

"I remember the first time you took your hat off and undid your tie." His chest vibrated as he chuckled. "It was wild and curly and... it reminded me of home. I remember thinkin' how each curl was like a crimson burn, winding and flowing, seeming without end, and Christ, I knew I was done for then." He rolled out from under me and hovered beside me to kiss my lips, trailing his own across my jaw and down my throat.

My eyes shut as he scattered more kisses over me. "And here I thought you put up with me at best. Bickering with me all the time—" My words come out high pitched as he found the spot over the pulse on my neck.

"Aye, because if I wasn't fightin' with ye, I'd want to be touchin' ye, to bury myself deep inside of ye." He grazed his hand down my waist to the hollow of my hipbone. "Had to release all my pent-up energy somehow."

The moment his fingers brushed my sensitive core, I huffed out air. "I thought we needed to get ready because William would be back soon. I wasn't trying to seduce you with my hair."

"Red, dinna ye understand yet?" he whispered into my ear before he took my earlobe between his teeth. "By bein' in the same room as me, you're seducing me. I can think of naught else than what it feels like to be inside of ye."

"Pi-pirate…" He was using his thumb in the way that sent fireworks up my body. "S-Savage." I gasped, back arching, eyes flitting closed.

He nuzzled my neck and hair. "I love watching ye come undone for me, *mo ghoal*."

I lost all semblance of control. The embers he prodded with his words, with his fingers, transformed into a full, raging fire. A fire I could no longer contain, and I cried out as a peak of pleasure coursed through me, my body shuddering at the waves every stroke of his fingers brought.

As my panting slowed, I peeled open my eyes to see a smug smile on his face. I arched a brow. "So sure of yourself, aren't you?" I pushed him back onto the bed and climbed onto him, my legs straddling his hips. "I can also undo you, husband."

He muttered in Gaelic as I raised my hips and eased him inside of me. I rocked my body over him, my head dropping back before I looked at him underneath me. The way he regarded me made me feel powerful, beautiful, and cared for in a way I hadn't felt in a long time, if ever. Secure. Safe. Like I finally had someone other than myself I could rely on.

For a moment, our gazes locked, and I drowned in the depths of his eyes filled with unsaid words, little truths we had yet to share with each other.

But we had time. We had each other.

I bent down and kissed him, my hair like a red drape around our faces. I brushed strands of hair off his forehead. "Alexander..."

"*Mo ghoal.*" His eyes were hooded, and he grasped my hips, fingers digging into my skin, before he cupped a hand around one of my breasts. "Tell me ye feel it, too. The way our bodies fit together like they were made for each other?"

As an answer, I pushed myself into his hand as I burst into a million blazing stars of ecstasy. His own groans and grunts preceded the warmth of his own release. I was soon sated and relaxed.

Sated, relaxed, and—happy. I climbed off him, breathing hard. "I do feel it too."

He tucked a strand of my hair behind my ear. "We *do* have to dress ourselves."

I nodded. "Yes." I smiled. "I should like to commission a riding habit before we leave."

He was already tugging on his breeches, and he stopped to crinkle his eyes. "Going somewhere on horses I dinna ken about?"

I rose and slid my shift over my head. "I was just thinking about what would be practical for ship life. It is a long voyage back to Europe. And stays are impractical. And the materials of most gowns are too delicate." I gave a pointed stare. "Well, I suppose I could always put my breeches back on?"

He laughed, pacing toward me, and slapped my arse. "I do miss how they hugged this so." He rubbed my behind before grabbing his shirt. "A riding habit seems very practical. And we do have a long voyage back across the Atlantic. But we will need at least one good prize ship. If I go back to Europe without Mr. Pilkington's investment return, he'll have my head." Adjusting his stockings, he tugged on his boots. "So we are in agreement, then. When William comes back, no matter what he has learned, we will tell him we dinna want to ken and tha' we've decided to return to Scotland?"

I turned my back to him and swept my hair away, and he dutifully moved behind me before I even asked, helping me with my buttons. "We are in agreement, Mr. MacLachlan."

"Mr. Lock, ye mean. I am still wanted by the Crown, technically. Just not by Cobbe." He smirked.

I raised my shoulders up to my neck, hands clenching, my lips pulling into a large smile as I squealed. "I cannot wait. Should you think Violet'll like me?"

He kissed the back of my neck and put my hair back in place. "Ye mean even though ye're English?" I faced him and smacked his chest, and he caught my hand and kissed my palm. "She'll love ye because I do." I stilled. Wasn't quite the proclamation, but it was close enough. He licked his lips and continued on like he hadn't said something that made my heart crash like waves in a storm. "And because you're Mistress Lock, *mo ghoal.*"

He leaned in and gave me a kiss. This was what it felt like to be truly cared for.

Alexander stalked toward the door. "That'll be William." I didn't make out the knock at the door, my head up in the clouds.

My bottom lip curled under my teeth. "I'll pour us all a *wee dram.*"

His hand on the doorknob, he paused, eyes sparkling. "Dinna do your awful Scottish accent in front of her, though." The door opened on squeaking hinges. "Ah, William, come in."

William's usual easy smile was missing from his face. "Good morn'."

"Here, I poured us a drink. Sit. We have some things we wish to discuss." I smiled, but his eyes had dark circles underneath them, and he pinched the skin of his throat. Alexander pulled out a chair for me. I sank down, not taking my eyes off William nor he taking his off me.

He licked his lips and sat across from me before Alexander sat at my right and grasped my hand.

Alexander exhaled, a small smile on his face. "William, we—"

"Are you quite all right?" I searched him for any visible injuries. "You look unwell. Are you hurt?"

"I'm not hurt. I..." He rubbed his lips together, eyes flicking between me and Alexander. "I discovered some information."

"That's what we wanted to discuss." My husband leaned on the edge of his seat, his hand squeezing mine. "Emme and I decided we dinna want to ken whatever—"

"Emme." His gaze was wide, eyes bulging. "Your husband, John, he is alive."

24

William's chest heaved up and down, his breathing loud. I blinked a few times, and Alexander stiffened beside me.

I shut my eyes, massaging the tension between my eyebrows before I reopened them. "I'm sorry. Did you just say John is alive?"

He tucked both his lips completely into his mouth. "Yes."

A dry laugh escaped my lips, and I shook my head. "You mean John Clark?"

"Yes, your"—he took a quick glance at my new husband before his gaze settled back on me—"your husband."

Alexander removed his hand from mine, and I straightened, my breath shallow. "This isn't a funny jest, William."

He closed his eyes for a moment, chest caving. "Emme, this isn't a jest. It's the truth."

Alexander's face was blank. He brought his dram to his lips.

"No." I grasped the edge of the table. "You're wrong. The information isn't accurate." Why did he want to ruin everything? I rose and paced the cabin. "Why would you say such a thing, William?"

He raised his hands. "I am just the messenger here, Emme."

"I'm sorry. You're right. I—" My breathing turned shaky. "Alexander. Say something. Tell him he's wrong." My voice was higher pitched than usual.

My husband didn't say anything at first, and he exhaled loudly. "Emme..." Hesitation licked at every letter in my name.

I paused my pacing and balled my hands into fists. "No. No, Alexander Grant MacLachlan." He stood and eyed me, brows pushed together, his lips thinned into a line. I shook my head fast. "Don't you do this to me."

He looked at the ground and tapped his palms on his thighs. "At the tavern, the sailor said his friend's death wasn't recorded with the Naval Board. You said Cobbe hadn't recorded John's either. That was why you came on the *Bluebell* in the first place. It's too big of a coincidence. Maybe his death wasn't recorded because he is actually—"

"Don't say it." I pressed in close to him and grabbed his hands. "Don't. It'll ruin everything." Warmth pressed against my eyes as my vision blurred.

"*Mo ghoal*, even if I dinna say it, it doesna make it any less true." He squeezed my hands.

A warm tear fell from my lashes and rolled down my cheek, slow like sap from one of the evergreens outside lining the harbor. "Let us leave. Our plans don' need te change." My practiced accent began to slip in my panic, my learned facade crumbling. "Take me home to Scotland."

He cupped my cheek and swiped at a tear from my face. He

shook his head.

"Please." I clutched the front of his shirt between my fingers. I wasn't above begging. It may have made me the most horrible person on Earth. I should have been elated that John was alive. But I didn't want to lose Alexander. I didn't love John. I loved Alexander. *"You're* my family now."

"I ken, Red." His eyes glistened. His warm hands still embraced my cheeks. He leaned in as if to kiss me, but he stopped himself short. "But I'm no' you're husband. Not in the eyes of the law or even the Lord himself. If we were found together... Adultery is a felony. With the law on his side, John could punish—"

"Fuck the law!" I shut my eyes for a moment. "You've been a wanted man for a decade, and in this, you draw the line?"

He jolted away from me and twisted his back to me, his hand running through his hair. "Ye're another man's wife. It isna right."

"A man who left me time and time again. Do I have no say in my life? You'll damn me to unhappiness and abandon me because of some sense of moral obligation? You committed treason, fought for your country. Yet you won't fight for me? Fine. Leave me here. But I bloody refuse to go back to him." I stomped to the table and picked up my cup and threw it at the wall. Embarrassment coursed through me for a minute, but I realized William wasn't in the room anymore. At some point, he'd slipped out. I faced Alexander again. "I see what this is. An excuse. Now you have an out of our forced sham of a marriage."

"Red, how can ye say such a thing to me after what we've shared?" His entire body was quivering.

I picked up his cup from the table and threw it at him, and he dodged it just in time, but brown whisky sprayed across his cheek. "Words to get me into your bed."

He shut his eyes, inhaling. "If ye recall, ye were in my bed from night one." He smiled, trying to lighten the mood.

"You rutting bastard." I searched the table for something else to throw at him. "Fine. Go ahead. Abandon me like you abandoned her. Sophie." I regretted the words the moment they ripped out of me. I slapped my hand over my open mouth.

He stilled, his face blanching, like I had actually hit him with something.

I shook my head. "No. No. I'm sorry." My tears transformed into sobs tearing from my chest. "You're my husband. You can't leave me. Please. Don't leave me."

I sank to my knees, tears streaming down my face, body shaking.

"Christ, *mo ghoal*. Ye're making it hard to do the right thing." He wrapped his arms around me, climbing to the floor in front of me.

"Then don't do the right thing. Instead, just love me." I grasped his cheeks, fingers splayed as if I could physically keep him in my hands. "Please."

His eyes were filled with emotion. "Emme, I *do* love ye—that's why I am tryin' to do the right thing."

I grasped the neckline of his shift and kissed him. "Then nothing has to change. We'll leave today." I peppered kisses over his lips, his cheeks, his neck, anywhere I could place them and climbed on his lap, sliding my hands underneath his shift.

"Christ, Emme ye canna just—"

"I know you want me." I licked my tongue down his neck and sucked at the skin over his pulse. He grumbled incoherent words. I rubbed my hands over the planes of his chest before I lifted the hem of his shirt and relieved him of it entirely. He thickened beneath me, his pants taut over his length. I ran my hand over him through his pants, and he groaned again. "I know you want me," I whispered again into his ear. "I'm here. I'm yours. Have me."

He grunted and wrapped his arms around my waist and lifted me, carrying me to the bed.

I wrapped my arms around myself as the chill breeze on the main deck pushed at my skirt and hair. I looked out at the bay. In the distance, there were too many green, tree-covered islands to count. Could one of those be Oak Island?

John could very well be on one of them. In danger. And I was leaving.

Turning back toward the ship, I blew out a restless breath. The crew shuffled around the deck, loading in new casks of water, crates of fresh fruit, bags of grain, and the like. The Danish flag on our main mast flapped in the wind.

I swallowed as I paced the deck, waiting for my husband to return. Alexander. Though technically not my husband at all. I rubbed the back of my neck and sighed. I had to make good with this decision since I'd live with it the rest of my life.

Although love wasn't what John and I had shared, he hadn't been cruel. He'd taken care of me financially. If I was honest with myself, I had been more in love with the idea of John and the life he could provide than in love with him. And my life in London wasn't what I'd hoped it would be, either.

Still, I was consciously leaving him now, leaving him to unknown dangers. The pit of my stomach clenched.

I exhaled in relief the moment my gaze landed on the tall Scotsman pacing down the boardwalk, his curl in place on his forehead. I had half worried he wouldn't return, that he might instead go and do something foolish.

Once he hiked the gangway, he came to me and gave a small smile. Things were a little tense between us, even after he'd agreed to continue with our plans. The sooner we put sea between us and this place, the better. Everything would return back to normal with some distance from the so-called Oak Island.

He brushed his thumb on my cheekbone. "Havin' second thoughts?"

"No, I was just thinking about earlier." I leaned into the crook of his neck and my voice dropped low. "About how you did that thing with your tongue."

His lips curled up, and he kissed the top of my head. "We are nearly ready to disembark. Waiting for William and Jacques to return from shore. Knowing Jacques, William is waiting for him impatiently outside of a brothel." He kissed my hair again. "I'll let ye ken when we're ready."

I nodded and peered back out at the harbor. The *Glory* in the far distance caught my attention. Its half-naked siren at the prow stood in all her large-breasted splendor. What was Cobbe doing? What did he need men for on that island?

And why John? He wasn't a skilled fighter. He dealt with

logistics and building weapons. If you wanted him to tinker or fix anything, he was your man. But brute strength didn't come to mind. Odd.

But I'd never know.

Stomping feet on the gangway made me turn back. Jacques was running up it. Good. We could finally leave this bloody forsaken place behind.

I searched the dock. William wasn't behind him. I froze on the spot, surveying the dock again. My pulse picked up in pace. Jacques bolted toward Alexander on the other side of the main deck.

I rushed over. An emptiness squeezed my gut. "What's happened?"

"They took 'im!" Jacques was panting.

Alexander dropped the rope he was holding. "They took William?"

His chest heaved up and down. *"Oui,* Captain. Four o' them, led by the commodore 'imself. Said they saw 'im snooping around and they know he overheard something 'e shouldn't 'ave. They said come with them to work or meet the end of the musket."

My mouth dropped open. Christ. They took William.

"Were ye seen?" Alexander's face was grave, his lips thin.

"Non. I was finishin' up with a whore and saw them and 'id behind a cargo load. I'm sorry. There were four of them and only one of me." His eyes were wide as his gaze turned distant.

"No. 'Twas for the best ye stayed hidden." Alexander nodded.

"Where did they go? What direction?" I asked, bouncing on my toes. "We could follow."

"They loaded him on a long boat and 'eaded out the bay." He paused and gave a deflated exhale. "I stayed 'idden until they rounded the corner due south."

I met Alexander's gaze. "What do we do? Follow them?"

He shook his head, exasperated. "I dinna ken. We have no idea how many of them are on the island, and what exactly it is they're doing. It could be suicide."

I rubbed my palms on my skirt. "So, what then? We try to find more information?"

He nodded. His eyes dipped to the ground before they landed on me, deflated. "Aye. Back to scheming and sleuthing."

My stomach dropped. We wouldn't be leaving, and John would loom over our heads for that much longer. I'd barely convinced Alexander to leave, and now he'd have time to change his mind.

26

"What did the man look like again?" Alexander usually didn't wear a hat, but today, for the fourth day in a row, he'd donned a three-corner hat, pulled low to shadow his face.

I, too, had my hat on and my hair tied back—and wore breeches again. We didn't want to be easily recognizable when we returned to the tavern.

I searched the faces of all the men in Navy uniforms, analyzing them. Were any of these men the one that William had spent the night with? "Umm… dark wavy hair, clean cut, and piercing blue eyes."

He arched a brow. "Piercing blue eyes, eh?"

Batting my hand his way, I smiled. "You asked for a description, didn't you?" I scanned the room again. "I'll know him when I see him."

He scratched the scruff on his chin. "What was his rank?"

"I don't know." Rolling my neck each way to ease the tension in my shoulders, I nibbled on my lip. "He had one of those funny-looking hats with the emblem that looks like it's made of neck ribbons."

He laughed—the first real laugh he'd given in what felt like days. "I'm sure the tough sailors would be happy to hear you think they wear neck ties on their hats." He rubbed the back of his neck. "Maybe he won't show up here again. He could've heard people were asking about him."

The door slammed open, hitting the wall behind it. I sat on the edge of the bench. Could we be so lucky, and William's lover from the *Glory* would walk right in? But gold epaulettes on his shoulders glistened in the light before I ever noticed his face. Cobbe. I blanched. My hand hovered over the flintlock pistol in the holster around my waist. At first, I thought it had been superfluous, and I had told Alexander just that, but now I was glad he had insisted on my carrying it, and I found comfort in its heavy weight at my hip.

I had half a mind to use it on him here and now. But sailors throughout the tavern rose to attention and saluted. Even some soldiers, from other branches stationed here, in their redcoats, saluted. He *was* a commodore. My body blazed with energy, like I'd combust at any moment. Cobbe waved the men to stand down before choosing a table with one sole chair to sit at.

"Let us go before we draw too much attention to ourselves. He'll have seen the *Bluebell* in the port and could be here to find us. I don't want to find out whether his word is true or not and end up arrested." He threw down some pence on the table and rose before nodding in the opposite direction of the commodore. "The side door."

I stood, teeth gritted, unable to keep my stare off the commodore, hoping the dimness of the taproom would shroud me enough that he wouldn't recognize me as we traversed through tables and sailors. So far, he'd held up his end of the bargain—he hadn't approached the *Bluebell* since the wedding.

The wedding. My steps faltered as red-hot heat burned through me, and I came to a complete stop, feet wide apart. "He knew."

"Red," Alexander whispered. "Let us make haste."

My nostrils flared as shallow breaths ripped from me. "I knew it was too easy."

I twisted toward Cobbe. He was preoccupied with sailors chatting and cheering others. He was completely unaware of the way he had dismantled my life. My entire body, from my toes to my head, shook with rage. He forced Alexander and me to marry knowing John was alive. Knowing it'd be illegal. Knowing it'd somehow come to torment us.

All for his perverse viewing pleasure.

I acted on instinct as my hand slid to the holster, my fingers grazing the handle before I yanked it from its pouch.

"No." Alexander was in front of me, his body pressing the gun to my stomach. "They'll kill ye. I willna let tha' man take another person I love from me. Slide it back into your holster before anyone sees."

My blood rushed in my ears. The grip I held on the gun was so tight my knuckles ached. After a deep breath, I nodded and shoved it back into the holster. Once safely tucked away again, he slid from in front of me. He grabbed my arm and tugged me toward the door. A quick peek back told me we had captured some attention—their stares still lingering, but the commodore hadn't seemed to even glance in our direction.

The icy night air cooled my too warm face the moment we stepped outside. Alexander still had a hold on my wrist as we stormed out of the tavern and around the corner. The cloudless sky displayed a blanket of thick stars and a bright, full moon that illuminated our path until he steered me into a shadowed alley between two log buildings.

Once tucked away deep enough, he let go of me and dragged his nails through his hair. Just barely able to make out his form, he paced in front of me. I leaned my back against the side of the building and exhaled.

He snapped in my direction. "What the hell was that, Emme?" His voice was sharp and loud.

I straightened. We'd bickered and argued, but he'd never talked to me like that. My cheeks warmed as I stared at my boots, the tips sticking out in a slice of moonlight. "I-I'm sorry. I reacted without thinking."

"Do ye have any idea how close ye were to having us killed? Getting yourself killed?" He shouted the words.

My jaw clenched. "Don't yell at me! I didn't think—"

"No, ye didna think. And I almost paid the price for it. I would have died for ye. Stepped in the line of fire for ye. But ye didna think about that." He pressed in close to me and settled an arm on either side of my head on the wall behind me. "Did ye?"

My eyes heated. "I'd never want to hurt you. I wasn't thinking. I'm sorry. I don't know what else I can say!" My brows furrowed, half angry that he'd have the audacity to talk to me like this, and half anguished at the near misery I could have caused. If he had been harmed because of my foolishness—I didn't think I'd have survived it.

He shook his head. "If ye died because of that man…" His breathing was quick and heavy. "Are ye trying to rip my heart out, Emme?" His large hands landed on my cheeks. "I already am not truly your husband. Are ye to have me hammer the last nail in your coffin, too?"

I couldn't fully see his face in the shadows, and I wished I could. "I said I was sorry! What more can I do? How can I make it right?"

"Ye canna make it right." His voice was thick.

A coldness rolled over my skin. "Why do I think this isn't just about the tavern?"

He didn't answer. I didn't think he would until at last he said, "Because it isna. Ye ken, if we find this Oak Island, find William, we'll verra likely find John. Your *true* husband."

A sob like sigh emanated from my chest. "I know. But it won't change anything."

He placed his forehead against mine, his pupils shining in the moonlight between his rapid blinks. "But it will, Emme. What d'ye expect?" Tearing away, he turned his back to me. "'Hello, darling. Nice to see ye're alive, but I've remarried now. Good bye.' Christ, Emme."

I swallowed a thick, burning lump in my throat. "W-why not? I don't love him. I love *you*."

I thought he shook his head again, but the light shifted, and it was nigh impossible to see anything but he must have turned back around because he pressed his head against mine again. A warm drop landed on my cheek. A tear. "Ye're killing me, Red. We can't work like this."

A sharp pain pierced my chest at his words. "What, do you want me to leave?"

"I want ye to be mine. Truly mine." His lips were a breath away from mine.

"Don't you see that I am yours in every way that counts? I am yours, and you are mine, Alexander Grant MacLachlan." I ran my fingers through his hair and steered his face to mine to close the gap between us.

Our mouths crashed together in a ravenous wave. Our hands were a blurred frenzy, each of us reaching out to one another to obtain the touch, the feeling we needed from each other. Taking and giving what we hungered for—the validation of our feelings for one another despite the damned complicated circumstances that pummeled our lives. The feelings we couldn't yet put into words, couldn't perhaps even fully understand or realize.

But there he was, and I was willing to give whatever was left of myself to him and he to me. I fumbled with the buttons on the flap of his breeches, and his grunts as his hands tugged and pulled at mine told me he was having just as much trouble. At last, I got one side free before I hurried to the other side. Once released, I pushed down the waistband enough to release his erection.

His hands still worked on the buttons of my breeches as I worked my hand up and down him, his skin like silk over hard iron. My body ached for him, my breasts tingling and heavy behind my shift.

"Hell, the skirt is easier." He yanked down the waistband of my breeches over my hips, giving up on the button, a ripping sound following his action. He tugged them all the way down to my ankles and hiked one of my legs around his waist, pressing my back further against the wall, before he thrust into me, fast and hard.

I gasped and dug my nails into his hair and neck. Every thrust, my back hit the wall as a shock of pleasure, stemming from deep inside me, rolled through my whole body. I breathed into his ear, and he moaned. "Tell me that you are mine."

He chuckled. "I am yours, Emme MacLachlan, always and forever."

The fact he called me by *his* last name was enough to make me shatter into endless pieces around him. After his pace picked up and with a final, deep thrust and groan of pleasure, he sagged against me. Both of us panted, and a sheen of sweat coated my body. I unwrapped my leg from around him and picked up my breeches. One seam had ripped apart a bit, that side sagging on my hips.

I kissed him, but caught the corner of his lips, still unable to see him fully in the shadows. "Remind me to anger you more often."

"Dinna ye dare ever do something so foolish." He kissed the top of my head. "I have to take a piss."

"Despite the breeches. I've never been able to relieve myself as easily as you men do." I jutted my head to the well-lit street. "I'll be over there."

As I paced toward the street, the shop I commissioned my riding habit from caught my eye. An elegant gown was in the window display. One of the benefits of staying here longer was that I'd be able to pick up my order.

Sighing, I leaned against a lamppost just as a sailor stopped in front of me. My eyes widened. "You!"

He slapped his hand over my mouth and dragged me around the corner. I thrashed against him, digging my heels into the ground, and screamed into his hand.

Bending to my ear, he shushed me. "Be quiet, they'll see us."

My heart hammered against my breastbone, and I tried ripping his hand from my mouth, my nails scratching down the top of his hands, his skin gathering underneath them. But he was stronger.

"Lass, stop. I promise, I'm not trying to hurt you." His breaths in my ear turned my stomach upside down.

I flailed my arms, my hand brushing against the gun. The tip of my fingers ran down the handle as Alexander shuffled from the shadows. Before I could reach it, five sailors pressed off the building and closed in around him. I screamed into the man's hand.

Alexander froze, hand close to his gun before he slowly raised his arms. The man nearest to him, short and very stout, removed his sword and flintlock.

I sagged into my assailant's arms, eyes wide, my blood rushing.

"Hush or they'll grab you next," the sailor with the piercing blue eyes said into my ear.

I nodded, having no other option but to trust him, his voice barely audible over the sound of my pounding heartbeat in my ears. He removed his hand from my mouth just as Commodore Cobbe slithered from the shadows, standing in front of my husband. I jolted forward, but the sailor clenched his hands on my shoulders.

He rounded in front of me, his blue eyes wide. "Go. They're coming for you next." My gaze flicked to Alexander, the two men holding each of his arms. "Go now."

Instinct drove my feet, and I pushed off the cobblestones, running into a crevice between two buildings just wide enough for me to squeeze into. But my heart was outside of my body, being dragged away by the traitorous men controlled by the commodore.

Cobbe stalked across the street to the blue-eyed sailor. My palms were slick with sweat, and I tried to quiet my panting breaths as he eyed the man who'd rescued me. "Private. Did you see a redheaded lad with a hat running around here? Or perhaps she could have changed back into a dress. We're searching for the wife of that very large Scottish traitor over there." He pointed to Alexander. "She often dresses in men's clothing."

The sailor shook his head. "Nay, sir. In fact, I saw the Scotsman exiting the brothel down the lane. There was no wife that I saw."

Cobbe sniffed in that odd way of his, and he peered in either direction. "I swore I saw her earlier." His nostrils flared again.

The sailor seemed to shrug from my angle, but his back was toward me, making it difficult to tell for sure. "I'm sorry, sir. I didn't see anyone else."

Cobbe's thin lips drew to an even thinner line. "Very well." He about-faced toward my husband once more. "Take him away."

Alexander's gaze seemed to search the area around him as the sailors pushed him forward.

The second they rounded the corner, I exhaled and climbed out of my hiding spot.

I looked at the man with the blue gaze, my legs numb and tingling. "They took him."

"They took him," I repeated, voice shaky. I ran to the sailor and gripped his coat's lapels. "They took my husband. What are you playing at?"

"Mrs. Clark. Please lower your voice before they hear you and come back for *both* of us." His eyes were wide, imploring me to listen.

I peered at my hands, my knuckles blanching, clenched on the lapels of his jacket. I released him and stuck my head past him to ensure they were gone. Should I follow? Christ, I didn't know what to do. I swallowed a thick lump in my throat, unsure of my next steps. Snapping my gaze around in the other direction, I pushed past the man and headed down the street. "I need to go back to the ship. Gather men."

"Mrs. Clark. Wait. You can't go to the *Bluebell*. You know too much. They'll look there for you first," the man called after me.

My feet stopped, rooting me in place. Facing him again, my mouth hung open. "Wh-what am I to do then?"

He scratched his chin. "He's a commodore. Run away while

you can."

My brows crinkled together. "What's that supposed to mean? He's a commodore, so give up? That's the end?"

"Hide and then stow away on a ship and go far from here." His eyes softened, but his lips were in a grim line.

"Leave my husband to that man?" My jaw slackened.

He backed away from me. "If you mean Captain Lock, he's not really your husband."

I jerked, shaking my head. It was as if my heart was beating outside of my body, and was in the hands of that man, the murderous commodore. I swept my gaze down the sailor from head to toe. "I will not abandon him." I narrowed my eyes. "Did you know that John was alive in Iceland when *your* commodore forced me to marry another man for his own entertainment?"

He sucked on his bottom lip. "Mrs. Clark—"

"Mrs. MacLachlan." My lips pursed. "And what about William? He has him too."

His eyes shut for a moment, corners crinkling, his hand pressing over his heart as if it pained him. "I know. But there is nothing a sole private and a lady can do. He's too powerful."

I stomped my foot on the ground. "I refuse to believe that. And even if it is true, I'll die trying. What do you know of Oak Island?"

"Oh, Christ." He scrubbed his palms over his eyes. "You're going to get yourself killed, madam."

"What do you know of Oak Island?"

"Mrs.—"

I yanked out my gun from its holster, cocking it, and pointed it at him. He raised his hands. "What do you know of Oak Island?" I said every word from behind gritted teeth.

His chest heaved up and down. "I—I… it's a fantasy. The man is delusional. Swears there's some Scottish pirate's gold there. Said when he was stationed in Scotland, he heard stories, rumors, that some pirate, called Captain Kidd, stashed his gold on Oak Island."

I lowered the barrel, the gun lax in my hand. "Gold. The man is hunting pirate treasure?" He wanted riches? It seemed unlikely that was his sole reason for the whole scheme.

The sailor looked around before leaning in. "Put that bloody thing away. I'm trying to help you."

I arched a brow before returning the flintlock to my holster. "If you betray me or try anything, I will kill you."

His mouth opened and closed it before he responded. "Good Lord. John had said his wife was a gentlelady."

Meeting his eye, I frowned. My brows knitted close together. "You knew John?"

"I *know* him. Aye. That's how I started learning about this whole thing. Our hammocks were next to each other when he was a lowly private." He placed his hand on his chest. "We became friends."

"What's your name?" The cool night wind snapped across my face.

"Weston Pierce, at your service, madam." He tipped his bifold hat with the odd necktie ribbons.

Wrapping my coat tighter around me, my eyes were wide. "You're John's friend? He never mentioned a Weston Pierce."

He stared at the ground. "Honestly, he didn't mention you much either. I didn't know he had a wife until after years of working together."

Because he didn't care enough to say anything about me. "He really is alive?"

"Aye. One of Cobbe's 'loyal' privates snuck a letter from him to me, telling me everything he knew. He said Cobbe has him using his knowledge of powder and explosives to blow up old caves and tunnels excavated there nigh a century ago. There are booby traps and puzzles to solve, and it apparently takes a team of men to try to excavate the aforementioned treasure."

I shook my head. "Cobbe would be a turncoat, lying to the Crown, for money?"

"No, I don't think the commodore is just after treasure." He tugged me deeper into the shadows. "In his letter, John said he met with a man with an aristocratic air, wearing French clothes but who isn't French. A Mr. Sinclair. And he said Cobbe kept muttering, 'She would have wanted this.'"

My breath hitched, and I tapped my fingers to my lips. "She? She who?" He raised a shoulder in a half shrug. "You're tellin' me that the man who had me marry another man knowing my first husband was truly alive is doin' this for love?"

"The way John wrote it, it didn't sound like the lass was alive." Weston rubbed his brow.

"Well, did he give any information on where the island is? How many men? What we're up against?" My voice was shrill.

"He said it was south, and it took about three hours for the longboat to arrive—as long as they didn't purposely go in circles because he was blindfolded." He bounced on the balls of his feet. "I'm sorry, madam. I must go. I booked a small boat to smuggle me onto a trade ship. I know too much."

"What? You're leaving? But…" I waved my hand between us. "How will I help them? What about William? Don't you care at all?"

He averted his eyes from me. "I do. But, madam, if you had any sense, you'd get on the boat with me. You really think any of them would want you to risk your life?"

"No. But I bloody don't care. It's what you do for those you love. Your family." My gaze filled with heat. "And if you won't help me, then get out of my way. I have people relying on me." I shoved past him.

"But whose love, madam?" he asked after me.

Pushing past crowds on the street, I stormed away from him, with no idea where I was headed. I focused on lamppost to lamppost, walking around each circle of light to avoid any of Cobbe's lingering sailors who might identify me.

I had no money to pay for an inn, and, apparently, I couldn't return to the *Bluebell*—and I had no skill to speak of to rescue Alexander. Or William. Or even John.

Slinking in the shadowed alley that had given me so much pleasure not an hour ago, I paced back and forth. What was I supposed to do? I was a lone lady.

He was gone.

Commodore Cobbe had won. This man dismantled my life months ago, leaving me with no assets, no access to my jointure— but now he had completely eviscerated me. I had thought that money, land, our townhouse was everything. But they were things. Meaningless.

And now I truly had had everything, and he took him too.

What if the worst had happened? A sharp pain in my chest dropped me to my knees. If Cobbe had killed him or arrested him to be hanged…

I survived hunger, survived neglect, but I would not survive losing him. My heart would be ripped out and torn to shreds. Even if he was alive and working on this asinine treasure hunting plot, if I couldn't save him from this mysterious Oak Island—it would be as good as death, anyway.

Sitting on my knees in the alley, hot tears streamed down my face. I wasn't enough to save him. There was no way.

Maybe I should have followed Mr. Pierce, the damned coward, onto his boat. Dull pain radiated throughout my body, and I wrapped my arms around myself.

I'd gone this far only to lose it all. Maybe I'd never deserved Alexander or the life I had in London. Maybe that was why my father drank and my brother left for war.

I was undeserving. And this was how it would always be. To be left with naught. To be nothing.

To have no one.

28

M y mouth was dry. I needed water. Or whisky.

My husband was gone. Both of them. Heaven forfend. I snorted a sardonic laugh. Was I to be left by the men I gave my heart to, over and over again? From the very first man who was supposed to love me, my papa, to the man I'd never seen coming who had absolutely stolen my heart?

The stars faded as the purple hues of dawn overtook the black night sky. I'd sat in this damn alley all night long, nigh freezing to death, while crying until I had no more tears left in me to give. I scrubbed my eyes with the base of my palms.

I needed to... to do something. I couldn't very well live out the remainder of my life in between these two buildings.

I loved him. Leaving him here to an unknown fate—I would never allow it. Maybe I could go to the authorities about what I knew of Cobbe and Oak Island.

But would they believe me? Would they care? A man who was wanted by the Crown being taken by a commodore sounded far-fetched. Not to mention, they likely wouldn't care about a Highlander turned privateer if it were true.

Alexander and I had asked around for days after William was taken—no one knew anything about an Oak Island—or at least anyone who was willing to say so.

There was no other option. It had to be me.

And I wouldn't abandon my husband.

I hopped to my feet. Damn it all to hell. The bloody pirate savage had to go and get himself captured, leaving me to rescue him.

But where to start? A secret island with pirate treasure sounded like utter madness. I froze. It had indeed sounded like lunacy when I had first read about it in the captain's logs on the *Bluebell*.

Bloody hell, how had I not put two and two together until now? It was right in front of me. That captain had been mapping out locations. He'd never found it, but at least I'd know where *not* to look.

The log was on the ship, though—and where Cobbe and his men would be waiting for me. I peered down at my breeches and shift. I was already wearing a costume, but this one was spent. They'd seen me in it at the tavern. And they'd seen me as a woman. My hair was too recognizable.

But I had no money. I couldn't buy something new. I snapped my fingers. I already had something to wear—my commissioned riding habit.

Bouncing on my toes, my heartbeat picked up its pace. But my damned hair. I could powder it and my face. Look more genteel. Would that be enough? In the early morning light, a man with a wig and a fine embroidered suit strolled by the alley. He oddly reminded me of Mr. Pilkington.

A wig. Yes. A wig. Plus some white powder and rouge. Still, the lack of money posed a problem.

My wrist brushed the cold iron of the gun. I couldn't. I gnawed on my cheek. Well, I could. Oh Christ, I'd been living with pirates for too long. It was one thing to pickpocket or steal for survival—but it was an entirely different thing to hold a man at gunpoint.

I exhaled hard, breath steaming around me. My heartbeat pounded like a galloping horse's hooves. Ripping at the hem of my shift, I tore off a scrap of fabric and wrapped it around my mouth and nose, leaving me a thin slice to see through.

No one was around yet, unless I counted a passed-out man in the gutter a bit down the road. Either it was too early in the morning for most to start their day, or they were still fighting off hangovers from the night before. Either way, but luck was on my side.

Shaky energy rolled through me, blood rushing. The man was half a block away now. Lord, forgive me. I'd be going to Hell for this. Blowing air out of my mouth, I pressed my boots off the ground and darted after him on my tiptoes so the smacking of my heels wouldn't alert him to my arrival. He stopped at a little shop door. I arched a brow when the sign came into view. No wonder I thought he looked like Pilkington—this man was a lawyer, too.

He fiddled with an iron key ring, and I shoved the barrel of the gun against the small of his back. He froze. Dropping the key ring, he raised his arms in the air.

I cocked the gun. "Don't move." I used the deep voice I had

practiced on the *Bluebell*. Could he even understand my words between my panting breaths?

"There is no money in the office. I bring it to the bank daily. All I have is my coin purse." His voice was shaky and clearly British.

"I don't want money. Give me your wig." Shite. I'd need some rice powder. "Actually, I need a shilling too. If-if you don't mind." Bollocks. I nudged the gun harder against his back. "I mean, give me a shilling." What if I needed to buy something else? Or food? I didn't want to do this again. "Make it a few shillings."

"Lad, just take the whole purse and be on your way. P-please." His broken plea made my stomach clench. "It's in the front pocket of my coat, left side."

With my free hand, I patted his coat and slipped my hand into his pocket, fingers brushing against the velvet. My head was in the crook of his neck, my body pressed against the back of him. It was close, and such an intrusion.

I closed my eyes tight for a heartbeat, trying to gather myself. My palms broke into a sweat until I at last clutched the purse and yanked it out.

"I'm so sorry." Dammit. My voice sounded more feminine than I intended. "The wig now. Keep your hands where I can see them and remove your wig."

With one hand, he removed the wig, revealing a bald head with stray white hairs poking out wildly.

I grabbed it from his grasp. "I'm sorry. I will repay you. Stay here in this spot with your back to me for two minutes. If you so much as move, I'll shoot."

I backed away, the heel of my boot catching on an uneven stone. Falling backward, I pulled the trigger. The bullet shot toward the roofline of the building. "Fuck!"

The man fell to his knees, hands still above him. "I won't move! I won't move!"

Poor man. Probably scarred him for life. I ran as fast as I could to get away from anyone who may have heard the gunshot. I ripped the material off my face and replaced my gun in its holster as my feet thudded against the cobblestone. Unsure where to go, I kept running and running until I physically couldn't run anymore. I stopped at the tree line to the forest just past the main part of the town. My side burned as if I were wearing stays.

I wrung my wrists out as if they were wet and rolled my shoulders. It was fine. The man was fine. I was fine. And I'd return the money. With interest. Fine. Everything was fine.

Which my husband wouldn't be, if I hadn't done that.

I took off my hat, placing it under my arm, and rubbed my hand through my hair, the weight of the stolen wig in my other. The shop I'd commissioned the riding habit from wasn't too far from the lawyer's place. If I had picked up the clothing before the wig, its location wouldn't have been an issue. Now I'd have to return to the scene of the crime. The constable could be there by now.

I tapped my toe over the blanket of brown pine needles covering the forest floor. I couldn't wait too long; the longer I waited, the more likely Alexander would be... my chest burned. I couldn't even think of the word.

Well, I'd have to change my appearance. Again. Eyes darting

around, the trees all looked the same, and shadows covered everything. I had no choice but to leave the wig, gun, and my hat here and hope I could find them again.

Stashing my things at the base of a tree, I searched for physical markers to help guide me back. The nearest building was the backside of a general store. There was a cluster of boulders straight ahead. I took some of the dried pine needles and covered my belongings. My hair was down, and I combed my fingers through it, and pinched my cheeks. I tucked my shift into my pants, trying to hide some of the torn hem. There. As presentable as I could be under the circumstances.

As I traversed the town's dirt and cobblestone roads, I wound around and in between the log buildings, keeping my gaze averted to the ground. The morning sun had warmed the crisp air, and not a cloud was in sight. Early risers pattered around me. Horse-led carts carrying goods and redcoats on patrol meandered through the streets. I slipped through an alley to avoid most of the people and cut through to the street with the dress shop and nearly pissed myself when a dog popped out into the passageway, blocking me. I froze, hand over my heart, until he sniffed the air and scampered off.

Sighing, I continued through the rest of the alley unscathed. At the edge of the buildings, I peered in each direction, my eyes falling to the lawyer's office immediately. Nothing seemed amiss. Stretching my limbs, I dashed across the street as fast as I could, but slow enough I wouldn't draw too much attention to myself. Once at the shop, I shoved open the door, the bells ringing making me jerk.

For goodness' sake. They were only bells.

I went to the counter. The woman who had taken my measurement wasn't inside, nor was her husband, the tailor. I tapped my fingers, ready to call it quits, when the woman appeared.

"Oh! I'm sorry, madam, I didn't hear the bells." She ambled forward, her silver hair tied in a bun at the nape of her neck. "Mistress Lock." Her eyes swept down me, her mouth open. "You-you look quite peculiar. Are those breeches?"

My pulse doubled in pace. "I-I... was robbed. Asked me for my gown. It was odd. Left me to my shift, and a soldier was kind enough to fetch me breeches to wear until I could pick up my order."

Her brows drew together, her mouth dropping open even wider. For a moment, I didn't think she believed me because she said nothing. "Oh, you poor thing. It's the queerest thing, Mr. Jones, the lawyer here in these parts, was robbed just this morning. Said the lad wanted his wig only."

I blinked and smoothed my features, swallowing. I was practiced in masking myself in tranquility. It wouldn't fail me now. "Bizarre indeed. Do you suppose it could be the same *man*? Going around stealing clothin' and the like?"

She paced around the counter and grasped my hands. "You must be rattled. Let me grab you some tea. And where is your handsome Scottish husband? If I remember correctly, he was a sight for this old lady's sore eyes. Don't tell my Mr. Doyle that." She placed her hand on her hip and fanned herself with her other one. "Back in ol' England in the thirties, I courted a Highlander. Clan Lindsay. The best kisser of my life. Don't tell my husband that either." Despite my urgency, I laughed. "I dare say by the look on your face when you two had come in, that seems to be a Scottish trait."

I nodded. "You would not be wrong in your assumption. But I'm afraid I must decline tea. Mr. Lock is on the ship, waiting for me. So if you wouldn't mind, I'll take the outfit only."

"Are you preparing to leave today, then? I was hoping to make alterations and ensure everything was to your liking."

"Regrettably, we don't have enough time. And could I dress here? I must make haste, and I'd like to surprise Mr. Lock with it." I gave what I hoped to be a pleasant and not a forced or overly anxious smile.

She nodded, eyes sparkling with warmth. "Of course, my dear. Let me fetch it."

When she disappeared from sight, I browsed the shop. Bottles of perfume, all different shapes and sizes, ensnared me. I opened one and took a sniff. Lavender and vanilla. How long had it been since I had perfumed myself? I replaced the lid and continued perusing the items on the shelf. Tins of powders and rouge, oils and balms. All things I'd long ago forgotten when I had taken on this voyage of mine. I grabbed a tin of rice powder and paced back to the front. What was taking so long? I shifted my weight from foot to foot, waiting.

A line of Navy sailors walked down the other side of the lane. I gasped and sank against the wall of the shop and peered out from the shadow of the building. The stout sailor, strutting through the street now, had most definitely been one of the men from last night. The others were looking around, eyes snapping in every direction. They stopped at the entrance of the alley I had come out of and paced while the others stood at the street, seemingly on lookout. They were searching. Most likely for me.

Oh God. Would they start going into shops?

"Here it is, Mistress Lock." I jumped at her voice. "Oh, you poor thing. You must be frightened after your whole ordeal. I wonder why your husband would let you come back here alone? To be sure, the ship could spare him for a moment whilst he attends his wife." She had the royal blue habit in her hands.

"He... he couldn't." Her head tilted to the side as if in question. "I mean, he..." Heat rose to my neck and chest, a drop of sweat rolling down my neck. "He was a Highlander, too. Fought at Culloden. He is wanted by the Crown. The commodore from the naval ship recognized him." Her mouth opened for a moment of shock, before she leaned in closer to me and placed her fingers to her lips, intrigued. "You understand the danger, I presume?"

She seemed to analyze every inch of me before she lifted her chin with a rebellious air and nodded. "Well, c'mon, dear. Let us get you dressed and out of here before they close in on your ship."

The blue habit was exactly as I had pictured it'd look like. I powdered my face heavily. More than I would have even at home for the Mayfair district. It had a tall hat to match. I powdered my hair, but it was still obviously red. Until I could get back to the wig, this would have to do. Sighing, I turned away from the looking glass and paced around the room divider to head up front.

The bells on the shop door jingled.

I halted my steps, and every muscle in my being locked for a breath before I shook my head and dove behind the partition.

"Good morning, madam."

My breath ripped from me in quick bursts. A man's voice. I searched my surroundings for something I could use as a weapon. Wait. I uncurled my fingers from the tight ball they were in. It could be a man here to pick up clothing or commission—

"Good morning, Captain?" Mrs. Doyle's voice seemed almost shaky.

"Commodore actually, madam." His voice was cold. The tone sent a shiver down my spine.

"Commodore, I'm begging your pardon, sir. Back when Mr. Doyle served, the Navy men still wore red coats. I'm not knowledgeable in the different ranks of these uniforms. What brings you in today? Uniform needing a mending?" Her voice sounded further away, like she had rounded the counter and neared him.

My palms were sweaty, my ears ringing. I stayed rooted to the spot. Oh Christ, she could very well be whispering to him about me right now.

"Unfortunately, I'm not here for your services today. There's a privateering ship here that we learned is captained by a wanted man. A tall Scotsman, dark hair. You wouldn't miss him if you saw him in a crowd. We fortunately have detained him, but his wife has seemed to be a little more elusive. She's English, bright red hair. She might have even disguised herself as a man."

There was no back door I could find from here. They'd look behind this partition, to be sure. I put my head against the wall and stared at the ceiling. Something metallic gleamed. A latch to a hatch in the ceiling.

"A tall Scotsman and a redhead? I have not seen anyone with their descriptions. But this was an old Scottish settlement. It's not so odd to hear the brogue around here," Mrs. Doyle said.

I could kiss the woman.

"Do you mind if we have a look around? She could be hiding in any of the area's buildings." His drawl was calm but authoritative.

I peered down at my hand and regarded my wedding ring. It may not be my true wedding ring, but tell that to my heart. I would do anything for the man who gave it to me. I shut my eyes tight and pushed off the wall.

"Well, of course not, Commodore. I'd feel much safer if you did." Her voice came louder, as if to warn me. Going as quick but as quietly as I could, I snuck toward the stairs leading to the loft. "Is your ship that giant, regal looking frigate that arrived a week ago?"

"Why, yes. That's us. But she's a man-o'-war." Was he closer than before?

My hands tensed. I couldn't waste any more time. I began climbing the stairs, slowly, one foot at a time so as to not make too much noise on the wood. About halfway, a particularly loud creak emanated from the floor. Dammit. I froze, my next foot still in midair.

"A man-o'-war? Excuse my ignorance, but how exactly is that different from a frigate?" Oh, bless her heart.

I hiked up the rest of the stairs without incident and aimed for the hatch. As I jogged toward the roof door, I caught a glimpse of the main part of the store. Cobbe poised, feet wide, with his hat under his arm, his brown hair tied back into a low ponytail. A knot formed in my throat, as if I were choking, and I dropped to the floor in a crouch behind some bolts of fabric. If I saw him, did that mean he had seen me, too? I needed to keep moving, so I crawled toward the hatch and slid my hand out to unhook the latch as booted footsteps pounded on the wood flooring. I pushed open the hatch, inch by inch, praying the hinges wouldn't squeak. Once open enough for me to slip through, I climbed over the threshold and pushed the door back, but with less than a half-inch left, I didn't know how to close it without a loud noise. I'd just have to let it go and run. Indeed, that would be the best solution, the only solution.

I dropped the last of the hatch into place and twisted myself toward the street. Losing my footing on the shingles, I slipped and slid down the side, my boots kicking off shingles as I went. Jutting off the side, I fell on my arse on the dusty street in front of two women promenading. They jumped back with screams, eyes wide.

Ignoring the radiating pain in my backside, I hopped to my feet and ran as fast as I could out of the town square, back toward the trees. No slinking and stealth, instead an outright run, going the shortest distance possible.

Once I hit the tree line, I kept running until I was sure no one would follow. A babbling stream with foamy white water coursed over moss-covered stones and fallen branches and tree trunks. I sank to the ground, catching my breath next to it. After a few moments, I splashed the icy water on my face.

Now all I'd need to do was sneak back onto the *Bluebell* and grab the journal.

It'd be easy, to be sure. Yes, like everything else always was in my life.

29

The wig smelled of pipe smoke and greasy hair. It definitely was fashioned in a man's style. But hopefully, with my riding hat, no one would notice that. And hopefully with the fine habit and reapplied layers of rice powder, no one would recognize it was me.

The sun dipped lower and lower into the horizon before it illuminated the entire sky with burnt oranges and pinks and purples. That was my cue to leave the forest. A loud rumble gurgled from my stomach. Maybe I'd be able to snatch some water and food from the galley on the ship. Stars winked across the blackening sky, and from here, the town's windows glowed with candlelight. The ships in the port started lighting up like beacons on a lonely night. Walking down Privateers' Wharf, a few provocatively dressed women sashayed and approached men. Like they'd done every night since we'd arrived. I unbuttoned the front of my habit jacket and pulled down the top of my shift to reveal my shoulders and the swell of my breasts. Enough to show off what I was selling, but not so much they'd see the gun tied around my hip. Dressed as a whore once more. Why did I even bother purchasing clothes? At this rate, I'd never again dress how I wanted.

I stood at the top of the dock, prostitutes eyeing me like I was stepping onto their territory. The *Bluebell* was berthed a few ships down. A pang of sadness struck me. It'd felt like home as of late. I shook my head. No. Alexander felt like home. The ship was merely where we slept.

By now, they'd know he was gone. Maybe they didn't care. With Alexander and William gone, the next in charge would be... the first mate. Jacques. I grimaced. The French scallywag with three missing teeth.

I paced down the dock and stopped in my tracks. A couple of men I didn't recognize stood on either side of the gangway. They had to be lookouts for Cobbe. I slipped behind a dock post, my back angled toward them, and peered over my shoulder. A sailor and a whore, arms wrapped around each other, stumbling drunk, walked past me toward the *Bluebell*. One of the men guarding the ship whistled toward the couple while the other lookout made kissing noises.

I chewed on the inside of my cheek. They no doubt hated the fact they were stuck here, outside of the ship, waiting for a lass when they could've been out having fun like other sailors. I drummed my fingers on my thighs before rushing back to the wharf.

I stopped in front of one of the prostitutes, a round and robust woman, heavily powdered, with a fake, black beauty mark above her lips.

She folded her arms across her chest and arched a brow. "Ya new around here? I innit ever seen you."

"I have money." I stood tall, chin high.

Her brows crinkled together. "Sorry, doll, I don' take lassies. My frien' Sheila over there will be willin'."

I laughed, cheeks heating. "No. I need two men down on the dock distracted. Long enough to sneak on to a ship. If you and your friend Sheila are willing, I will pay you two shillings each and another two if you succeed in distracting them long enough for me to get on and off."

She leaned back, lips pursed. "If we succeed in distractin' em? We are professionals."

I adjusted my slackened shift's collar. "Then it shall be easy money."

Her head tilted, her lips moving from side to side. "Make it three each for after. If we *succeed,* tha' is."

I rolled my eyes. "Done." By Jove, I hoped there was a coin purse still in my trunk or in Alexander's.

"And if they ask who paid? They'll know we don't give nuthin' for free." Her high bun flopped in every direction when she talked.

I inclined my head. "Tell them the commodore sent you for remaining loyal and dedicated to him."

I followed them several paces behind. The lanterns on the dock were far apart, so I remained mostly in the dark. They stopped in front of the men, and I hid in an unlit part of the dock amongst some netting and ropes.

I couldn't quite make out their words. Sheila said something like '*hello gents.* 'The women slid their hands down the men's chests and arched their bosoms into their faces. One of the men waved off

Sheila, and I almost panicked that they wouldn't be distracted, but then she whispered in his ear and a wide grin spread across his face.

Now or never. A fisherman strolled by. I stepped out of the shadows and linked my arm with his. "Evenin' fine nigh', innit?" I matched his stride down the dock.

"Sorry, not interested." He tried to shake me off his arm.

"Oh, I'll give ya the best rates in town." I caressed his arm, not letting go until we were right in front of the *Bluebell.*

"Sorry." He rolled his shoulder, and I let go right in front of the gangway.

From the looks of it, Sheila already had her skirt pulled up. I probably didn't even need to pretend with the fisherman at this rate. Could've walked right on by. I ran up the gangway to the main deck. Once on the other side of the railing, I exhaled.

The familiarity of it eased something in me, loosening the knots in my stomach. The slippery deck and salty air, and the lacquered wood... my shoulders relaxed. The *Bluebell.* Warmth pressed against the backs of my eyes despite the cold night breeze numbing my cheeks and nose.

I didn't have much time, so I made a break for the staircase down onto the gun deck. There weren't many lanterns lit, but after weeks on a dark sea, my body knew where to go without them. Passing the quartermaster's cabin with a heavy sadness pressing on my chest, I twisted the handle to the captain's cabin.

I winced the moment I took in the room. It still smelled of him: oak, salt, leather, musk. My chin trembled as I paced across the room, feet heavy. If I didn't succeed... I ran to the navigation table and tore everything off, looking for the mad captain's log. The brown leather cover was falling off, dangling slightly. I'd know if I saw it, to be sure. Scouring every surface with haste, I came to the conclusion that it wasn't here. I pushed off maps and unfurling parchment. Nothing.

No. No! A tear escaped my eye. It was my only clue. The only thing that could possibly help me. I slashed my hand over the table, shoving off the contents. I wouldn't let him down.

I trudged toward my trunk, and my toe hit something on the floor. The sight of camel-colored leather ripped a sob from my chest. I grabbed the journal and went to my trunk, and gave a shaky laugh. My leftover pin money was still in my reticule next to the letter Cobbe had written me, *certifying* John's death, and the letter we'd found on his sister-in-law after he'd killed her.

In Alexander's trunk, in search of an extra pistol and powder horn, I stopped short. Flowing plaid fabric covered all of its contents. This time, it wasn't a tear rolling down my cheek. It was a whole damned river.

I brought the material to my face and breathed in the familiar scent. I shut my eyes. For a moment, it was like he was right there with me. His sporran was underneath it. I grabbed it and put the journal and my reticule inside. I found the extra pistol and a powder horn and a few balls and placed those in his bag, too. Unable to refuse myself, I wrapped the tartan around my shoulders, tying it like a shawl, and rose.

With difficulty, I pulled myself away from his trunk and left the room. I descended to the next deck and sipped a few ladles of water, then stowed some hardtack and apples in the sporran. I climbed back up to the main deck. A few men were sitting and drinking.

I caught a familiar French accent from across the deck. Jacques. He was in the corner next to a lantern talking to someone with their back to me. I ran up toward Jacques, his eyes crinkling in the corners, when his gaze fell on me. Then his eyes widened in recognition, and his face blanched. He gave a slight shake of his head. I froze. Without moving, he flicked his eyes back to whoever was talking to him.

I backed away slowly, quietly. They were blocking the path to the gangway. The man shifted, his form hitting the light, highlighting his distinct navy-blue frock. My back hit the rail on the other side of the ship. The jolly boat was just attached to this side. I swung my legs over the rail, sitting on the top. The gap between the rail and the boat had to be nigh two feet. It hadn't seemed that far from the deck. The Royal Navy man started to turn, and I sprang for it, landing in the dark boat with a thud. I laid out on my belly, stiff as the wood below me as the jolly boat swung.

I could release the boat into the water, but it would make a huge, loud splash. If the sailor on the deck didn't hear, the men on the dock would. Although, they still might be thoroughly occupied. Thumps around the deck made me freeze.

"Feel free to search the ship. As I said, you'll find nothing. Would you like to start 'ere or down at the 'ull?" Jacques called, maybe feet away from the railing.

"From the bottom up, so those who are hiding may escape above me? I shall start here. Every level will be thoroughly searched, I can assure you." The sailor seemed further away.

"So we'll be up 'ere a very long time, then?" Jacques' voice was loud. Much louder than it needed to be. For me.

"Yes, frog eater. Do I need to spell it out for you?"

"*Non.* I'll *ring the bell* to call all the men to the main deck if it pleases you, sir?" A distraction to hide the sound. Oh, he was quick on his feet. I would kiss him the next time I saw him, despite his missing teeth.

I perched on my elbows, searching for the way to release the pulley that'd let me lower the boat—to no avail. The ship blocked any moonlight, and most of the stars were covered by clouds.

No other choice but to stand and feel my way around. I paused, inclining my ear toward the ship. No voices I could hear from here. It was as good a time as ever. I inched up, my arms stretching out to balance on the wobbly boat hanging on its ropes.

What had William said about the jolly boat on the night of the storm? A lever on the inside could release the davit in an emergency but it'd free fall.

Brushing down the sides of the coarse ropes, my fingertips grazed the sanded wooden wheel of the pulley. I pressed around it, searching for something lever shaped. At last, I smoothed over a rectangle, pushing the tips of my fingers on its underside. I tugged it just enough to see if it was a movable object. After a bit of resistance, the lever raised, and the boat jolted a smidge. I exhaled, ready to yank it at the first ring of the bell. My stance was wide, bearing down and holding unnaturally still, my fingers buzzed in anticipation.

At the first clang of the bell, I pulled back the lever and dropped to a crouch as the rope slid fast through the squeaking wheel. I braced the sides as the boat free-fell, waiting for impact. Within seconds, it collided with the black water, sending up a large splash, icy water spraying over me. The loud clanging bell still rang from the main deck, but if the whores weren't doing their due diligence, the men at the dock would be here any second.

I yanked one oar out and then the other, heart racing, fingers fumbling, and pressed them into their oarlocks. Sweat coated my palms as I wrapped my fingers around the oars, my grip slippery. I exhaled as I pressed the oars forward, propelling the jolly boat and slicing it across the pitch-black water. Again and again, I pushed and pulled the oars as fast as my arms would let me. Clearing the *Bluebell,* I continued on, prayin' that nobody saw me and was chasing after me. I cleared the other ships and rowed toward the bay. My arms burned from the effort. Once I rounded the corner, the wharf completely blocked from my vantage point. I stopped rowing, letting my arms and shoulders sag.

As my muscles relaxed, my body slowly cooled, the chilly air even colder here. I tugged the tartan closer to me. Here the moonlight was unobscured, its wide beam glowing over part of the bay in a stream of white, its nearly full circle reflecting in the shimmery water. On either side of me, the coasts were lined with more of the giant pine trees.

I was absolutely alone.

But I didn't feel the pang of sadness in my chest I usually felt when I realized I was totally alone. Nor that slimy uncomfortable feeling that pressed on my shoulders and raised the hair on the back of my neck when the dark place in me whispered *you're not enough.*

Instead, a feeling of tranquility and clarity washed over me. I closed my eyes and tipped my head back. John was gone. William was gone. And now Alexander was gone.

But I wasn't abandoned. Because I always had myself. And I'd never given up on her once. I wasn't the same woman I was when I had started off on this journey. I was more.

I was enough. Enough to change the circumstances of my life, and enough to control my own fate.

And I wouldn't abandon Alexander. Because he was my fate.

30

I blinked my eyes open, beams of rainbow-colored circles shining against my gaze. I blocked the sun with my hand as I adjusted to the light. My back and neck were stiff from sleeping on the boat. Alexander's tartan was wrapped around me, but my ears and nose were bitterly cold and numb. I steamed the air with my breath as I gathered my bearings.

I'd floated to a shoreline on one side of the bay. The boat was stuck in place by an uprooted tree that had fallen into the bay. Well, I hadn't been sucked into the middle of the Atlantic, at least.

I ran my hands over my face, grimacing when they came back white. Dunking them in the water, I splashed water on my face, scrubbing them. My hands were pale and numb by the time I'd finished. My face burned icy hot.

I hopped on the tree log, balancing my way across it, before splashing down into the low water near the shore, and yanked the boat up the beach. Heaving, I dug my heels into the wet sand, the tide lapping at my boots. The damned thing was heavy. Once the hull was far enough on the sandy bank that I didn't think it'd float away, I hiked to the tree line and sank down at the base of a pine, my back against the trunk.

My mouth was dry and my stomach squeezed from emptiness. I opened the sporran and found the apple. Biting into it, juice sprayed in every direction.

All right. I'd eat, read the journal, and then save Alexander.

The captain's log had the ramblings I remembered from last time. But I re-read the pages with a new critical eye. Some entries were clearer and made more sense than other pages that were a complete array of unconnected thoughts. As I continued to the pages I hadn't read, my shoulders slumped lower and lower. The man sounded as if he'd fallen to lunacy.

It could be that the man in the journal wasn't even talking about the same island as Cobbe's secret project. And as if to confirm it, three-quarters of the way in, in a particularly lucid entry, there was the name—*Smith Island.*

I sat straighter. It was the first time the man had used the name. I was so sure they were the same island; the area and location were too similar.

17 April 1720

As I drank at the inn, another Scotsman, Finlay Oglivy, was heavy into his ale. When he had heard my accent as I ordered a drink, he shouted to me in Gaelic. The Scots in the French colony had been dissipating, but he'd said his granda had settled here, and eventually he'd come over after the failed uprising in '15. After some shared stories about lairds and brawls, I'd dared to ask—had he heard of the secret island? He said Captain Kidd had been rumored to be dead now for nigh twenty years, but his story was a legend around here amongst the leftover Scots, and those who'd heard the story of the Scottish pirate, even back home in the Highlands. Smith Island, he called it. Said he had searched for it too, him and hundreds of Scots by now. The Spanish ship the treasure was claimed to be from was rumored to be an entire year's worth of taxes from Florida. Said it would be enough to fully fund a war with England and many were eager to be the one to bring it to the Stuarts.

Apparently, there were two secret treasure islands here. I tapped my chin. Coincidence?

Captain Kidd's treasure. A *Scottish* pirate—Cobbe could have heard the story in his time stationed there. Could he have mistaken the name of the island? Had the rumors changed over time like they tended to do? A Scotsman did love to share a good story. Placing the journal in my lap, I scratched the back of my head.

Talk about the irony if it *were* true. The commodore was after treasure once sought to finance the very rebellion he helped dismantle. The very rebellion that had led him to kill his ex-lover and Alexander's wife.

I flipped the pages, reading on. More useless ramblings until—

2 May 1720

On the precipice of nigh giving up after another three days of failed attempts to find Smith Island, I stopped in the newly established settlement in the La Baye de la Toutes Isles, *to a settlement the French exiles call* Acadie. *Most of the people are fishermen. We all drank together, tearing apart our common enemy, the English. We'd swapped stories, and one of them asked of the Jacobites. I told the tale of the hapless mission I was on. I asked if they had ever heard of a supposed Smith Island with treasure—I was giving up, what was five more fishermen hearing the tale to matter? One said he had never heard such stories about Smith Island, but they had heard them about an Oak Island. It was supposedly not far from here—but the fog always made it nigh impossible to see the tiny isle. They said it was told to be the shape of an* éléph*ant. I asked if any had tried to go. One made the sign of the holy cross and shook his head. He said there was a* malédiction. *Every man that tries to excavate it dies.*

I stopped breathing. This was it. The same island. I re-read the last line again. *Every man that tries to excavate it dies.* Well, that was ominous.

Now, to get myself to *La Baye de la Toures Isles,* to *Acadie.* To save my husband.

And my other husband.

And my best friend.

31

I rowed out to the middle of the bay, hoping the next ship I encountered would be leaving Halifax and not heading toward it and the waiting Royal Navy.

Leaning back in the boat, I regarded the white, fluffy clouds floating across the azure sky above me. *"What do you do with your mate full on rum?"* I sang. "Oh, that one looks like a horse." I was at sixes and sevens and possibly losing it. *"Ain't got his senses come mornin' sun!"*

What seemed like hours later, all my hard tack and water gone, at last, a small fishing boat rounded the corner from the port.

I stood in the boat, trying to maintain my balance and not fall into the water, and waved my arms to flag them down. "Help me, help me! Please!"

After a few minutes, they neared and tossed me a rope. It took a couple of attempts but I fished it out of the water. I tied it to one end of the jolly boat and they tugged me in toward the bow of their small ship.

Gathering my belongings, I tied the tartan around me like a

shawl again and put the sporran over my shoulder. A man gave me a hand to help me into their small ship. They spoke French. The captain, or so I assumed from his hat, muttered so quickly I couldn't translate.

Dammit, it'd been a decade since I'd last spoken French. *"Je-je ne parler pas bonne."*

One man grimaced. Hopefully, I hadn't said something insulting. *"Anglais,"* he said, facing his crew, their eyes widening, their weight shifting from foot to foot.

The apple and hardtack turned sour in my stomach. "I am Scottish. By marriage." I didn't even know if they spoke English. "They hate the English too."

One sitting down on a crate started laughing. *"Oui.* They do."

"You speak English?" I licked my lips. "Please, my ship. There's been a wreck, and—"

"What's in the bag?" He jutted his head toward my shoulder. His accent was clear, like he'd spent a lot of time speaking English. The other men circled behind me.

I raised my hands up. "A'reet." Bloody hell, there was my accent slipping in. "There are weapons in my bag." Despite being half frozen the last few days, sweat broke out on the back of my neck. "I grabbed what I could. But I swear, I'm not here to hurt you." My voice broke. "I—I just want to get to my husband." Warm tears plopped on the deck as I blinked. "Please, I just want my husband."

The fisherman who spoke English narrowed his gaze. He was a type of handsome with his soft, delicate features. He didn't look like he was a fisherman. After a heartbeat, he nodded and said something to his comrades in French. "Where will he be? Your Scotsman?"

"A rural settlement in *La Baye de la Toutes Isles* called *Acadie.* Do you know it?" I gnawed on my cheek.

"Aye. But it's no longer *La Baye de la Toutes Isles.* The English call it Mahone Bay now. We will sail right by it. About an hour. I'll assure your safe arrival." His gaze swept down me as he seemed to scrutinize every detail of my outfit. "Did your husband fight in the Battle of Culloden?"

"Your English is good." Too good. I peered around me as men shifted, but they simply started working again, and the ship started to move in the breeze.

He pursed his lips. "I went to school and university in London. But rest assured, Mistress—"

"Lock." I placed my hands on my hips.

Squinting, he raised his chin. "Mistress Lock. I hate the English. No offense. Lock. A *nom de guerre.* So, I'll assume he *did* fight in Culloden." Smirk in place, he arched a brow. "Lock. A MacLachlan, I'd wager." He nodded. "Good men."

"He is a good man." My throat burned. "Please, do you have any water?"

"Where are my manners? Please forgive me. We have food and drink." He rose, the edge of his cloak billowing, revealing a fine suit under.

Once I chugged water and nibbled bread, I eyed the man again. The ship cleared the bay and sailed south. The smaller ship was quick, the wind snapping my hair. "Thank you for your hospitality, Mr.—"

"Mr. Sinclair." He smiled. "We should be arriving soon, Mistress MacLachlan."

"Thank you, Mr. Sinclair. I'll be glad to see my husband." I clenched my hands in the plaid wrapped around me.

"Oh, I didn't even notice the tartan. Since Culloden, King George forbade the Highlanders from wearing their plaids." He leaned on the edge of the crate. "You and your husband must be loyal to the Jacobite cause."

Blinking, I hugged myself. "My husband was. But there is no Jacobite cause left. They were defeated. The British always win."

"There are many in France who support the Jacobite cause. And they're currently at war with England." He adjusted the tie of his cloak that pressed against his throat.

"They are? So you're not French?" Unease coursed through me, and I gnawed on my cheek.

He leaned back, crossing his legs with an obvious air of self-inflated importance. I was surprised there wasn't a footman offering him a cup of tea and feeding him grapes. "Sinclair is actually Scottish."

My eyes widened, my mouth parting. Something was off, and I couldn't place my finger on it. "Oh. The name *had* sounded familiar."

I flinched when he raised his hand to point past me before I smiled and smoothed the skirt of my habit, trying to remain calm. "There it is. Mahone Bay, and that is the French exile settlement. For now. The English have their eye on it."

It looked like everything else around here—dense green forest. But sure enough, a few rural log buildings stuck out between the trees with smoke rising above them. Some of the knots in my stomach unfurled, knowing it was close, and I'd be off the boat soon, away from this odd man. I went to the railing, clenching it.

His footsteps thumped across the deck before he leaned against the railing beside me. "You know, if the French have the opportunity, they will invade the borders of England."

I leveled my gaze at the settlement, unwavering. We'd be there soon and I could get to Lock. "To be sure. It is war."

In my peripheral, I caught his head tilting as he watched me. "Some believe the French and Scottish would be natural allies. The Scottish invade from the north, France from the sea borders."

I looked at him, truly looking this time. "Forty minutes, Mr. Sinclair." One of his brows rose high. "That's how long it took for the Jacobite rebellion to end. It took forty minutes for my husband's family to be destroyed, his century long traditions washed away, his entire life decimated. It's over. It'd be with great difficulty that the *French* would find enough Scots willing to join them for a successful invasion."

His nostrils flared, and he pursed his lips. "And what about loyalty? The Stuarts are the rightful heirs to the throne."

"Mr. Sinclair... most people are trying to survive these days and have no energy to focus on anything else. I don't know what else to tell you." There was no dock in the settlement. Luckily, the jolly boat was still floating behind the fishing boat so I'd be able to take it to shore.

"There could be enough gold as an incentive." Mr. Sinclair tapped his fingers on his lips, seemingly talking to himself rather than me.

"Madame Lock." A fisherman offered me his arm to escort me to the back of the ship.

"Well, thank you all for your hospitality." I gave a tight-lipped smile. Mr. Sinclair tipped his hat, saying nothing more.

The fisherman walked me to the stern. "I forgot to ask... umm. *Tu sais island*, umm…"

"I speak uh, some, a little English." He smiled.

He helped me step into my jolly boat and squatted down to untie the rope. "Oh, thank God. Do you know of an island around here, supposedly shaped like an elephant?"

His hands froze, his eyes widening. He dropped the rope altogether.

Shite. "Never mind. If you could release my boat now."

He rose. Without thinking, I took the oar from the boat and swung it at him, sweeping his feet clear off the deck until he fell in the water with a loud splash. Adrenaline coursed through my veins. I finished untying the knot and rowed like my life depended on it— which it very well could. The man was flailing, trying to swim back to the ship, shouting in French.

I kept pushing and pulling the oars, my arms burning and tired. Cracks of gunshots rang behind me. The blood rushed in my ears as fast as the waves crashed in a tumultuous storm. A musket ball shot past me, air whooshing close to my ear, hammering into the empty bench seat in front of me. The sand was twenty feet away. Row. Keep rowing. Another blast of the gun made me duck before I pressed on. Feet from the shore, I hopped into the knee-high water and booked it to get out of the range of the gunfire, not bothering to bring the boat on the beach. I zig-zagged to the tree line as the men on the fishing boat fired more shots.

Once the line of the shore disappeared, and I was shadowed in heavy foliage, I slowed to a stop, chest heaving.

What the bloody hell? There were secrets on Oak Island, and I'd wager there were more than my dead husband being alive. Whatever was happening was the Crown's problem. All I wanted was my husband.

A shout from shore made me stop panting. I placed my back against the wide trunk of a tree and peered over my shoulder.

No. I pressed my palm to my chest. The men from the fishing boat had rowed to the shore.

The bark dug into my back as I dared not to move from the spot, one of my palms bracing the jagged wood on the side of my hips, the other wrapped around the handle of my pistol. They had spread apart. I'd run as far as I could before they began to close in on me. I had just enough time to pour in powder, wrap a ball, and prime it.

What was the big mystery of Oak Island? What could be so significant, of the utmost importance, that they'd hunt down a lone Englishwoman?

Crunching pine needles made me hold my breath, hand sweating on the hilt of the gun. Shooting a target that stood in place without my life looming over my head had been hard enough. I didn't think I could hit a moving target, especially one that had a gun pointed back at me. I should've grabbed an oar—I'd have had better luck.

A lone man rushed past me, and I hopped behind him, pressing the gun to his back, cocking it. God's teeth, how many men would I hold at gunpoint?

I took a soothing breath. As many as I needed to find my husband. I would do this over and over again until I found him.

"If you scream, I'll shoot." My voice was steady despite the buckets of sweat pouring down my nape. Hell, *I* almost believed me. *"Comprend?"* He nodded. "Drop the musket "

It fell to the pine-needle covered ground. Voices still came from rather far away and seemed to be fading deeper into the forest.

"Hands up and turn around. Slowly." He could easily overpower me and disarm me when he saw what he was doing. I bounced on my toes. "Wait. Don't move. Keep facing that way."

For Judas's sake, I was horrible at this. He stiffened when I shoved the barrel harder against his back. "Walk. To the beach, back to the boat. You're taking me to Oak Island."

F orty minutes.

It took forty minutes to clear the Mahone Bay from the rural *Acadie* establishment to Oak Island in a jolly boat. And these forty minutes were as important as the forty minutes were for Alexander in Culloden. My life would change, if not end, because of these forty minutes. What did fate have in store for me?

Being so far north, the sun was already dipping behind the mountain, and the briny fog crept in as the French fisherman rowed while I pointed the gun at him.

Oak Island was larger than some of the others in the area, though it was hard to see through the dense fog. A few lanterns glowed on beached longboats tethered to trees, so there *were,* in fact, people here.

I wanted to vomit. I had to face reality—I had absolutely no clue what to do, and it might already be too late. I kept my chin high. "Take us further down, away from the other boats, so they don't see us."

The fisherman did as he was told. From where he stopped, the lanterns down the shore were just visible. I hopped into the lapping tide on the sand, barely able to see where I was going in the growing dark of the night, and tugged the tartan tighter around my shoulders. The man climbed out and heaved the boat up far enough on the sand that it wouldn't float away. And then he stopped in place, looking at me expectantly, blinking.

What the hell should I do with him? I scratched the back of my head. I'd need the boat to leave. And I couldn't let him go off and alert anyone to my presence. To be sure, I didn't have it in me to kill him.

I eyed the boat, adjusting the sporran I'd taken to wearing around my shoulder. "Grab that rope." His eyes widened. "I'll let you go once I have my husband. Promise." I had no clue how much English he understood, but our communication thus far had seemed to work well enough.

His chest heaved with a heavy sigh as he grabbed the coiled rope out of the boat.

I jutted my head to the forest. "To the trees."

Once I'd adequately tied the fisherman to a tree, I continued down the beach, keeping within the shadows so as not to be seen. Though the thick, dense fog hazed most of it, the light of the full moon shone bright white, and I wasn't taking any chances. Traversing the woods in the dark was a challenge. Gnarly roots and loose needles caused me to trip and slip. I'd banged up my knees, and the base of my palms were scuffed up. It was like being a bairn again, every speck of me bruised, knees eternally scraped from playing too rough outside. My riding habit caught on branches and bushes, and a distinct tearing sound made me wince. Dammit, I had really loved this outfit.

As I crept toward the boats, I found a temporary wooden wall that'd been erected. Sideways sticks, woven almost like a basket, and globs of mud holding 'em together. Primitive but effective. It seemed to form a boundary around something. I crouched low against the foot of the wall, following the perimeter.

I stopped short. Some ten feet away, a sailor stood guard, a flaming torch next to him. I couldn't be sure, but in the dancing flame light, it looked like he wore a Navy uniform.

I froze. Next to him, wooden thatches were cut out in a way that made me think it was a door. Could I sneak past him? Even if I managed to, God only knew what was on the other side. More soldiers could be waiting for me.

Unless...

May as well finish this the way I started it.

For one last time, I would be donning breeches.

I stole one of the oars from the longboats beached on the sand and waited for a good moment to make my attack. The man was large, so my strike had to be hard and true on the first attempt, or there'd be no more attempts after that.

When he meandered past the glowing circle of torchlight, I perched on my toes, ready to pounce. He unbuttoned his trousers, taking a piss. I inhaled and charged—he didn't even turn his head as I bashed the oar over it. A loud thump, and the man keeled over.

His hard skull reverberated down the oar, radiating pain down to my elbows. I dropped the oar and paced to the pile of man. I scoffed. Served him right—it was the stout, robust man who'd disarmed Alexander. Didn't know the Royal Navy fed their soldiers so well.

I grabbed his wrists and tugged. The body didn't budge from its place. Digging my heels in again, I yanked as hard as I could.

Christ. Well, I'd have to leave him here. At least he was in the shadows. I removed his breeches and coat—a nigh difficult task as moving him was, his limp body nothing but dead weight. Once I had the clothes, I jogged back toward the trees.

The breeches were swimming on me, and the coat reached to my knees. I stashed my riding habit—after folding it with care—within the trees. The one positive of the too loose clothing was that I could hide my belongings underneath it. The plaid still around my shoulders added a fake bulkiness with the sporran under the coat, and I tied the two pistol holsters around my bare waist under the breeches. The coat reeked of sour body odor and the hat was still damp with sweat as I put it on my head. I grimaced.

This was as good as it was going to get.

I was ready to uncover the secret of the mysterious Oak Island.

The door's hinges creaked. I paused, angling my ear out, my gaze narrowed. No one came running, so I continued.

It was still too hard to see, despite a lantern glowing on the far side of the area, but there seemed to be rural log huts, similar to those in the Acadian settlement. But much more rudimentary. It gave me the distinct feeling none of this was meant to be permanent.

I walked on tiptoes, trying to decipher the shapes in the shadows. My knee hit something hard with a painful thud. I jumped back, bouncing on one foot, holding my other knee in my palm. Hands waving in front of me, I paced forward until my fingertips brushed against the object. Tracing the edge, it was a perfect circle. A barrel of some kind. Running my fingers over the top, I found the thumb hole and pulled up the top and stuck my hand in.

Small granules coated my palm. Gun powder. And from the fine feel of it rolling between my thumb and forefinger—primer. The extra flammable kind.

As if my thoughts willed it, a loud explosion shook the ground.

33

I screamed and fell back onto my bottom. What the bloody hell?

I snuck deeper into the gated area, following a trail of torches through the fog, but stayed far from the actual glow of the light.

Past more trees, the trail opened up to a glowing clearing. The fog had lessened here, further from the shoreline. Hundreds of torches lined what seemed like a pit, several of Cobbe's soldiers patrolling its perimeter.

As I neared, the pit became clearer. The men had picks, hammers, and shovels.

The blood drained from my face. William was there, hammering away at the earth with his pick. I slapped my hand over my mouth. Maybe I could catch his attention.

I surveyed the pit. Good lord, Cobbe *was* doing this for treasure? There had to be at least a hundred men digging, and at the far side of the pit stood the entrance of what seemed to be a mine shaft, nigh collapsing upon itself.

I searched the faces of every prisoner. *He* wasn't here. My brows furrowed as my heart sank. Men walked from the mine entrance back toward the pit.

Every muscle in my body tensed. Shallow pants escaped me. John. I was still a good distance away, but it was undeniable—there was my husband, my true husband, back from the dead.

He had a large piece of paper in his hand, and he tore off a corner and balled it up, tossing it behind him. The little ball of paper rolled back into the shaft before John folded up the larger piece, scratching his brow. It'd been months since I'd last seen him. He had a patchy brown beard and seemed thinner. Dirt and soot marred his skin. How long had he been here?

A soldier rushed to him, and John shook his head, his arms moving animatedly. The shoulder aimed his musket toward him, and John backed away. They seemed to be arguing.

I needed to get closer.

Hoping my disguise was good enough, I strode toward the pit with my spine straight and my head high. *Yes, nothing to see here, gents.* To my relief, no one seemed to pay me any attention.

John's voice was raised. It jarred me, making my steps falter. He never shouted. How often had I wanted his voice to wrap around me and finally say all the words I'd yearned to hear over the years? And when I'd found someone who did say those words, I couldn't keep him, because I was married to this man who'd cared more about his work than me.

"... I'm telling you, we cannot afford another explosion. The shaft is filling with sea water." John gritted his teeth.

The soldier pressed in against him with his gun. "And I'm telling you, we aren't stopping until we find the gold. The commodore says too many people have been asking. We're on a time limit. Any day now, the Crown will become privy to his plans."

"I don't know another way to clear more debris until the water dries or is pumped out. How am I supposed to ignite gunpowder if it's wet? Do you have a solution you'd like to offer?" He folded his arms over his chest.

I paced by the pit, acting like I was on patrol.

A man working keeled over, groaning. A soldier ran up to him, gun pointed. "Keep working."

The poor man coughed. "Water. I need water."

The soldier used the butt of his gun to hit him on his back. A fleshy thud followed by a cry turned my stomach. "Keep working, otherwise ya won't be needin' any water when I'm done with ya."

I continued my marching. Blinking, fighting back tears, I wondered if William had been treated so poorly.

The soldier ordering John pushed him with the barrel toward the entrance. "You're the supposed expert in powder. You figure it out."

John shook his head and stalked toward the mineshaft.

I continued "patrolling" the perimeter of the pit. A soldier hopped in when a man a few rows away stopped working. That would be my way to William.

I climbed down the ramp to the pit, marching past rows of digging men and past William. I stopped and did an about face. "What did you say to me?"

It took a moment for William to register that I'd spoken to him. He stared up long enough for me to catch the sunken look his face had taken on, but he gave no sign of recognition. He looked exhausted. "I didn't say nothing, sir." His voice was weak.

"Don't lie to me. I heard you!" I wanted to grab him out of the pit and take him far from here. Fighting the urge, I swallowed and leaned close. "William, it's me. Emme."

He stiffened, eyes wide. "What are you doing here?"

"Rescuing you and Alexander." My breath was shaky. "Where is he?"

"Christ, Emme. Ya're going to get yourself killed, or worse— captured and forced to dig." He kept slamming his pick into the clay while he whispered the words.

The fact that he thought staying here to dig was worse than death was very telling of what had been happening to these men. I swallowed a lump of nausea. We could unpack that later, but he couldn't heal if he wasn't free of this place. A soldier from above was eyeing us.

"Work faster!" I shouted before lowering my voice to ask, "Where is Alexander? Have you seen him?"

"He refused to work, injured some of Cobbe's men, and killed two. They had to restrain him. They dragged him to one of those log huts." He grunted as he hacked away at the clay.

"God, I must've walked right by him." I shoved him, pretending to get him to work harder. "You call that working?" I leaned in towards him again, looking in either direction around me, and dropped my voice. "Here, take this." I yanked a pistol out and shoved it in his hand.

He placed it under his shift in his pants' waistband. "One gun isn't going to—"

"I know. There are boats beached on the shore. I'll make a distraction long enough for you to escape. You'll know it when you see it." And hopefully, I would too.

A soldier stomped over. "Everythin' all right here?"

I kept my gaze lowered. "Yes, just teachin' him a lesson." I met William's eye before I marched back up the ramp.

Once back at the top, I waited for an opportunity to sneak from the others without drawing attention. After a few minutes, I strode toward the side of the pit from where I'd come, and I peeled away from the perimeter toward the dark tree line.

"Soldier!" someone called from behind me. I froze and peered over my shoulder. "Where are you headed?"

I said the first thing that came to mind. "To take a piss." It'd worked well the last time I'd used it.

"Well, hurry up. The air feels restless tonight."

I didn't look back as I rushed away, following the trail of torches once more, past the clearing and into more wooded darkness, the fog growing heavier. Once I neared where I started, I took the last torch from the trail with me.

The handle of the torch was warm in my hand and formed a circle of light a few feet in front of me, fog still seeping against everything. Once I was at the gate, the structures and objects took a little more shape than they had with the addition of the torchlight. There were several log structures, though I had no clue what was on the inside of each one.

Heart pounding as fast as the men had excavated the earth, I pressed open the door of the first room, nearly dropping the torch because my hands were so sweaty. Empty save for a pile of what seemed to be coconuts.

In the next, I found a man tied around a post in the middle of the room. He slowly raised his head to the light, groaning when I entered. Haggard and weak, he looked like he was a blink away from death.

My stomach dropped. I couldn't leave these people here. I'd have to help them.

Both his wrists and ankles were bound. My pulse raced as I clenched my teeth. How long until someone would come by here? This man was a stranger, and I could be missing my chance to help Alexander. Bloody hell. I couldn't leave him. Placing the torch on its side on the dirt ground, hopin' like hell it wouldn't stop burning. I dropped to my knees, fingers fumbling over his wrists, trying to figure out where to start.

"Wh-what are you doing to me?" The man's voice shook.

"Shh. I'm trying to help you, sir. I'll get your hands, but you'll have to untie your feet. When there's a distraction, make a break for it. There are boats on the beach." Finally, pushing through the loop, I unwrapped the rope from around his angry red wrists. "Good luck."

Snatching the torch off the ground, I opened the door, peeked my head out, and ran to the next structure. On an inhale, I yanked open the door, unsure what I'd find. Loud grunts coming from within made me freeze. Slowly, I raised the torch to the inside.

Alexander, despite his bound ankles, was on his feet, ramming his back hard against the post he was tied to, the middle of it cracking. He stopped the moment the light hit him, furrowed his brow, and tilted his head away from the brightness.

I ran in and shut the door quickly behind me.

I faced him.

He cursed in Gaelic. "Christ, tell me I'm fantasizing from lack of water, and you're not really here, Red."

My brows crinkled. "You think you'd fantasize about me dressed like a lad?"

He laughed. Despite the circumstances, it was deep and rich. "I think ye ken ye wouldna be dressed at all. What are you doin' here?"

"Rescuing you!" I dropped the torch to the ground and ran to him. "What are you trying to do?"

"I'm escaping, to get back to ye." His eyes swam over my face.

I cupped his cheeks and kissed him. He winced. Upon closer inspection, purple bruises peppered his face, and his bottom lip was split.

I gently brushed my thumb over it. "Christ, Alexander. Let me untie your wrists."

He twisted his back toward me and I started to work on the rope.

He laughed again. "Hell's bells, Red. Ye're a madwoman."

"I've nearly got the knot." There were voices outside. I froze.

Alexander shook his head. "Go. Pretend you're on patrol if ye run into anyone. Come back when they pass."

Black spots speckled my vision. "No. I won't leave you."

"Ye're not leavin' me, ye're hiding. They'll see the torchlight in here. Go." His eyebrows drew together.

Damn it all to hell. My heart thrashed against my chest, half from the thought of leaving him and half from fear. I grabbed the torch and peered out. Seeing no one, I slipped out. But the torch was a beacon in the darkness. I ran for the trees as coverage, hoping that between them and the fog, it'd be enough to conceal the flame. A patrol of men came and went, looking like ghosts holding floating lanterns and torches in the dense fog. I couldn't tell if it was more soldiers or not.

If I couldn't tell, then *they* couldn't tell I wasn't really a soldier.

About to return to Alexander, I neared the tree line just as I caught sight of a lone soldier patrolling the area around the front of the structures. How would I get them out of here? I'd need a distraction. Something big that'd make them all come running.

The gunpowder!

How big would the explosion be if I lit the barrel I'd seen on fire? Maybe too big and kill us all. Or too small and not enough of a diversion. There were no other options—I had to take my chances.

How far did I need to be away from it to safely ignite it? I'd just have to eyeball it.

Leaving the torch in the forest, I slipped past the soldier with the lantern. I went right up to a barrel, felt the top of the lid, and found the thumb hole again. As I began to tug it upwards, the lid made a sound like a cork being freed. I stopped raising it. The soldier froze before rotating in my direction. I held my breath. He raised his torch, moving his arm in an arc. After a minute, he twisted back around, continuing his patrol. Once he was far enough, I exhaled and lifted the top completely off. He paced around a few hundred yards away. Too close to Alexander, but far enough for me to continue with the gunpowder.

I could make a trail of it to the tree line and light it there once Alexander was out of the structure and far enough away. I shoved fistfuls of the powder in my pockets, filling them to the brim. Regarding the sentry again, I dug my toes into the ground and attempted to push the whole barrel sideways. It didn't budge.

After rolling up my sleeves, I paced backward, eyes on the shadow of the barrel. I charged toward it as hard as I could and shoved it to its side, granules spilling out like an avalanche of gunpowder. I trailed powder between my fingers, walking back to the tree line. Once there, I doubled back, having no idea how thick it needed to be to catch fire and burn up to the barrel.

Satisfied, I brushed my hands off.

Voices from around the other side of the perimeter wall urged me forward. I ran on my toes so my footfalls wouldn't alert them to my presence. I'd have to wait for them to pass. A trio of sentries strode past my spot in the trees, kicking up my trail of powder before they stopped in front of Alexander's building.

No. No. My blood was loud in my ears as I rubbed the back of my stiff neck. Their lanterns disappeared into his wooden hut. I'd need a big explosion, but not too big—I didn't want to harm my husband. But the men inside could be hurting him.

I walked back toward the structures. Right as I cleared the trees, the men left him. My foot hovered in the foggy air, frozen in action, before they passed by. Once they were gone, I ran the rest of the way back to him.

I shoved open the door and closed it behind me. "All right, let us make haste. I have a distraction that'll allow William to escape, too." I hadn't grabbed the torch again, his silhouette just visible.

His eyes were hooded under a heavy brow. "It's a trap."

"Wh—"

A gun cocked behind me. "Mistress MacLachlan." The voice, instantly recognizable, sent a chill down my spine.

Raising my hands in the air, I slowly turned around. "Commodore Cobbe."

"You couldn't have left well enough alone?" Holding a lantern high, his gaze swept down me. "You do look good in blue, but I daresay those breeches are far too big for you."

He shook his head. "Why couldn't you two stay out of trouble?" Cobbe strutted in, followed by another man with a lantern. I noticed the finely embroidered breeches first. My breath hitched. Mr. Sinclair from the fishing boat.

"Emme…" Alexander's voice was low. I backed away from the men at the door, bumping into him.

"You're imprisoning men, taking your own soldiers, faking their deaths—all for what? Some legend about pirate treasure? Money?" My back pressed into Alexander, providing some comfort to me.

Cobbe's head angled to one side, his nostrils flaring. His dark blue uniform, in utter disarray, was crumpled and dust covered. A few gold links of a chain in his epaulette seemed to be missing. "I'm not doing this for money. I'm doing it for her. For her memory." His eyes flicked to Alexander.

My brows knitted together as Alexander tensed behind me.

"Don't you know who this is?" Cobbe waved his hand at Mr.

Sinclair.

"Aye." Alexander's deep baritone rumbled his chest. "That's bonnie Prince Stuart."

34

"Bonnie Prince Stuart..." I eyed the man. "As in the—"

"As in the true heir to the throne." He swaggered forward, his cloak gone, and a wig now on his head. He looked more a member of royalty than a fisherman.

My gaze snapped from him to Cobbe. "You're working with a Stuart? For what?"

"For her." Again, his eyes went to Alexander. "It's what she would have wanted. We aren't treasure hunting to become rich. We are hunting for gold so we can once again fund another Scottish Jacobite army."

"It's what *who* wanted?" My back pressed harder into my husband, and his hand snaked around my hip from under my coat. A knot in my stomach uncoiled. He had slipped his hands from their bindings after I'd loosened them earlier. For a moment, he palmed my lower belly and thighs, and I had the grimly humorous thought that he wanted to caress my body one last time before we died, but instead, he grasped the gun hanging around my hips.

"Sophie," Alexander said from behind me, his gaze set on Cobbe. Sophie, his first wife.

My mouth opened.

"Yes." Cobbe stalked forward, his brows drawn, and his eyes glimmered like oil in the lantern. "I loved her."

"Then why did you kill her and my son?" Alexander's voice was thick and hoarse.

Cobbe's lips drew into a thin line, his head shaking. Strands of his hair had fallen loose from his ponytail, and dark circles wrapped around his sunken eyes. "It wasn't supposed to happen. It was just supposed to be a patrol." He stomped toward us. "I loved her! I'd never harm her!" His voice was low, dangerous.

A chill ran up my arms to my neck. He was mad.

Cobbe's gaze landed on something, becoming unfocused. "We were looking for Alexander. I was just waiting until it was long enough where she'd give up on him and choose me. She had loved me once. We"—he peered back at Alexander—"we were in love before you came along. I was waiting it out until we found you and you were hanged. I hunted you, just so she could be free to..." He shook his head. "But we had to do our due diligence and ask her. When the patrol said we'd torch your house, it had been to scare her. But she refused to say anything or come out and a private tossed a torch. I screamed and ran toward the house, but the moment the flame hit the thatch..." He shook his head again, nostrils flaring, his haunted stare glued to my husband behind me. "It was too late."

My mouth hung open, nausea pressing up my throat. "Good Lord."

Alexander's breathing in my ear was shallow and erratic. I dared to peel my eyes off the men before me and glance behind me. His face was slack and vacant.

Cobbe sniffed as his head bobbed up and down. "Yes. Yes. You think me a monster?" He laughed, a cold sound that made goosebumps erupt on my skin. "I think me a monster, too. Which is why I have to do this. This is what she wanted. Half of her family died in Culloden. She wouldn't want it to be for naught.

"But you couldn't leave well enough alone. I picked men for this project who I didn't think would be missed. They could go missing and no one would know. But I made a mistake. I didn't know John had a wife." Cobbe's face flushed, skin mottled across his neck. "When I took him, he said to tell you he died."

I sucked in a sharp breath. "W-what?" Alexander gripped my waist.

"Yes. When I found out, he was already here, and when he mentioned you, he said to tell you he was dead—that he'd do the work without protest if I did." The commodore's gaze narrowed.

"Why?" My stomach clenched.

His head inclined, with his eyes wide and curious like an owl. "Because then he said he wouldn't ever have to return home when this was all over."

I jolted back like he'd physically hit me. "John said that?"

"Yes. So when I came to you, I figured you'd be some haggard, fat wife he wanted to get away from... and instead I found you. But you didn't cry. Widows always cry. And then there you were, with *him*, in Iceland, in love. It was fate. And an offering of redemption."

He sniffed again.

"How did forcing us to marry offer you redemption? You knew John was alive. You're sick." My heart fluttered irregularly.

Sinclair, or Stuart, snorted a laugh. "Oh, good Lord, you have two husbands?"

"No. No. You don't understand." Cobbe's chocolate brown eyes dug into Alexander's face. "I wanted you to know I was done hunting you, that she wouldn't want that. And you two looked at each other with a raw passion."

I exhaled. Had we looked at each other like that then?

"It was the way I looked at Sophie. And I knew Alexander needed to move on. I owed him peace." His eyes landed on me. "And if you were in love and happy with your new husband, you wouldn't go on asking about John, the two of you living in ignorant bliss for the remainder of your lives."

His eyes narrowed to slits. "But you were too loud. Asking too many questions. Sending crew from the *Bluebell* around. I wanted Alexander to find happiness, but I will not be hanged for treason."

"I do say, this is all very exciting. Who knew that the wild English creature in the bay would provide such a story to tell?" The prince gave a smug smile.

I wanted to slap it off his face. "You're imprisoning men. Working them to death. And you're a murderous traitor. I saw you kill your sister-in-law in Limerick." Cobbe's eyes widened. "Did you kill your brother, too? The former commodore?"

"Red." Alexander said his name for me from behind clenched teeth.

"He'd begun piecing things together. I didn't want to do it," he shouted, his hair flicking back and forth with his words. His proud air, his pristine appearance of a loyal commodore, was crumbling apart. "But there are no rules in war. This man is the rightful heir, and I'll fight for him. We have already met with a French colonel. Together, we can defeat England. For her." His voice lowered as he inched closer to Alexander, a breath away from him. "Sophie would want you to keep fighting. She wouldn't want her and wee Alexander's deaths to be in vain. Don't you see we're on the same side?"

"Dinna say their names! Ye dinna deserve to even speak them. It's over. Another Stuart will never sit on the throne. I willna lose everything to this cause again." He inclined his head to the prince. "Ye barely fought, and ye fled. My clan, my family, was nigh destroyed." His voice strained with barely contained fury. "And ye expect me to fight for ye again? For any Scot to risk their lives and family anew? It's over."

"I dare say!" The prince's brows drew together. "God has chosen me. It was when I was in exile in France, holed up in a medieval castle, and I'd heard of this trove of treasure left behind by a Scottish pirate. It was then I knew I needed to come to this place. And as if God sent me his blessing himself…" He dug into his pocket and raised a rudimentary lead cross up before us. "I tripped over something in a hallway and found this cross. They say it was forged by the Knight's Templar themselves. It was a sign. Have you no loyalty to the rightful heir? To me? To God's will?"

"Fools. The both of ye." Alexander's hand holding the gun

hidden beneath my coat seemed to quiver. "I'll never fight for ye again."

"Loyalty. Of all people, I'd think you'd remain loyal, MacLachlan. You left your wife, your son, to die for the cause, and yet you cannot muster the courage to..." Cobbe clicked his tongue as he shook his head. "Well, that is unfortunate. You both know too much."

"*Ye're* the reason they're dead." Alexander's voice was a harsh whisper. "There's loyalty, duty to the Crown, and then there is outright murder of innocents."

"I didn't mean... I'm making it right." Cobbe shook his head erratically.

He was sick, his mind gone. I balled my hands into fists. "You're a treasonous murderer. You have guilt over Sophie's death, yet you readily killed your brother and sister-in-law. What about them? What about *their* children? You've left them orphans."

Cobbe visibly trembled in unabashed fury, his chest heaving, breaths coming in loud, short bursts. "Perhaps it is true. I am a murderer. There may be no redemption for me."

"There isna. Ye canna undo what ye've done. And I ken, in my heart, ye'll burn for eternity for your sins." A pregnant pause followed Alexander's declaration.

Cobbe stared with a vacant expression. "That may be... but, nonetheless, I will not be hanged for treason."

He raised his musket, but before he could shoot, Alexander pushed me down and fired the pistol. The loud bang filled the structure with a bright white flash, making my ears ring. As the smoke cleared, the toppled lantern illuminated the commodore's fallen body. Cobbe's blood oozed from his chest, his whole body spasming, before his muscles stiffened, and he went completely slack. Alexander offered me a hand, pulling me up and away from the commodore.

"Good Lord." The prince put his hand over his heart, eyes wide, before he whimpered and ran out. The lead cross he had been holding thumped to the floor.

Panting breaths heaved from my chest as the tight knot in my throat released, relief washing over me. It was over. Cobbe was gone. Dead. A swift death he didn't deserve. I hoped my husband was right, and that this man would burn for eternity.

My reprieve ended too soon.

"They'll have heard a shot." Alexander tugged my hand, pushing open the door. He peered down at Cobbe. "That death was too easy for ye."

"Run to the tree line. I have a distraction planned." I passed him the spare balls and powder, and he began reloading the pistol as he limped toward the wooded area. Once at the trees, I reclaimed the discarded torch, the oil tip still burning, and gave a smug smile. "Get ready to run to the beach and watch this."

Pressing the tip to the powder trail, it illuminated in sparking snaps, running down the trail faster than my eyes could follow. And then it stopped halfway. What the—

I growled. "Damn those men who kicked it!"

"We'll have to run. The soldiers are coming." He angled the gun toward the approaching soldiers, but there were too many, and his arms trembled as he tried to aim. It was then I realized how badly he slumped, and how low his shoulders drooped. He seemed weak, like he'd been starved or deprived of water on top of his obvious injuries.

My Highlander warrior couldn't make an appearance today.

Oh, bloody hell, that meant it was all up to me.

"Here." I snatched the gun from his hand. I planted my feet, my stance wide, lined my eye up down the gun, and aimed for the powder barrel. As the group of soldiers ran near, on an exhale, I pulled the trigger.

35

The explosion erupted with a loud bang, billowing flames reaching high into the sky. The pressure pushed Alexander and me down as ash and debris floated around us in the smoky air. My ears rang, and my head spun.

Alexander's hand grasped mine, and he yanked me to my feet. I didn't even know how he could walk, let alone help me after the explosion. We stumbled, holding onto each other, running past wounded and unconscious soldiers. The dizziness and ringing slowly began to dissipate, and I found my bearings.

"William!" I shouted over the ringing. "We have to wait. He'll be coming."

He nodded, holding me upright. Or maybe I was holding him up. As if on cue, men crested the hill, past the now burning structures, chasing a few straggling soldiers with their pick-axes. One soldier fell, landing on his belly, and a man slammed his pick into his back, an arc of crimson spraying around him. A shot fired, and a soldier fell to his knees before us. Some feet back, John stood holding a smoking pistol. William clenched his arm, struggling to stay upright.

A large gash of red slit through the front of his shift.

John helped William hobble forward.

I tugged on Alexander's arm, and we stumbled toward them. Between the smoke, fog, fire, and men running in all directions, it was all disorienting. Men swinging pick-axes nigh missed us and a musket fired right near our heads. I jumped back, and Alexander squeezed my hand.

A man with a pick, a gash on his forehead with a trail of blood dripping from it, hopped in front of us. Soot covered his face. "You're a dead man, you bloody soldier!" His words sounded as if they'd been muffled by quilt batting.

I stiffened before I jumped back. "No, I'm not a soldier. I'm a woman." Alexander tugged me behind him. The man's eyes widened, and he jogged away. A structure right in front of us caught fire, the flames growing higher and higher. At least we could see a little better with the flames offering light.

As the inferno roiled, burning embers landed near three more barrels of powder. My body trembled. We were too close.

"Mac!" William shouted as he slouched on John.

I braced Alexander's hand with mine, panic flooding through me. "William. Make haste! The powder—"

"Red, go. I'll wait for him." He tried to free my hand from his.

"You're a bloody fool if you think I'll leave you. Have you learned nothing?"

"Ye'll be the death of me. But I'll gladly hand ye my sword to do me in with." He kissed me hard, deep. God, how I'd missed his kisses.

And when he pulled back, William and *my husband* were standing in front of us.

Alexander ran to William's other side to help carry him, despite barely being able to walk himself. "We have to go. Quickly. The powder's going to blow."

"Follow me to the beach." I jutted my head toward the gate and ran.

"Emme?" I thought I heard John say.

We careened past the threshold of burning wall and onto the beach area. Right as we cleared the wall, a giant boom followed by two more shook the ground. Sand and debris shot everywhere. I fell to my knees in the sand, disoriented and dizzy, catching sight of the man on the ground I'd stolen the clothes from.

Alexander helped me to my feet. The boats were already full of men disembarking as others chased after them, trying to catch one of the departing vessels.

"The boats are gone. We're trapped here. We must hide." Alexander pointed to the forest.

"I have a jolly boat down the shore. You can't see it from here." Running in that direction, the men followed. I kept at a sprint down the shore, but I didn't see it. "Christ, where is it? It was right here. The other men couldn't have possibly made it this far."

Plumes of smoke and flames, taller than the trees, rose in the air, illuminating the sky. Dawn was near, as the black sky gave way to purple hues. Any surviving soldiers would be able to find us all too easily in the daylight. We stopped on the shore.

"Stuart. He'd have snuck away first." Alexander bared his teeth.

"Stuart? As in…" William's eyebrows nigh disappeared into his hair.

John ambled forward, his spectacles askew on his face. "I'm sorry. Have I gone completely mad? Or Emme, is that you dressed as a man?"

William, Alexander, and I all snapped our heads toward John.

My heart tugged in the opposite direction, but I strutted toward him, unsure. "John. I—"

"What are you doing here? How did you get here?" He wrapped his arms around me, pinning mine to my sides. "Christ, Emme."

My gaze met Alexander's as John embraced me. His lips were in a flat line. My breath was shaky, and my chest ached. "John, I—"

He leaned back, and his eyes snapped to Alexander. "Wait, did I see you kissing my wife?"

Alexander's chest puffed, his fingers curling into a fist.

William limped between them. "Since our lives are in mortal danger, I'll save us some time. Alexander, meet John, Emme's husband. John, meet Alexander, Emme's other husband." I glared at William, a smirk on his lips like he was going to enjoy this, and he shrugged when he met my eye. "If we all live, we shall have time to resolve this later."

The sun painted the horizon in yellow as it began to creep up higher in the sky. Unease stirred in my stomach. "What, we wait here until more of Cobbe's men find us?"

Alexander stood straighter. "Nay, we'll craft a raft with wood and—"

"The Royal Navy will have seen this smoke, even from Halifax."

John pushed his glasses back up his nose, one lens cracked. "They'll rescue us."

I took him in. He wasn't his normal clean-cut self, with quiet features that took a moment to convey his handsomeness. Instead, he was jarred and disheveled.

"They'll rescue us? They caused this." Alexander's gaze narrowed on John.

"Cobbe isn't the navy, and he isn't the Crown." John clenched his jaw.

"Excuse me if I willna trust a redcoat ever again." His nostrils flared before he grasped my hand. "I'll leave ye to findin' your own route, then."

John grasped my other hand. "I do believe I can escort *my own wife* to safety. Good luck with your raft."

Alexander paraded in front of me, chin high. "I'll be takin' her to safety, seein' as ye asked Cobbe to tell her ye died in the first place."

I yanked my hands free of both of them. "Or, Emme will find her own way to safety, seeing as she was the one who saved all three of you." I paced to the tree line. "While you argue about how not to die, I'm going to find my riding habit. This coat smells like an animal died in it."

After a futile search through the trees, I went to where William sat on the sand. The rising sun glowed against his ochre skin. I sank down next to him. In the near distance, Alexander was hacking away at the wood with a leftover pick.

"What is my husband doing?"

William lifted a brow. "Which one?"

"Oh Christ, I should never have rescued you." I folded my arms over my chest, still wrapped in the smelly coat. My riding habit was long gone.

He laughed. "Sorry, love. Mac is trying to build a raft, and John is building a fire to create a smoke signal." He winced and placed his hand on his stomach. "I know ya love Mac, but ya're still married, and if John chooses to enforce the law, ya're *his* wife. His property. Could have Alexander hanged for kidnapping, and you held in a pillory for days as an adulterer. If you love Mac, ya may have to let him go."

"His property." I scoffed. "I'm a person."

His gaze became unfocused. "I know the feeling."

I sighed and reached for his hand on his lap, squeezing it. We sat in companionable silence, watching the sun rise.

"Shite. Mac won't be happy about that." William pointed to the end of the bay. A large military ship rounded the corner, a British flag floating on the main mast.

The captain of the *HMS Halifax* paced in front of us.

"Captain. I was the former captain of the *HMS Glory* before…" John paused. "Before all of this happened. I'm prepared to give a full account of what happened here. The Scotsman wasn't involved in this act of treason."

The captain stopped his pacing and gave us a scrutinizing stare. "There were reports of a Scottish pirate and a redheaded English woman asking all about the treasure of Oak Island. And there are reports of a Mr. Sinclair, the same name Prince Charles Stuart used after Culloden, meeting with a man. And you'll have me believe the Highlander savage, now known as Xander Lock, has nothing to do with it?"

My hands balled into fists. "He had nothing to do with it. It was all *your* commodore."

His eyebrow arched as he inclined his head. "That is quite a brilliant shade of red, isn't it?"

The implication was obvious.

John snaked an arm around my waist. "Allow me to introduce my wife, Mrs. Clark. And I assure you, the Scotsman was held captive with me and a hundred other men, not the other way around."

"And Cobbe is a murderer. He murdered his own brother and sister-in-law to keep the secret of Oak Island," I growled.

The captain's heavy stare landed on me. "The few remaining soldiers have a different story. They place the pirate Lock within the burned-down structure where the commodore's remains were found." He glanced at John. "You'll forgive me, sir, but I must do my due diligence with a thorough investigation with the Crown. He'll ride in the brig until we reach Halifax."

"I understand." John nodded.

My mouth dropped open. "What? No, you—"

"Emme. Please." John squeezed my shoulder. "Once they know he helped rescue all these men, he will be let go."

"Fine. You should know, there's a man tied to a tree somewhere over there." I pointed in the general direction and stomped toward the water. The captain's eyes went wide.

A navy soldier paced forward to the captain. "Sir, shall I send for the scribe so you may dictate your account while we investigate?"

"No, Lieutenant McInnis, we can't afford to record this and end up with pirates or treasure hunters; the king plans to colonize this area. Send the order to bury everything and all proof of its existence." The captain paced down the beach.

"Everything? Even the tools and—"

"Everything, McInnis," the captain said over his shoulder as he neared a beached boat.

My heart skipped a beat as my gaze found Alexander, wrists shackled behind his back, sitting in the jolly boat to head back to the *HMS Halifax*. Our eyes locked, my lips parting, wanting to say every word I couldn't... That he was my husband, no matter what, and that I wouldn't give up on him.

And that I was absolutely madly in love with him, and he'd altered my life forever.

36

"Emme." John's voice was hesitant as he paced behind me.

We had spent the last week in a cabin in Halifax. Me, barely moving from the rocking chair, looking out the window, with Alexander's tartan wrapped around my shoulders.

"Emme." He tried again when I said nothing. "Your new riding habit came. I didn't even know you were particularly fond of riding."

"Do you know anything I'm fond of?" I wrapped my hands around a warm cup of tea.

"I deserve that. I know. I haven't been the best husband." He walked around the chair and leaned against the wall, sliding his hands into his waistcoat pockets.

"Did you ever care for me? Was it all horrible for you?" I didn't look at him as I asked.

"Of course I cared. In the only way I knew how. Financially. That was all that mattered to my family. It was how we showed love. But I never wanted to be a husband." He paced to me and squatted in front of my chair. "My family pressured me to marry, despite knowing my desire lied elsewhere. I'm a soldier. Through and through. When I met you, I knew you weren't the typical woman."

A scoff escaped me, and I frowned. "Because I was poor?"

He gave a light and airy laugh. "Because you would be fine without me. You survive, Emme. I could give you a life you wanted, and I wouldn't be forced to give up what *I* loved. Because you didn't need me there. You're the strongest person I know."

The knot in my stomach untightened. "You really believe that?"

"I do. I thought if I were believed dead, you could have your jointure, and you'd be free of me to find someone who really deserved you and the life you wanted, and I wouldn't have this guilt weighing on me every time I saw your face when I was about to leave." He rose to his feet. "Look at you. You're brilliant. Christ, you're in Nova Scotia right now. You saved hundreds of men and stopped a potential plot of treason. If the prince had gotten that gold…"

I nodded. "Aye. But men will keep hunting for it. I fear the island won't have seen the last of its treasure hunters. And Stuart knows something is there. He could find another devout follower willing to help." I shook my head. "How did they manage not to see an aristocrat rowing into a small Acadian settlement?"

"Well, after some investigating, there were some locals who'd seen a *woman* in a blue riding habit there the morning after everything." He folded his arms across his chest, and he tapped his fingers on his elbows.

"That was my habit!"

"I have news." I held my breath, waiting for his next words. Had

Alexander been released? "I've accepted a promotion. I am the new commodore."

My shoulders dropped. "Congratulations."

"I've never wanted to move up. So much brings you back to London and parliament and the politics I've been running from my whole life." He pushed off the wall. "But I have sway with the governor here. And the ability to ask for pardons for prisoners."

What was he implying? I couldn't dare to hope.

"If he was here, standing next to me, and both of us asked you to come with us, me to take you back to London and him back to... wherever, who would you choose?" He scoured his gaze over my face. "Truthfully?"

I bit my bottom lip, and my heart thudded hard against my breastbone. "I... You've given me so much and I will always care for you, but..."

"But." He nodded. "In truth, you've resented me for not giving you what you really needed. Time and time again you asked me to quit, and I never listened. I refused. I haven't been married to you. I've been married to my job.

"And now you've married another man. The way you looked at him... you've never looked at me like that and I've never looked at you that way either, Em. It was fine. Marriage is not always a love match." His chest heaved with a large sigh. "Time was of the essence. I had to accept this position because they didn't do an investigation, and they're quick to condemn traitors, especially ones with a history of piracy. He's scheduled to hang at noon."

I gasped. "What?" A sharp pain shot through the very core of me.

"But he'll be freed. And cleared of *all* charges. You told me the reason you boarded his ship in the first place was to procure the letter from the commodore certifying my death to access your jointure. Well, turns out, the letter in the commodore's own writing was the very proof of evidence the governor needed to believe the whole story. Your daring adventure has liberated the man. He can return home to Scotland as a free man." He arched his brow with and gave a challenging smile. "If you can get there in time."

For the first time in a very long time, I looked him in the eye, truly looked, my heart erratic.

All my daring to obtain the damned letter was the thing that'd freed the love of my life.

John extended his hand, placing a parchment paper with a wax seal in my palms. "It's signed with witnesses. The pirate chap who's been eavesdropping this whole time in the next room followed me to Governor Cornwallis's house and back and knows all the details. I may have failed you in the past, but I hope this makes up for it. A royal pardon."

I rose to my feet, heart leaping out of my body.

"And I regret to inform you that your true parentage has come to light." He had a smile on his face. "When we wed, your benefactor had claimed that you were of noble birth. And now that I've found out you're a miner's daughter—"

I scowled, taken aback. "What? You've always—"

"There's no denying it, Emme. I know the truth." He had an odd expression on his face. "I consented to marry a noble lady. And such a thing as lying about breeding counts as marriage of error or fraud, as such, the Parliament can grant a full divorce. Meaning we can both—"

"Remarry," I finished for him.

He gave a small smile, rubbing the back of his head. "Yes. If we choose."

"John..." I covered my mouth with my hand as warm tears pricked my eyes.

"The petition requesting the divorce is on the table. Once Parliament receives a copy in a few weeks and a large amount of my inheritance, they will review it. It'll be public, and you already know London's perspective on divorce. But seeing as you have become a pirate, I don't think you'll care too much about the court of public opinion. Consider this pardon and our divorce a way to make up for taking the last six years of your life. Horses are ready out front. At least now you'll have a real reason to wear your new habit." He waved his hand toward the entryway where William had been waiting to meet with me. "Now go to Fort Charlotte. It's on George's Island. Go. Before it's too late and he's put on the gallows."

I placed my hand over my heart. "John..." My voice came out shaky. "I don't know what to say."

He rushed to me and placed a hand on each of my shoulders, twisting me toward the exit. "Say nothing. Just be happy."

I nodded and gave him a final embrace.

William and I mounted horses, galloping amongst the tall pine trees and through town in the early morning sun, racing to the royal dockyard.

Another bloody island.

At the dockyard, we tossed a man a purse filled with coins to take us to the island. Twenty minutes later, we ran into the fort's courtyard, where they held public executions.

The moment the gallows came into view, I stopped breathing. A man was hanging, body swinging in the air, the sky dark and gloomy behind him. I clutched my chest, suddenly sick. The storm in my body was as ferocious as the one brewing on the horizon.

Behind the gallows, a line of men stood waiting for their deaths. I exhaled, nigh crying out. It was impossible to miss the tall Scotsman. Grime and scabs and bruises covered every inch of his skin, his lips thin and grim. His hair was wild, for once the perfect curl on his forehead in disarray. His unshaven face made him look like the pirate I had expected at the start of my journey.

As if he could feel my stare, his gaze snapped to me. His face looked stricken, as if he was more pained than relieved to see me. His Adam's apple bobbed before he stared at the ground, shoulders slumped. Then his sight landed on William, and he gave a less than pleasant look, as if to say, "Why did you bring her here?"

"Alexander Grant MacLachlan, otherwise known under the alias Captain Xander Lock, of the Danish privateering frigate, the *Bluebell*," a soldier called out as another with a quill recorded his name in a thick register. "Charged with treason, kidnapping, murder of a commodore of His Majesty's Royal Navy. Come forth."

He stumbled forward, a swell of emotions matching the dark sky behind him in his eyes.

I didn't peel my gaze from him—the stirrings in my stomach as rocky as the sea in a storm. I cleared my throat, pinned my shoulder blades together, and channeled, once more, the gentlewoman I was all those months ago. The woman I fought so hard to be, but had long since abandoned. The woman who no longer felt like myself, no longer felt comfortable—a woman I no longer wanted to be. "I demand that Alexander Grant MacLachlan be released immediately."

Several redcoats and Navy men snapped their heads toward me. I sauntered toward the platform, every step haughty with an air that exuded importance. I marched to the captain.

His brow arched. "Madam, this man is a pirate and will be hanged as such—"

"Privateer. And this man revealed a treasonous plot, the murderer of the original, late commodore, and ensured the release of a high-ranking officer, the former captain of the *Glory*. He shouldn't be hanged. He should be rewarded for his loyalty to the Crown." I slapped the parchment against the man's chest. "A letter. From the *new* commodore. The one who's only alive because of this man. The aforementioned former captain."

"Who are you, madam?" His mouth was agape, appearing incredulous.

Who was I? Well, I suppose, in the eyes of the law, for a few more weeks, I was Mrs. Clark. But after today, I would never be her again. I'd made my choice long ago. But in this one last thing, would I assume the role of the wife of John Clark. "Who am I? I am Emme Clark. You may have heard of my husband. Commodore John Clark—your new commanding officer."

The man cleared his throat and opened the letter, the parchment curling at the top. His eyes roved across the paper, widening and narrowing as he read. He peered up again before licking his lips. "A harrowing tale, it seems. We will have to verify the authenticity of the letter. But I assure you, we will investigate, and if the pardon holds true"—Alexander's eyes widened, and his posture straightened—"he will be released. Guards, take this man back to his cell."

I pursed my lips. "I'm sure the new commodore will appreciate your aid in the liberation of his savior, Captain..."

"Blake. Captain Blake." His white wig slipped back, revealing his natural black hair.

"Ah, yes, Captain Blake. I'm sure my husband will appreciate a speedy investigation as well." I smiled, fake sweetness imbued in my thinly veiled threat.

"Yes. Of course." He nodded.

I tried my best to not follow my husband with my eyes. Watching him go back into the garrison was like letting my heart itself go into the fort. But I had to contain myself and maintain my faux sense of confidence and authority. So, I fixed my glare back on the soldier. "By the end of the day, then?" The captain's eyes widened. "My husband will be most delighted to hear all about it during supper this evening. And, of course, you can send one of your men to the port to release the *Bluebell* back into the custody of the ship's quartermaster, so he can ready the ship and find a crew in time for her captain's return?"

The redcoat's patience had nearly run out, his eyes giving a slight roll before I arched a brow and pursed my lips again. "Of course, Mrs. Clark. Lieutenant, head to the port with Mrs. Clark and this *quartermaster* and relay this information to the soldiers guarding the ship."

I strolled from the courtyard, William at my side. "Do make haste, lieutenant."

My legs bounced as I sat on the edge of the bed in the captain's cabin. William paced from lantern to lantern, lighting them with a tinderbox as the sun dipped below the horizon.

A pressure coiled tight around my ribcage. "Oh Lord, shouldn't he be here by now?"

"He'll be here. They won't deny a royal pardon." William uncorked a bottle of rum and poured us both a cup.

Soon, the moonless night sparkled with twinkling stars.

My stomach gnawed on itself. Oh God. What if they'd gone through with the execution? "Should we go back?"

William sipped on his third cup. "No, let's wait a little—"

The door to the cabin slammed open. Alexander limped in, still covered in dirt and grime. His gaze snapped to me sitting on the bed, his brows furrowed.

Well, that wasn't the homecoming I was expecting. I hopped to my feet.

"I'll ready the ship." William ran out without looking back.

Alexander's gaze narrowed on me. "And what are ye doing here, Mrs, Clark?"

Tears sprang to my eyes. "How dare you ask? As if you bloody well don't know why I'd be here. As if I have no right."

"Ye're no' my wife." His eyes shimmered in the lantern light. Unshed tears, perhaps.

I straightened. "Do you love me?"

"Do ye no ken yet that I love ye? I'd die for ye. But the idea of another man so much as lookin' at ye, let alone touchin' ye, guts me. Ye're married. And it isna to me." His voice strained, his face reddened under the purple bruises peppering his face.

"I'm not your wife, as you bloody well made clear. But—"

"No, you're not my wife. And I love ye more than anythin' but *Mrs. Clark,* you *are* married, and it 'tis not to me." He opened the door. "I do appreciate what ye did for me, but I'm not keen on getting re-arrested for kidnapping."

"Stop." I rose, slammed the door, and slipped my arms around his neck. "You Scotsmen sure love to talk. If you'd let me get a word in, then you'd learn that I am not Mrs. Clark and haven't been for a long time. I chose you long ago, but now it's bloody official, you fool!"

"What? Something happened to John? Ye didna kill him?" His brow arched.

My mouth dropped open. "What the bloody hell kind of question is that?"

"I saw ye wi' the gunpowder." He shrugged.

I dropped my hands to cover my face. "Christ, there's no living with you. We will be granted a divorce. I'm on this damned ship because I want you. Because I love *you.*"

His brows furrowed over his wide eyes as he leaned away to evaluate me. "Ye're choosing me, and this life, willingly? Ship life is dangerous and uncomfortable. Are you mad?"

"Quite possibly. Am I scared of what the future could hold, the unknown dangers? Yes. Will I let that fear keep me from you and the *Bluebell*? No." I placed my hands on my hips. "I didn't save you to let you sail away without me. Now, will you please just bloody tell me you love me and kiss me already?"

He laughed. "Christ." He grabbed my hands, leaning in but stopping short of my lips. "Although, when ye look at me like that, I dinna ken if ye want me or... I'm a wee worrit for the family bagpipes. I'm quite fond of them."

Even through the grime and bruises, his damned grin weakened my knees.

"I remember you being quite fond of them, and you have every reason to still be worried for them after how you burst in here ready for war, *after* I rescued you. Again!" I laughed before I crossed to the bed and sat, tapping the space beside me. "Come here, you fool." As he neared me, I grabbed his collar and claimed his lips. "I love you."

He cupped my cheek with his hand. "Even though I'm a pirate savage?" He planted a kiss down my neck, over my pulse.

"Especially because you're a pirate savage." I gasped, and my head fell back.

"I love you too, Red." He sucked my bottom lip into his mouth.

"Forever?" I pushed him back onto the bed and scanned his face.

"Aye, until my heart stops beating. And even then. I'll haunt ye as a wee ghostie, *mo ghoal*." His sideways smile could melt me like snow in summertime.

My ear-to-ear smile had to look silly. "All this time you've called me that. What does *mo ghoal* mean?"

His lips curled up. "It means *my love.*"

Christ, I was done for. "Whatever will I do with you?"

"I've a few ideas in mind." He raised his head up to kiss me.

But I pressed my hands on his chest, stopping him.

His brows crinkled. "I ken I'm covered in dirt and probably smell like a chamber pot."

"No. Well, yes." I arched a brow. "But it's not that. I've one more thing to ask of you."

His eyes narrowed. "Am I already in trouble again? I've just returned."

I grasped his hand. "Alexander Grant MacLachlan, will you marry me?"

Our life at sea had transformed from gray skies and chilly air to sunshine and clear, turquoise waters. Alexander said we could sail year-round in the West Indies without fear of ice, but storms in the late summer months were something fierce.

Anchoring in the sea, we rowed to a tiny uninhabited island with a cove and a beach. I'd never seen such absolute beauty before.

Sailing through the Indies, it had been my great delight to be able to jump into the warm sea daily and cleanse myself. It wasn't a hot bath, and the salt dried on my skin and hair, but it was far superior to the grime and dirt scrubbed off with a bucket of icy ocean water. As an added benefit, the crew smelled much better, too.

Though the sea water here was so salty it burned my nostrils, it was easier to float in. But my shift still weighed me down. Even now, its skirt pulled and pushed each way as I floated in the small cove. But having grown up in a port town, I'd learned how to swim with the currents and was a strong swimmer for it.

I laid back and bobbed atop the water. With the warm sun as company, I let myself float over the gentle, rolling waves. My ears were submerged, so the only thing I heard was the rushing water and I saw only the blue sky with puffy white clouds above me. Utter bliss. A serenity I hadn't enjoyed since Oak Island.

Three weeks later, we were far away from there. But Alexander seemed like his head was still there from time to time.

But for now, this was peace and I'd revel in it.

That was, until something grabbed my foot, and I was yanked down. A scream escaped me before I was pulled under the surface to find my sea menace was only a large Scottish arse. Bubbles poured from his mouth as he laughed. I gave him the vulgar *bras d'honneur* before kicking up to the surface.

Once he came up too, he was choking and coughing between laughs.

"Serves you right, you rutting bastard!"

His deep baritone laugh made my toes curl. "I'm sorry, Red. But you shoulda heard your scream. I've heard pigs slaughtered scream quieter than that."

I punched his bicep. "Did you see your life flash before your eyes? Because you're a dead man."

He was completely nude and the *very* clear water didn't do much to conceal the fact he quite enjoyed scaring me. Rivulets of water trailed down him, curving around under each curve of his chest, down over the mounds of muscles in his abdomen before streaming down to the particularly enticing V-shaped muscles above his groin.

"Well, if ye keep lookin' at me like that, I'll never see it coming. Too distracted by your beauty and those pale pink pebbles poking through your shift." He waded through the water, closer to me. "Too distracted knowing what's to come."

He bent down to kiss me, but I placed a hand on his chest, stopping him. "You're so sure of what's to come? After you've scared me half to death?"

"Half to death?" He used the hand on his chest to tug me closer before lacing our fingers together. "I better finish the job then. There's a reason the French call it *le petit mort.*" His lips left a wake of fire as he trailed them down the column of my neck.

Le petit mort. The little death—as in the loss of consciousness after a climax. I shivered.

"Where's the rest of the crew?"

"I sent them back to the ship. Canna have them seeing my wife in this translucent shift." He fingered the strap sticking tight against my skin.

"Isn't that an abuse of power?" A shrug was my only answer before he showered me with more kisses. "And it's hardly fair. They're permitted to bathe in the nude while I nearly drown with this sopping wet thing on."

"Oh, a dangerous situation, to be sure. Allow me to remove it for ye." He splashed water as he headed toward shore, pulling me along with him.

"Where are you taking me?" I ambled through the water, not nearly as graceful as he.

"Away from prying eyes. There's a cleft in the rock over there that forms a wee cave of sorts." His head jutted toward the rock in front of him.

Making love on the beach was quite an idea. I raised my brows.

"I dare say, you were quite sure of what's to come if you've already scoped out a spot."

"Aye." Once on the warm, golden sand, he peered over his shoulder at me. "It was the verra first thing I did once we dropped anchor."

His confession brought a smile to my face. "You have your priorities in order, I see."

My hand in his larger, warm one, he dragged me across the shore to a jutting rock formation. "I did tell ye I'd put ye first those months ago when we handfasted." His lopsided smile as he winked at me was enough to melt me then and there.

I'd follow this man anywhere. Especially his muscled backside. Like two glowing, white, full moons that flexed with every step he took. "I had no idea that'd entail such *carnal* activities as well. And now I'm not even technically your wife."

"A handfasting is as good as the paper." He steered me into the shade in the cleft of the giant rock formation. "And it was those activities I particularly meant when I said I'd do *anything* for ye."

My lips curled upward. "You've a depraved mind, husband."

"The filthiest." Climbing down to his knees on the wet sand, he tugged me down with him, laying me on my back. My damp hair splayed around me, mixing with the fine sand. "But ye like it."

"Pirate savage."

"Christ, will I ever have enough of ye and your red curls spread around your head like a crimson crown? I'm so madly in love wi' ye, I canna think straight if you're next to me, and canna think when you're not next to me because you still possess my mind. Ye beguiling creature." He brushed his lips over mine.

"How you undo me so, husband." Sand stuck everywhere on my sodden shift. When he hauled up the skirt, it was like sandpaper grazing my thighs. "So much for returning to the ship clean—"

He interrupted me with a deep kiss before sliding himself inside of me.

I gasped. "Oh, God."

"Ye can just call me Alexander." His smile was cocky.

A playful smack on his shoulder quickly turned into me digging my fingers in his skin as he thrust deep. We both reached our climaxes, a quick and primal taking of each other. Our panting breaths mixed with the crashing sounds of the ocean. As the foaming tide rose, warm water splashed our feet. Despite the sand that'd be stuck in places that should make me blush, it was quite a lovely spot, indeed.

His powerful arms on either side of my head gave way and his heavy weight sagged on me. I squealed.

"Sorry. Jesus. Ye made me dizzy for a moment." He pushed up and tilted his head to brush his lips across mine, our bodies still connected. "I could stay like this forever. But alas, duty awaits. The sun is almost down. It'll be supper soon. And we're on a tight schedule."

"Schedule?"

"Aye." Offering me his hand, he helped drag me upright.

I fixed my sandy, wet shift as he rotated around, his buttocks covered in sand. "Let us rinse off before we return."

After scrubbing the sand off me anew, we climbed into the jolly boat.

He passed me his tartan. "If any of the men were to see ye in tha' translucent shift, I'd have to kill them."

I wrapped it around my shoulders and breathed in his scent.

His gaze roved over me as he rowed us to the *Bluebell*. "Ye look verra bonnie in a tartan. But I'm afeard ye'll no' be able to wear it when we go home."

I ran my hands through my salt-crusted hair. "Home?"

Back at the ship, he helped me into the hatch door from the jolly boat. "Home. To Scotland." I held his hand as we traversed to the ship and then to our cabin. Once inside the captain's quarters, he planted me with a wide stare, emotion covering his face. "I never thanked ye for not giving up on me. For coming to Oak Island. And for giving me my freedom back. Because of you, I can return to my family. With my beautiful wife on my arm."

I changed into a fresh shift and an emerald riding habit and skirt. "You don't need to thank me. It's what you do for love."

He nodded, biting his bottom lip. "Let us go to the main deck, pull up the anchor."

On the main deck, I tugged down the front of my hat to shade my eyes from the burnt orange sunlight dipping into the endless turquoise waters. The breeze whipped strands of my hair around my face.

The crew was pushing the capstan, four men at a time pressing the wheel around. As they did, they sang a familiar tune. *"What do you do with your mate full on rum?"*

I smiled widely as I watched Alexander tugging ropes and William discussing something animatedly to him, his arms flailing about.

"Leave his sword in water 'til she's rustin'."

Alexander stalked over to the helm, his gorgeous gaze landing on me, and he nodded for me to come over. He slipped his arm around my waist, his other hand on the wheel. "Shall we?"

I looked at him, a wide grin splitting my lips, and he peered down at me, a similar smile on his own lips.

"Take me home, captain."

Acknowledgements

To my Writer In Motion family—thank you to my WIM family for support, encouragement, or reading various parts or all of this book from re-write 1 to re-write 1000. All of you have helped me in numerous ways and have been the best cheerleaders!!

About the Author

Jenna Mandarino is a historical and fantasy women's fiction writer usually incorporating romance and your favorite tropes. She is a freelance content editor having formerly worked at small publishing houses. By day, she is a Teacher on Assignment and specializes in behavior interventions and is attending school for her Doctorate in Education. She lives in Southern California where she can often be found drinking champagne, cooking, speaking French, trying a new TikTok organization method, and with her husband chasing after her two sons.

Jenna also writes under the pen name JM Jinks. Her urban fantasy series can be found here:

https://www.amazon.com/dp/B07JMCGNM6/